the key

jo morgan sloan

The Key

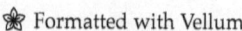 Formatted with Vellum

To all the boys who wondered why they saw girls in the mirror,
to all the girls who thought being a boy was just a phase,
to all those in between who never had words to define it,
everyone's welcome.

goodbyes

. . .

Tabby

THE OLD ME WAS DEAD. She'd never be seen again.

It wasn't like I didn't have a good life. I did. But so much time was spent trying to figure out what I wanted, once I knew, it was too scary to do anything. Prissy makeup, frilly dresses, well-done hair and nails—all the shit that made up who I thought I was supposed to be, how I was supposed to look—was icky like caked Vaseline on my skin, impossible to wash off.

No, I was more than that. *Different.*

It started with a few books and my counselor. Some art and scattered conversations with people online. An LGBT message board or two, which I used late at night after Mom went to bed. All my confusing, impossible questions were answered in a resolute yet painful truth: my body didn't feel like mine. It didn't match who was inside. To be happy, I needed to show off the person screaming at the top of his lungs to get out. If not that, he wanted to at least be acknowledged. I'd have to come clean and stop trying so hard to be the pretty girl everybody else saw.

But putting that thought into action? No way.

Mom and I moved around the country a few times, landing in Colorado when I turned fifteen, at the start of my self-exploration. In school, I fit the bill for the good girl next door: debate team and high honors, though I didn't like sports. Time in gym class only highlighted my dysphoria and discomfort spending time around girls, who didn't match me at all. The sign on the locker room door, a stick figure in a dress, represented me just as poorly. I never changed clothes for class in the open, even though we all shared the same parts. Teenage life was a prison of secrets.

Things changed when I met him: the skinny, shy boy who came out of his shell to tell me he liked the Akira anime pin on my backpack. We met in an after-school club for students who stood out for being a little bit strange; kids known for being heavily into art and out-of-the-box hobbies. Among the others, despite my private love for online gaming and obscure movies, I was still the odd man out. Jax appreciated the things no one else knew about, like my obsession with all things Japanese and the part of my eye that looked like a keyhole. I masked the coloboma behind heavy makeup and fake glasses, but he loved that part of me. He loved everything.

I loved him, too.

His dirty blond hair and his metal mouth charmed me, though it didn't really matter what he looked like. Beneath it, he was a hopeless romantic, a boy who gave his heart away to anyone who'd take it. It sat pinned to his sleeve, just waiting to be crushed. If not by me, then by the next pretty girl, who would surely take him for granted. Jax never missed a phone call and bent over backward to invent new ways to have fun. He lit the world with his presence.

My care for him complicated things all the more. Now I was gay, too. Two closets to leave.

Against all of Jax's love and perfection, my fractured self longed for a clean slate. Mom's new job in San Francisco became an opportunity for escape. I would start a new school, a new name, a new life. Coming out around people I knew was too hard and too terrifying; what if everyone rejected my new identity? What if they hurt me? What if I chickened out and detransitioned just to please them all? I was a determined boy, ready to sacrifice what I wanted now to get what I needed for the rest of my life.

The first casualty was my love for Jax. I had to leave him behind.

Pretending to be adults, we discussed our breakup. Very practical. Long distance wouldn't work because we both hated the phone, knew we were young, could appreciate what we had for what it was...and other bullshit we recited to make ourselves feel better.

For our last date, in a final gesture of romance, Jax took me to see the Nutcracker ballet on winter break. A cheesy tradition with my mom for years, I knew every note and tapped my fingers to the music. He didn't bother trying to stop me, and I savored his warm presence at my side. Just us, one more time.

Afterwards, hand in hand through the flurrying snow, we walked down the cobblestone street of the 16th Street Mall to The Cheesecake Factory. He looked like his father in a black suit and tie, finished off with an oversized wool coat. The green and black scarf I crocheted him for Christmas finished the ensemble nicely. I matched him in a forest green sparkly dress that itched terribly. Jax was worth every second of discomfort if it helped him remember me fondly. Even if he eventually forgot my bleach-blonde hair, my love of chewy candy, and my awful off-key singing, he'd remember how his first sweetheart was everything he ever wanted. At least, that's what he told me then, and I complied.

We spent an hour in the restaurant pretending we weren't falling apart. It dragged. He made no mention of how he was feeling—a gift borne of our last talk about the future.

"Promise me you won't make this some big deal, Jax. Please. It'll just make it worse."

He sighed. "If that's really what you want, Jamie. Okay."

If we ripped off the Band-Aid, it wouldn't hurt. We'd move on. Happy memories alone.

But after dinner, Jax stopped on the sidewalk, tugging my hand to turn around. "I have something for you."

"Yeah?" I sucked in my cheeks to rein the threatening tears.

Shaking, he knelt on one knee, sniffling as he pulled a velvet box from his front pocket. "This is a promise. No matter where you are, you're everything to me." He opened the box and held it up toward me, letting the creak of the hinge fill the space where his emotions wouldn't let him speak at all. "I'll never stop loving you, even if you say no. Please...will you stay with me? Stay mine, even when you're far away?"

"Jax..."

"Try it on. It has to fit. It has to." He fumbled and slid it around my left ring finger, trembling from nerves that ignored all the snow.

Like him, the ring was perfect. It had no jewels that made it look like an engagement ring or anything like that—he knew me too well and found something akin to a tree branch made of bronze and dark silver. It wrapped around my finger twice and made me feel like I belonged inside one of our D&D games, telling fantasy stories and pretending I was someone else. The open-ended design of the ring meant I could play with the sizing if I wanted to, but not now. He was right. It needed no adjustment and was at home on my hand.

I loved it, but keeping him meant hiding myself, and was that fair? Was he worth the minuscule chance that we'd still love each other at twenty? Twenty-five? Hadn't we already talked about this? I cried out of anger that he broke his word. I cried for the heartache of losing him. And I cried for the coward that beat inside my chest, begging to be released—*let me out!*—because I was too terrified to ask if Jax could love him, too.

I silently stared while Jax made his case. "You might never come back from San Francisco, but I wanna try long distance. Can't we at least try?" His glassy eyes gazed into mine, though all I could see were the twinkling red and green reflections from the Clocktower club behind me. Snow kissed his spiky blond

hair and light lashes. It was the picture-perfect image of a Christmas proposal from the movies, except I was breaking his heart. "This can't be it, Jamie. It *can't* be. We're too good together. You're my Hwa. I love you."

Hwa. One of Jax's and my special words that meant nothing and everything. He was one, I was the other. *Hwa-Wah: I love you. I need you like water.*

The wind bristling my ears amplified the cold. So many flurried evenings in Denver were like snow globes wrapped in a blanket of protection, but not tonight. My body was otherwise numb.

There was no point in trying to keep my composure. "Wah, I'm so, *so* sorry."

"Is it 'cause my braces are so bad? They're coming off soon—"

"Of course not. It's not your teeth. It's nothing you're doing or not doing." I wiped my dripping nose with my loose knit glove. "I just can't do it. You're trying so hard. I shouldn't take this."

"No—keep the ring," he said, cupping my hand over it and sobbing. "'Cause tomorrow you're gonna wake up and remember you love me."

"I *do* love you." I blubbered and hid my face from the eyes of the passersby. *Why'd you make this harder than it has to be?*

"Then you know you'll always have the key to my heart." He choked on the words but wasn't shy about saying them in public. "Maybe right now isn't the right time. Someday we'll meet again like those people in *Serendipity*, and you'll know it was meant to be. I'll look in your eyes and know, too. I'd know your eyes anywhere, no matter what you look like or how old you are." Jax kissed my hand one more time before wiping his face with the scarf. "Until the day I die, I swear I won't feel any different."

He was my first love. My so-called Romeo. Like the star-crossed lovers, we were only seventeen and barely knew better; I shouldn't have said yes to dating him at all, but our year as a couple was so wonderful. It was filled with late nights in my basement watching movies, dates to the sprawling bookstore downtown, even the few times we'd anxiously had sex. Regardless of who I became, he'd never be replaced. *This* tragic end was all my fault because I chose to avoid telling him the truth over having the hard conversation.

"I'll always love you, too, Jax. No matter what."

"Then if you can't do long distance, promise me the future. Say you'll give this a chance if we meet again. *Please*, Hwa. Promise me you won't disappear out there. Swear you'll look for me, and I'll look for you. When it's time, we'll know it, won't we?"

How could I say no when I hoped for the same? I didn't really believe he would still want me when the makeup was off, and I lived how I wanted. He might've thought nothing was insurmountable; he was wrong. It was a sweet gesture and a nice thing to say. Nothing more.

Still, I said the words. "Yes, Jax. I promise."

He kissed me under the falling snow. One last kiss that bid me farewell. The salt of his tears and mine lingered on my lips when I left him at the light rail station downtown. He was gone, and I never expected to see him again.

Such was the end of my teenage romance and the beginning of a new chapter.

Coming out wasn't a problem for my tiny family. Mom and I already talked about it at Thanksgiving. She didn't tell me she had her suspicions, but I guessed by the way she nodded when I told her that it wasn't exactly a surprise.

I was glad to leave the snow of Colorado for the sun and became a new person as soon as we stepped off the plane at SFO. In the bathroom by baggage claim, I pulled a black wool beanie over my head and tucked in any loose strands of my long hair—I planned to chop it before starting school. Foundation didn't cover my freckles anymore. Mascara in my brows made them look thicker. I ditched the fake glasses despite my coloboma; Mom said I could get contacts to cover it instead. Comfortable with how things were going, I was ready to say things aloud and move forward.

"Mom, I thought of a name," I said, not looking away from my reflection.

She tenderly put her hand on my shoulder.

A wish to honor Jax in my transition made my decision easy. I thought back on all the games we'd played, and warmth washed over me. I'd never felt more like myself than when Jax and I lived in our fantasy, rolling dice and being whatever we wanted. My favorite roleplay character was a cat-like creature, one that was curious, steadfast, and agile. Aware of everything around them, they were prepared for anything. Just like me. Lost memories of my father, who affectionately called me *tiger moth* before he died, made for the perfect choice beyond any other.

"Tabby. Call me Tabby. And I like masculine pronouns. You can also use they and them, okay?"

Mom showed her support by not letting love—or sadness, or disappointment—spill down her cheeks. It wasn't about her. I could be reborn. "Okay, Tabby. Son. Whatever you want, I love you."

I inflated my lungs with the sea-level air. My first breath in the world.

Goodbye, Jamie. You're dead to me now.

endings and beginnings

. . .

Jax

I HOPPED on the light rail train to the Littleton Park n' Ride from my errand downtown and bounced my legs without stopping. The jeweler got Heather's ring perfect, and it ate a hole through my pocket to be shown off. Part of me wished I'd used Shine Co., especially since I'd heard the ads my whole life on the radio. *Just off Arapahoe road...*

Who else was there to show but Chris? I had him to thank for meeting my girl anyway. We'd gone through everything together: met as freshmen in college at Boulder, got our MBAs at UC Denver, and worked together at our first jobs out of school. He thought he knew my type, so he hooked me up with Heather after a blind date with her didn't pan out on his end. He said he wasn't interested in her demure sweetness.

Lucky me. I loved to charm, and she soaked up every bit of my cheesy worship. Two years was long enough to know I wanted her forever. She deserved an extravagant, ridiculous, over-the-top proposal and with both of us pushing thirty, I was ready to kickstart the next chapter of my life.

Chris would temper my excitement and talk me down. He'd give me a beer and laugh about how he couldn't imagine only picking one woman for the rest of his life, and I'd counter by saying how grateful I was that I'd been picked at all. Predictable? Sure, but he'd be happy for me in the end, like he always was. My biggest problem would be convincing him not to do something too crazy as my best man.

I found my car in the parking lot and drove the ten minutes to Chris's place, cursing every red light for making me wait longer. My fingers drummed on the steering wheel out of rhythm with the radio. *Should I get down on one knee for him? Shit, he'd love that.* My heart rushed like I was about to jump off a bridge when I turned down his street and finally parked.

I took a deep breath to slow my pulse. "Chris, sweetheart, love of my life, will you marry me?" Chuckling, I pulled out the black velvet box and admired the prominent diamond surrounded by smaller sparkles one last time. I wasn't a big fan of the round cut, but that's what Heather wanted. This was all about her. All *for* her, the girl I loved. I imagined she'd chime with anxious laughter to see how I'd picked the one she described last year when I casually asked what her fantasy was.

I stepped out with a whistle and tossed my keys in the air while pocketing the ring box again. My fingers absently fumbled around my key fob to lock the car as I walked up Chris's driveway, but something down the street beeped at the same moment I pressed the button instead of my Subi's mid-pitch horn.

My brow furrowed and I did it again. *Boop-beep.* The extra key fob to Heather's Nissan wasn't too unlike mine, and I often got them mixed up. I pressed her button instead of my own. Horror in my hand.

I turned and did it a third time. The lights on her maroon sedan flashed from halfway down the other side of the street. Chris's silver Buick sat at the top of his driveway, as it always did.

My mouth watered. I wanted to puke. Almost did. What the hell was she doing here?

I locked my car for sure, then took slow steps to Chris's door. Ghosts of all the times we sat together on his porch yelling about the Broncos were permanently etched in the wicker furniture beside me. The four chairs and small table were my house-warming present. His barbecues were the best parties all year, and over time, I opted to stop going to local RPG meetups so I could hang out right here. His place was like the set of *Friends*, always flooded with people who laughed and pretended to be one huge family.

I hesitated before ringing the bell. Maybe I was wrong. Maybe she knew someone else in the neighborhood. Unlucky coincidence. I sucked in cool summer air through my nostrils and tried to convince myself that my nerves were talking too loud. When I couldn't wait anymore, I thumbed the button, and an obnoxious off-key melody sang through his house like a creepy ice cream truck.

Chris's voice came through an open upstairs window. "Shit, who's that?"

A girl answered, but I couldn't make out what she said, and she was too quiet to be familiar.

Please, God, be wrong. My heart beat so fast, it hurt.

Thumping echoed through the house. The peephole dark-ened and stayed that way for several seconds—longer than it should've. He stared at me. Processed me. Fought with himself about opening the door.

I rang the bell again without blinking.

He unlocked the house but left the screen door between us. "Hey, Jax—what's up?" His right hand drummed against the door jamb afterward. He never did that. Never kept me outside. His house was my house.

"You gonna invite me in?" I asked while commanding the shudder in my throat to stop.

He ran that same right hand through his receding brown hair and avoided my eyes. "What are you doin' here? Don't you have some fancy errand tonight? Said you'd be busy 'til eight."

"Got it done faster than I thought."

"Cool. Cool. Well, it's not really the *best* time for me right now, so—"

"I don't wanna keep you too long. Can I show you something?"

Chris absently licked his lips and puffed his chest up and down like he was out of breath, even though he stood in place. After an uncomfortable few seconds, he nodded quickly and stepped out of the screen door, folding his arms tightly. "Sure. Yeah. No problem."

I wanted so badly to ignore my gut and fake propose to my oldest friend. The ring in my pocket still wanted to be seen. Fate got to decide what happened next. I pulled out the first thing my fingers could find.

The keys won.

"Check this out." Pointing down the street, I pressed Heather's lock button again. "Weird, huh? That's Heather's car."

His face lost all color. He swallowed hard.

"Any idea why she'd be around?" I asked.

The way his mouth contorted was confession enough. He didn't apologize. Offered no excuses. Chris stared, and his body language pleaded the fifth. Guilty by omission.

I put my chest to his. "Hmm?" My instinct was to slam him into the sidewalk. We weren't super athletic, but we both tapped out at just over six feet. If I'd started a fight, it would've gotten ugly fast.

Heather came downstairs and froze when she caught my eye through the screen door.

"Hi, sweetie," I said with a cloying tone, not stepping away from Chris at all.

"Jaxson?" She tugged on the shirt wrapped around her body. Chris's black striped button-down. His lucky shirt. The one he *always* wore on dates and said he *always* got laid in. Now her lucky dress.

Chris slowly raised his hands in defense, looking pathetic in his sweatpants and T-shirt, and I bet underneath he wore nothing else since I'd interrupted them. "Look, it's not—"

"Not what it looks like? You fuckin' kidding me with this shit?" I shoved him backward, aching all over with betrayal. "Unbelievable."

As I stormed into the house with Chris close behind, Heather shrieked, "Jaxson, listen to me, please. Baby, I'm sorry."

"Bro, you don't...come on...."

Their voices became muddied and dull to my ears. I found her keys hanging by the door and took off the extra fob to my car and her house key.

She screamed, "What are you doing? Stop, please. Baby—"

"Can it." I dangled the orphaned keys in her face. "You're not coming back. I'll put your shit out tomorrow. And *you*—" I turned to Chris and let my anger erupt into spit as I spoke. "We're done. You hear me? I don't ever wanna see you again."

He got misty-eyed and fidgeted in shame. Didn't even try to cover his own ass.

Heather's loud sobs broke my heart, because as her boyfriend, I'd been programmed to hear those tears and comfort her. Not anymore. I deserved those tears. Every last fucking one.

"I just wanna know one thing," I said, trading glances between their lowered, shameful expressions. "How long has it been goin' on?"

Heather's mouth opened, but she said nothing and looked at Chris for guidance.

"No, no. Don't you dare do that shit. Don't come up with a lie together. You owe me this." I snapped my fingers quickly, adding panic to the moment. "Come on. Tell me. Spit it out. When did it start? *When?*"

"S-September," she spat, curling in on herself.

"September?" I asked, doing math in my head. "*September?* Nine months of this?"

Chris finally spoke up. "Jax—"

"How long after my birthday, you fuckwad?" I got close to him again. "When?"

He gulped. Silence again.

"Right. Jesus. I'm thinkin' of you at my Christmas table. Hangin' out with me and my dad. You looked me in the face and said I was closer to you than your damn brother. Would you do this to him?" My gaze turned back to Heather. "And *you*, 'too tired' on Valentine's Day." I let the false quotes linger in the air. "Said you had too much to eat for lunch and needed a break. Oh, I bet. I *bet*. Bet you had *him* for lunch that day, didn't you?"

She sobbed harder and hid her face.

I glared. "I bought a damn ring for you."

"What?" Her eyes shot open wide.

"You disgust me." I charged to my car, grateful neither of them followed.

After speeding up C-470 to the other side of the city and snaking south again through the stoplights to calm my nerves, I parked at the light rail station again. I'd spent the trip yelling, rehearsing any arguments that might come my way if they chased me down. Now I sat in numb silence. Things I'd never considered became grossly appealing.

I left a voicemail on my boss's line, doing everything I could to sound semi-professional. "Hey, this is Jax Grady from IT. We talked a few weeks ago about potentially relocating to California for the analyst position and I shot you down...I'm kinda hoping you'll say it's still open. I, uh, need to get outta here. If it's not with our company, I'll be looking elsewhere. Thanks, and talk to you later." I hung up and already regretted making the call in the first place, but Future Jax would have to deal with the consequences now.

As much as Heather and Chris's betrayal stung, I didn't shed more than a handful of tears. That's why I waited in the car for so long. The train of emotion was supposed to hit, but it didn't. What if I hadn't caught them? Would she have said yes? Would he have stood at my side as best man, then screwed her after our honeymoon?

I stared at the ring and focused on every jewel. It was incredibly ordinary. Pretty, sure—but the more I looked at it, the more I was sure. It might've fit Heather, but it didn't fit me. And she didn't fit, either. Not when I buried my desire to be wanted and looked at the facts with an objective lens.

I wanted to feel committed to someone. In the end, guess I didn't care who it was.

The velvet box made a satisfying soundtrack every time I opened and closed it. Creak open, snap shut. Creak open, snap shut. They had their own language, didn't they? Not the first time I thought that, though it had been years. The light rail train came and went, but I stayed. I even considered sleeping in my car and avoiding the house in case they came to find me.

While scrolling through bullshit online, my phone rang. The boss, returning my call already. My finger slipped, and I answered it by accident.

Shit. "This is Jax," I said, trying to infuse my voice with more life than I had when I left the voicemail.

"Grady, thanks for answering this late."

"No problem. I wasn't expecting to hear from you tonight. Sorry I didn't wait until tomorrow."

"No, no. We need to move on this position as soon as possible and haven't had any other takers. You mean it? You're willing to head up the new office?"

I sighed and nodded, though of course she couldn't see me. "Yup. I wouldn't really want anyone else's hands on the updated system if you're gonna move the hub out there."

"Great. Really, *really* great." The excitement in her voice was palpable, and I could just see the fist pump in the air that she normally did at meetings when she got what she wanted. "You'll get a pay bump of course, relocation costs covered. The expansion's going to be awesome for us, and you're not a small part in that, Grady."

It was an empty compliment, but one I needed in the moment. "Thanks."

"Have family out there? Friends? People to show you around?"

"Nuh-uh. I'm a Colorado native. Californians don't exactly... *excite* me. Silicon Valley can't be too bad though, right?" I squeezed the bridge of my nose and said a prayer that the weather wouldn't be too hot.

"That's the best part. We thought we would have to be in San Jose, but most of our investors are coming from Marin. We'll be in San Francisco proper. You'll love it there, and we'll help get you on your feet."

San Francisco. It stirred up my heart in an old way. A lost way. The same way the ring box did a few minutes ago. *Could she...?*

"Now, it's not cheap to live out there, so you might have a bit of a commute. We'll figure it out. Thanks for this. Really. I'm sorry for whatever's changed for you, but I can't afford to have you leave after all we've been through. Anything you need, just ask."

"Sure. Thanks."

I sighed when the call ended and waited for my heart to catch up to my brain and register what I'd just agreed to. Shock prevented me from feeling anything at all. I didn't want to chance getting no sleep, so I paid for a hotel room and stayed far away from my place. It wasn't exactly the kind of "new start" I was hoping for after I'd seen the jeweler, but it was certainly better than the dark hole of anger I felt when leaving the traitors behind.

DEALING with Heather's stuff was sticky at best. Told her she could keep anything of mine that she'd tainted. After only a week, I'd purged her from the duplex. As for myself, I packed the few things I wanted to take with me to California, and Dad said he would store anything else I wanted to keep.

Days before leaving, Heather drove up while I loaded the shipping cube on the sidewalk. The bass thumps from her too-loud pop music shook the whole street before she turned off the car.

Fuck, here we go. At least I don't have to listen to that crap anymore.

Dark circles under her eyes made her look older than usual. No makeup. Not trying. Her curly, natural blonde hair was piled in a messy bun on the top of her head. The only way she could've been more pathetic was if mascara streaked down her cheeks. To pour salt in the wound, she wore my old UC Boulder hoodie. "Jax, can I talk to you?"

"No." I kept pushing the bookcase to the back until it slammed against the side. *Dammit, I probably just broke something.*

"Please?" She sniffled. "I heard you're moving."

"Wow. Somebody's a genius." I rolled my eyes and grabbed the nearby coffee table.

Heather sighed. "I know you can't forgive me. That's not why I'm here."

"I don't wanna hear this." I leaned the table up against the bookcase and left it precariously balanced while storming back toward the house.

"Chris is really tore up," she said.

"I bet."

"Jax, stop it."

"What more do you want from me, huh?" I turned around from the raised porch two steps above her. "I gave you two years of my life, brought you into my house, and caught you red-handed with my friend. Stop pretending like that wasn't the worst fuckin' thing you coulda done to me."

Her chin quivered. "I said I was sorry."

"And?" I stepped down once, then met her level on the grass. "Why'd you come back here?"

She shifted her gaze to her strappy sandals, which she took off and slid back on. "Your blessing?"

I burst out laughing and looked to the sky with a sarcastic smile. "Christ. I shoulda known when you started working late nights at your firm. Still wanna say your tax clients were the problem?"

"Please—"

"Nah, I think you were just having Chris check *you* for hidden assets, huh?" I turned away from her and kept working, steeling myself to keep from imploding at her presence. "Sure. You have my blessing. You assholes deserve each other."

She blubbered like she did at Chris's house but still refused to leave. "I'm sorry, okay? I know I messed up. He does, too. We want to make sure you'll be okay. Where are you going?"

"San Fran." I threw boxes into the cube now, one after the other, too angry to set them up nicely as I'd planned.

"You hate California."

"No, I hate California transplants and seeing memories of you and Chris everywhere I go." Arguing with her finally beckoned the tears I'd done so well at holding in. I wiped my eyes fast and picked up another heavy box to pass it off as sweat. "Now, if you don't mind, I'm kinda busy. Please get off my lawn."

"You've been through too much with Chris. Please forgive him. I started everything, and he always felt guilty."

I lost my patience and dropped the last box while I yelled, "Is that supposed to make me feel better? That he screwed you and felt *bad* about it? Wasn't enough to stop either of you, and now you're here acting like you give a shit."

"But I—"

"You know something? The last time somebody broke my heart, they knew they were doin' it and actually looked like they felt sad for hurting me. Ripped off the bandage and ended things fast. *You* only feel bad 'cause you got caught. Same with him. I'm worth more than that." I sidestepped her and went to the house one last time, intent on shutting her out.

"Who are you more upset about losing? Me or Chris?"

A surge of adrenaline squeezed my insides as I turned to her. "Excuse me?"

She sniffled and tugged at the bottom of my hoodie as if her current torn-apart status was somehow my fault. "Are you in love with him? Is that why you're acting like this?"

"Wow." I shook my head and scoffed. "No, I'm not in love with Chris. I got drunk and told you I was bi, and now you're tryin' to hurt me with it. That doesn't mean I wanna fuck everything that moves; all it means is I care more about who a person is than what's between their legs. Turns out I shoulda cared more about what was behind your ribcage—it's nothing but a goddamn void." I slammed the front door and went to the basement, blocking her number and Chris's, too.

I needed something better than the vapid girl upstairs and the weak bond that wasted my time. Something real. Something permanent. I knew exactly what I was looking for.

Maybe this was my chance to find it.

settling in

· · ·

Jax

SAN FRANCISCO WAS another world compared to Denver. First thing I noticed was the food. Or, lack thereof. All the restaurants at the airport were...*crunchy*. Organic, vegan, paper straws, and sourdough. A new world compared to my comfortable green chili. Nothing was spicy and I didn't know the chains. Even the pizza was unfamiliar, covered in things I'd never dream of back home—things like artichokes and goat cheese.

Yuck.

My research into the layout of the city barely prepared me for getting around. There was absolutely no thoroughfare from one side to the other. A maze of stoplights separated the airport from the Golden Gate Bridge, which rose out of the mist in the north like an ancient, orange dinosaur. I knew it well despite never seeing it in person before. Unfamiliar familiarity. It reminded me of the time I went to New York City and knew my way around just because it was so popular in movies and TV shows.

The images I had in my head about San Francisco streets were pretty accurate, too. Hills reached up, up, up, and then crested like a roller coaster. Who the hell built a city like that on purpose? I missed the mountains, but now I had water. It was chilly and humid, even for late June, but the intense green everywhere was unreal. Hobbiton hills. Flowers I'd never seen blossomed on every street corner, and even the people were different. I heard new languages, saw new clothes and diverse skin tones, and reveled in the opportunity to expand my horizons and find things here I'd never considered before.

My boss told me to ditch my trusty Subaru and buy something new because driving a stick in the city was ridiculous. Once I saw those hills, I agreed. Public transportation wasn't too bad, so I bought a used Mazda but took the bus most days.

I found a guy who needed a roommate, and thank God I did. Nobody could move to San Francisco alone without a fucking trust fund. The apartment as a whole was small, but the kitchen was decent, and he'd covered the windowsill in potted plants that required a lot of attention. Roomie was perpetually out of town which is why he needed me in the first place—if I hadn't been there to water the greenery, they would've shriveled.

And so it was, my existence beyond the office was relegated to *Plant Babysitter*.

DAD CALLED AFTER A MONTH, right when I got off work. Took him that long to finally absorb the hour time difference. "Hey, kid. How's it goin' out there in Cally-forny?"

"It's good, Dad. Big city." I dodged somebody on the sidewalk and opted to walk through some shops a little, skipping the bus to avoid dropping the call.

"Uh-huh, right, right. Have you talked to your mom since you moved out there?"

"Nah, she's busy with…whatever the hell she's been up to, I don't know. Somethin' going on I should know about?"

"No, just curious." He cleared his throat on the other end, and I could see him running a hand over his bald head in my mind. His fishing for info on Mom's new husband, Brian, was obvious but unsuccessful. I never gave him fuel to beat himself up over losing her. Dad would've walked on the surface of the sun for Mom, and she no longer wanted to give him so much as a birthday phone call. She went through a midlife crisis, and we all knew it. Nevertheless, my poor father missed her and hadn't yet tried to find someone else, perpetually hoping she would come back.

I got the hopeless romantic crap from Dad, one hundred percent.

He came back to the line after the traffic around me lulled. "So, your old buddy Chris came by here yesterday."

"Augh." I shook my head and clenched my empty fist. "What the fuck did he want? You know what—I don't even care. Did you take a swing at him?"

"Nah. I thumped him on the temple like I did when you were a kid."

Dad was pretty passive, so if he really did that, it was saying something. "Better than nothing, I guess."

He sighed in that extra-long, extra breathy exasperation he always did whenever he had to say something difficult. "You know, he and Heather got engaged."

I stopped cold, even though my feet landed in a suspicious puddle.

Dad understood how the words paralyzed me even from so far away. "Come on, sport. I know you'd rather hear it from me than online."

"Yeah, that's why I've avoided all my socials. I can't fucking believe this." I wanted to scream, but I also felt an adolescent sense of being left out. What made me so easy to betray and cast aside?

"I wanted to tell you so you could, ya know...start movin' on. Have you met anybody?"

I groaned and kept walking, albeit at a much slower pace. "No. My coworker Jenny wants me to try one of those dating apps. I hate that shit. Life was so much easier when we had to be in classes together or working together and that's how you'd meet people. Now, everything's online. People can be whoever they wanna be, which would be nice, except apparently what most people wanna be is an asshole."

Dad laughed. "Well, that's what I told you when you were a kid. Don't be an asshole, Jax. The world has enough."

Hearing his lighthearted, rattly tone from his too-many-cigarettes and not enough sleep sunk my homesickness to a new low. "I miss you, Dad. It's so different here, it's like another country."

"What, like Boulder?"

I chuckled. "Something like that. When I tell people I'm from Colorado, that's the first thing they ask me."

"Maybe you can find an ex-Coloradan support group. If anything like that existed, it would hafta be *there*, right?" Dad's lingering snicker cut in and out. "Damn—that's work, Jax. I've gotta go."

It was over too soon but a gift anyway. "It's nice to hear from you, Dad. Enjoy chili night, alright?"

"Extra hot, extra cheese, extra crispy relleno, kid. Love you."

"Love you, too."

I pocketed my phone and wandered around Union Square while people-watching. For an early Wednesday evening, it surprised me how many folks were out. It helped quell my loneliness to feel like I was part of the city's pulse. Dad was right—it was time to start again.

CRUISING THROUGH CRAIGSLIST, I found a Thursday night call for RPG players downtown. I hadn't done D&D in over two years—Heather had no interest in it, and I internalized her comments about not wanting to end up with a nerd. It threw me back into being fifteen, teased relentlessly for my braces, gangly body, and taste in anime. All I ever wanted was to be accepted for who I was and what I liked without being made to feel like shit for it. Loneliness beat me down so much in my twenties, I no longer had conviction for that same acceptance when it came to Heather.

Oh, yeah. Lucky me.

When I found the call for D&D night, an impossible fantasy played out in my head. I'd show up, introduce myself, and maybe tell a joke or two. I wouldn't feel awkward or forced to like something I didn't, like a football team I knew nothing about. Dad taught me how to meet strangers and instantly find something we had in common, so I had a plan.

Behind me, fashionably late, my soulmate would appear. Someone who would share my love for puns and stale candy corn. A person who wouldn't cringe if I bought flowers and wrote poetry. Somebody who would know what they wanted and had dreams and goals of their own to accomplish. Someone who wouldn't lie to me.

Only one person in my life fit that whole bill before, though the fool's hope in my heart to rediscover her had faded. I purged the thought after years of disappointment when she didn't appear in any internet searches. Despite technology's pervasiveness, my first sweetheart left no footprint—if we were indeed meant to be, my interference made no difference.

Dragon's Lair was like any other game and comic shop I'd seen in Denver. Bright colors and posters adorned all the walls and stacks of Magic: The Gathering cards piled high in the front counter's case. It felt like home in a way—a haven for all those who wouldn't fit in where sports memorabilia was sold, like an adult version of the Diversity Club I did after school as a teen. High school wasn't exactly what I'd call the best days of my life, but it was still fun to relive the same kinds of excitement as an adult with more common sense to ground me.

In the far-right corner were five folding tables set up with rickety plastic chairs, and people of various shapes and sizes crowded around each other. Like Comic-Con, nothing was too outrageous. Unlike Comic-Con, I didn't feel like I was going to be quizzed in Japanese as a greeting, and I was certain their clothes were all clothes and not body paint. Everyone looked to be about my age, too, or maybe even a little older.

My people. So, they did exist.

"Just so you know, store's closing down for regular shopping in twenty minutes," the guy at the counter said. His lime green hair was like a bug lamp, and it looked extra bright against his black brows, beard, and exaggerated mustache. A punky pirate. He talked to the counter he was cleaning more than he talked directly to me.

"Um, about that—I'm here for game night." I glanced over the dice in the cabinet to avoid his eyes while forcing my introverted self not to back out. A set cast in contrasting gold and silver alloy practically waved at me. *If this works out, I'm taking you home.*

"That right?" He chuckled and slid down toward me. "I haven't seen you in here before. Do you know what group you're joining?"

I should've emailed first to find that out. What a dumbass. "I don't, actually. But if there's not any room for a new guy, that's—"

"No, no. We'll find a good place for you." He extended his hand. "I'm Ethan. This is my shop."

"Nice to meet you. Jaxson Grady."

After a few basic pleasantries, he told me to hang out in the store for a while so he could introduce me to people. I wandered through the figurines and paint for model making, even some comic book stacks. As for the single bathroom, instead of indicating gender as is customary, it had three crossed-out symbols: a boy, a girl, and a wheelchair, accompanied by a sign underneath that said, *We don't care. Just wash your damn hands.*

I chuckled. It might as well have said, *No assholes allowed.* I loved it.

"Ready to hop in?" Ethan asked, passing me to lock the doors.

I nodded and followed him to the game tables, shaky with nerves. My heart pounded like it was the first day of school, regressing in age for how self-conscious I was.

Of the five groups playing, the troupe against the wall where

Ethan took me was the largest. There were only four unoccupied seats—two at the end, and two on either side. He cleared his throat to get the attention of the folks chatting below. "Hey everyone, this is Jaxson. He's joining us tonight."

I raised my hand awkwardly. "Jax is fine."

The girl sitting against the back wall emerged from her black hoodie to greet me, lightly parting her ash-brown hair to show her face. "I'm Annie. Dungeon master." For someone who shrunk back into herself just as quickly as she said hello, it surprised me that she would volunteer to run the whole thing.

Another woman twisted to shake my hand. Her deep brown eyes, which matched her skin tone, were strikingly bright. The swirling pattern of her undercut mimicked the tight curls she had on top. She had an artsy feel about her that was rare in my Colorado circles. While she took me with a firm grip, she said, "I'm Cordelia, like the vampire slayer."

I wished I had a clever retort for her Buffy reference, but I was glad to understand the joke at all. "Nice to meet you."

"I'm Gavin," said the tanned man on the other side of the table, waving for my attention. An intricate Chinese dragon tattoo wrapped over his right shoulder in a rainbow of blues and greens. He squeezed the skinny guy next to him closer. "This is—"

"Ah, ah, ah," his boyfriend said, weaving his head enough to make his single silver earring dangle. The man's slight lisp and overall demeanor outed him. "Call me Hawk."

Ethan snorted. "Bullshit."

Hawk folded his arms with a huff. "What? He's new. Why can't I tell him a new one with no strings attached? I'm so sick of my old name."

"And *Hawk*'s the better choice?" I asked.

"If he's Hawk, I get to be Axolotl," Annie said.

"Oh, oh, call me Optimus Prime," Ethan said while doing a small robot dance.

Cordelia broke in, "Wait a minute, are we doing animals, or fictional characters? Keep it straight, guys."

"Impossible, Cordy," Gavin said, laughing so hard he could hardly breathe.

It was my chance to prove—to them and myself—that I could belong here. "Why not swing both ways, like me? I'll be Pikachu. No, Charizard. *Way* cooler."

"Ah!" Annie pointed at me. "This guy's got it. He can stay."

"Old school, I like it." Ethan gave me a fist bump. "You really bi?"

"Yeah." My cheeks went hot. *Wow. First time I just...said it out loud like that.*

"Excuse me," Hawk said, now fussing loudly like a carica-ture. He pointed his nose at the ceiling.

"Don't mind this one," Gavin said, squeezing Hawk to his chest. "Every week he tries to convince us to call him something else. Nothing's stuck yet."

"I still vote for Voltron," Cordelia said, winking.

Hawk replied in a know-it-all tone, "You can't *be* Voltron. You can only be one of the Paladins."

"Jesus, here we go," groaned Annie.

"There can only be *one* Highlander!" Ethan cheered, which made us all bust up louder, earning annoyed glares from the other four groups trying desperately to stay in their own private D&D worlds.

The front door to the gaming shop rattled, and two men peered through the window and waved.

"Gotta get that. Pick a chair, just leave these two on the end." Ethan left to let in the last of the group, and I settled next to Cordelia. Her linen clothing smelled like patchouli and Nag Champa incense, like my aunt's place in my youth.

Maybe it wasn't like my earlier daydream, but soulmate or not, I found my people at last.

nice to meet you

. . .

Tabby

"TOLD YOU WE'D BE LATE," Rob said, shaking the handle of the locked game shop for Ethan's attention. "They already got started without us."

I rolled my eyes. "We're only five minutes past closing. Chill out."

"You were the one who insisted on changing after work. You know nobody cares if you wear your scrubs."

"Except me. I care." I tucked the waist of my shirt—a beige button-up covered in bright-colored books—into my black skinny jeans. "Come on, I can't do fun things at work, and I'm there all day every day. Least you could do is support me wanting to get some use out of the rest of my closet once a week."

He puffed up in his red hoodie. "Is that a jab at me for not taking you out enough? You're the one who—"

"No, no. Not this again. I took an extra five minutes at my place to change. That's all. We're not going to let five minutes explode into a fight before D&D."

Ethan jogged to the door, unlocking it with loud clunks. "Sorry about that. We've got a newbie with us."

"Newbie as in new in town, or noob as in has no damn clue

what they're doing?" Rob asked, hugging Ethan quickly. Their years of gaming together before he met me made Rob somewhat of a snob for such things.

"New in town, I think. Hey, Tabby," Ethan said while bringing me into his arms next. "Nice shirt."

Rob grumbled. "It's the shirt's fault we're late."

"No problem, it's all good. We're still getting to know this guy. Come on." Ethan locked up again and brought us over to the table, where Gavin was showing off some of his character sheets.

The man sitting with his back to us was taller than Cordelia. Impressive. I surveyed him for signs to make sure he was safe. Couldn't be too careful with anyone new.

He passed the sheets back to Gavin one by one, careful not to crease any of them. His hands—gorgeous hands, strong and slender and wrapped in thick veins—were a gilded tone of natural tan, not orangey at all in the tell-tale sign of a spray-on booth. His forearms were lightly adorned with hair up to his checkered blue sleeves, which had been rolled up to his elbows. A good sense of style. His blond hair was severely parted from the front to the back, like an overgrown military cut, which made my heart jump a little—was he conservative? Bigoted? Brash? That wouldn't fit here. He was clean-cut from what I could see, but maybe his job kept him from dressing down, the same way mine did.

He couldn't be too far away from the rest of us, or Ethan wouldn't have let him sit down. I had to trust my friend's judgment before making my own.

"Hey, rest of the crew's here," Annie said while smiling at me.

Ethan patted the stranger's back as he stood to meet us. "Here's our newbie."

"Hey there," he said, extending a hand to Rob.

My ears suddenly rang, drowning out everything but my heartbeat. The world moved in slow motion. He wasn't a stranger, yet he wasn't a friend. I was caught in a lucid daydream. The face from my past—one I never thought I'd see again—struck a nerve in my soul that pulsed through the pit of my stomach. Tunnel vision surrounded him in a halo of light. His smile, no longer covered in braces, was bright and straight and perfect. His deep brown eyes, vivid and clear, squinted cheerfully while shaking Rob's hand. Not a daydream. Too real. With his square jaw, the light scruff on his chin, and the crow's feet that said he spent much of life smiling, I'd know him anywhere. Age couldn't hide him. Change couldn't hide him.

Wah…you've grown up. You found me.

"This is my boyfriend, Tabby," Rob said, putting his arm around me while I came out of the daze.

My tongue turned to jelly. Completely useless, much like my eyelids, which couldn't even blink.

"Tabby. Right. And I'm, what did we say? Oh yeah, Charizard." Jax tittered.

Oh, God. He knows. I gulped past the urge to throw up.

Ethan cleared his throat. "That's actually his name. None of that *Hawk* bullshit."

Jax's eyes went wide. "Oh, shit. I'm *so* sorry. We were just jokin' about Hawk wanting to be called a different name, and I figured—"

"It's okay," I said, still unable to move, but relieved his comment didn't mean he saw through me. What could I say? I wish I knew this was coming. Wish I had a chance to prepare. All the times I'd fantasized about seeing him again, I solved the issue before we met—my mom had told him or something like that—freeing me from the burden of an explanation.

He awkwardly scratched at his temple, then extended a shake to me. "Jaxson. Everyone calls me Jax. Again, I'm really sorry."

I trembled while reaching for him; then I remembered people were watching, so I took him firmly. *You taught me how to do this long ago. Straight wrist, firm grasp, quick end. Do you*

remember the lines of my palm the way I remember yours, even now?
They're familiar, like tracks in the land that I've cut to not forget my
way home.

"Nice grip," he said, releasing me.

"Uh-huh." I couldn't tear my eyes away. Like the last night I
saw him, I was otherwise numb.

He squinted, flitting his gaze over my face. "Have...have we
met before?"

"No, you don't know me," I said, hating myself as I did.

"So, are we ready to get started?" Rob shook my shoulder.
"Babe?"

"I'll be right back." Escaping before I lost my cool, I ran to the
bathroom and disappeared.

Catching my breath felt impossible. The man in my reflection
meant nothing to Jax. He had no idea. I now had a dark, defined
goatee. Hair that was no longer bleached and curled—instead, it
was auburn and barely reached past my ears, flipping forward in
a natural wave. I was bulkier, confident, not afraid to be who I
was and show it to the world. Tabby's eyes, *my* eyes, were
hidden behind rainbow-colored contacts that I wore to cover my
coloboma.

It was my only escape. Like this, even Jax's keen senses
couldn't guess. If my eye was covered, so was I.

"I'm okay. He doesn't know. He doesn't *have* to know. I'll tell
him when I'm ready, if I tell him at all. I don't have to. I can
just...go out there and act like everything's normal. It's fine.
It's—"

On my hand was my D&D ring. Jax's ring. The same ring he
gave me years ago. I wore it every time I gamed because without
it, my D20 rolls were low.

Is the ring lucky, or is it you, Wah?

As I stared at the twisted branch talisman on my thumb, a
tear spattered on my knuckles. "Dammit." I wiped my face and
sniffed back hard, then took a few deep breaths and cracked my
neck. An inescapable feeling of exposure came over me, and my

psyche and self were naked in a way I'd never been. The ghost of my past life returned to haunt me.

"He won't know you. Don't say anything." I took off the ring and stuffed it in my pocket, certain even if Rob noticed it was gone, he wouldn't mention it. "It's Tabby's turn to get to know Jax. So, there."

Outside the bathroom, Annie grabbed a can of Coke from the machine. "Hey, everything okay?"

Hell no. "Uh-huh." I raked through my hair and straightened my shirt once more.

She quieted her voice and stood close to me. "Are you and Rob fighting again?"

"Ugh." Standing against the wall, I hid my face a little.

"He's still giving you shit, isn't he?" Annie sighed. "When are you going to tell him—"

I mumbled, "It seems not telling people things is my new M.O."

"What does *that* mean?" she asked, putting a concerned hand on my shoulder.

"Nothing. Thanks for looking out for me, but Rob and I are fine. Let's go."

Everyone was laughing when we returned. I sat beside Rob and kissed his cheek. "Sorry about that."

"You okay?"

"Yeah. Forgot to pee in my rush to get ready. What're we doing?"

Cordelia cleared off the table in front of her. "It's a Battle Royale tonight. Since Jax doesn't have any character sheets, we're just gonna pick something and fight to the death. Last man standing sets the campaign for next week."

"Or last man standing declares Hawk's new name," Gavin said with a chuckle.

"Sheezus," I groaned, but winked at Hawk. It never bothered me that he couldn't stand his given name. Made sense to me, even if he only wanted to play around with us and not do it for real. Even my last name changed when I made things official, so I respected all of Hawk's efforts to redefine himself.

Jax helped unfold a large hand-drawn battle map that Annie brought, already armed with various pitfalls. "I really appreciate you letting me cut in. How long have you been running this, Annie?"

She cocked a brow and eyed me. "Actually, Tabby started the group four years ago. Rob joined a couple years after and brought Ethan, and they set up the regular game nights here. I just like being DM more than playing a character."

"Oh." Jax looked my way. "Hope *you* don't mind my being here, then."

"It's cool." I averted his gaze and focused on anything that could distract me from him. Impossible, but at least I tried.

"I'm sure you'll find a group that you fit in with soon enough," Rob said.

We all paused.

Hawk snapped, "Excuse me?"

Rob's patronizing tone threw a cloud over everyone. "Come on. He isn't exactly…one of *us*, if you catch my drift."

I tapped his shoulder and whispered, "What are you doing?"

"Did I…miss something?" Jax asked as his cheeks flushed.

Gavin leaned forward. "Rob's implying that we all have something in common. Did you notice?"

Jax's brow furrowed, and he met everyone's eyes around the table. "Um. Gimme a hint."

"Well, some of us prefer a little more *male* persuasion than others," Gavin said, hugging Hawk at his side.

"Some of us, *women*," Cordelia chimed in, looking at the map again to dismiss the issue.

"A few of us prefer a, uh, more complex *trans*action." Rob chuckled and bumped against me. While I normally would've found his comment funny, now I felt he used it to push Jax away.

Ethan huffed. "He's bi. One of us. Can we please drop this?"

Lightning shot through me. *Jax said that?*

"Wait, wait, wait." Jax leaned back and held his hands up. "I really don't get it."

"We're all queer, dude," Rob said flatly. "This is the LGBT D&D group."

Annie added with a groan, "Excuse me, add the A to the end of that, if you don't mind."

The blush creeping up Jax's face said he truly didn't notice. "Um. Okay?"

"But if you say you're bi…I guess we'll take your word for it." Rob sighed and arched his brows while shaking his head.

So, you don't believe him? Why are you being such an asshole right now? I wanted to defend Jax, but fear held me back. After all, I didn't know enough about him now to say anything.

"Rob, don't be a dick." Ethan snapped his fingers at Jax to get his attention. "Seriously, it's fine. You fit in great. Rob and Tabby are trans, you can guess who all's gay, Annie's ace, and I'm bi, but I think pan fits better—the labels are always shifting a little. Whatever works. You don't need to prove anything."

"Thanks, I guess." He folded into himself somewhat, losing a bit of the shiny excitement he had when Rob and I came in.

Annie passed out two trays for dice rolling. "Enough of this crap. To the death!"

new guy

● ● ●

Tabby

WHEN THE GAME was over and Hawk came out victorious long after the other four groups left the store, we cleaned up the table and said our goodbyes. Jax gathered our numbers and traded text messages until we were all on the same chat thread. He was a fine addition to us, regardless of my apprehension. I was simultaneously over the moon and panicked that he would be a regular at game night.

Jax lingered by me after Annie and Cordelia caught an Uber. His small talk was nauseating. "Is you guys's place close by here?"

We don't live together yet but I don't want to say that out loud because Rob will hear me and think I'm trying to force him into talking about it again and that's not something I want to tell you because you—

I halted the running dialogue in my head and kept things short to avoid saying something I might regret and shrugged instead. "Not really."

"Yeah, I don't live close either. I kinda wish I'd known how hard it was to get around in the city before picking my roommate. It takes almost an hour to get to work in the morning. Shit —I thought Denver's traffic was bad."

"Colorado, huh?" I did my best to pretend I knew nothing about him; how he'd grown up in Denver, how his Dad worked construction, how his mother used to take us to the Tattered Cover bookstore and let us run rampant through the stacks. "So, what brought you out here?"

"Work, *and* I had to get the hell out of there. They could've sent me to Mars, and I would've said yes."

He didn't say what I secretly wanted him to. It stung. *I'm such a moron. You didn't move out here for me. It's been, what, twelve years? Almost thirteen?*

"Why's that?" I asked.

"My girl left me. Correction, she cheated, and I kicked her out. Glad I found out before proposing." Jax pressed his lips in a thin line, then flitted his eyes toward me. "Sorry. It's not anyone's problem but mine. Don't mean to unload that on you when we just met."

How sad. "No, it's—"

"You ready?" Rob asked me, killing our conversation.

Ethan chimed in, tempering my irritation with Rob's harshness. "Thanks for coming in tonight, Jax. We'll be happy to have you as a regular. Next time, show up a little early and I'll let you pick a set of dice from the case, on me." He shook Jax's hand again.

Jax beamed. "Wow, that's awesome. I'd better head out. Rob, Tabby, real nice to meet you." He waved with a more suppressed smile as he turned to leave, then put an open hand over his head to protect from the rain.

"He's decent," Rob said, then grimaced when I glared at him. "What's *that* look for?"

"You know exactly what. Why were you such an asshole to him?" I folded my arms and stepped back to not be so close. "That gatekeeping *you don't fit in here* bullshit."

"Okay, you two," Ethan said, acting as peacekeeper, which he often did. "Personally, I think Jax is great. He lives by Golden Gate Park, but his roommate's never home. Seems temporary.

I'm thinking about asking him to move in upstairs so he's not as far away from everything. I could use the company since Carlos left."

Hawk sauntered past us. "I think Ethan has a crush on the new guy." He made kissy noises and squeaked before running out the door.

Gavin chased him. "Get back here, you! Later, everybody." They ran through the rain to the parking structure up the street.

I watched Ethan carefully, and he smirked on just one side while staring at the floor.

Oh, no. Not that.

"Come on. It's time to go home," Rob said, taking my hand.

I nodded and let him lead me away. The sooner I could forget about that night, the better.

ROB DROVE with the radio on and didn't try to chat with me. I was lost in thought and silent the whole ride back to my apartment. He pulled up to the sidewalk in front of my building and locked the door so I couldn't escape.

"You feeling okay?" he asked, sounding more soft and concerned than he had all day.

"Yeah. I'm fine, I think." *More lies. More hiding. I'm trapped in a new darkness.*

Rob rubbed my hand. "Tabby, look at me."

I turned but could barely see his olive eyes in the dark.

"I can tell something's wrong. You've been weirdly quiet all night."

"It's just..." I sighed, but Rob was being kind, like he genuinely cared about what I had to say and wasn't already forming a response in his mind before I finished. A nasty habit. "Did you happen to hear Jax say where he was from?"

Rob squinted. "No...?"

"He's from Colorado. Came from Denver. I used to live in Denver, remember?"

He chuckled. "Yeah, so?"

"It...brought back some memories, is all. I'm fine."

"So, you're upset because some dude showed up to D&D, and he's from Colorado?"

"No. It's not that." *It doesn't even scratch the surface. But I can't talk about this right now. It's better to just stuff it down.* "Jax isn't the issue; it's me. I have a lot on my mind, okay?"

"Babe, come 'ere." He graced the side of my face with the tips of his fingers, following the dark line of hair on my jaw. "I can stay over if you don't want to be alone."

I kissed his hand. "Thanks, but I have an early morning tomor-row and don't want to kick you out before you have to get ready."

"You know, I've been thinking about what you asked me last month." Rob closed in on me, leaning across the cocked emergency break to be in my space.

My heart pounded. Tonight was turning into a crossroads of my past life and my current one. *Are you remembering the same conversation?*

"Tabby, you were right. It would be nice not to have to sleep alone ever again." He kissed me softly, his bottom lip lingering against mine. "I wouldn't want to wake up with anyone else but you."

"Rob, really?" What a delightful distraction. My breath caught.

"Yeah." He nodded and pecked me again. "My lease is coming up in ten days. I'll start moving stuff in next week. More than a drawer this time."

I let out a prolonged sigh. "Can't wait."

"I love you, babe." Rob squeezed my earlobe when he kissed me once more. In a switch from his annoyance at my taking time to change, his affection brought me back to why I loved him in the first place. The gift of our future was exactly what I needed to bring me back to earth.

When I got to the door of the building, he beeped his horn

and winked at me, then drove to his apartment five miles away
—one of the last times he'd ever do so. Life wasn't what I
thought it would be when I was seventeen, but this was so much
better. Wasn't it?

satisfied

. . .

Jax

I DIDN'T STOP GRINNING the whole ride home and scream-sang at the top of my lungs to anything on the radio. I was high. Getting to know people in an environment that felt like it belonged to me was freeing. My body buzzed with adrenaline, and falling asleep at a reasonable hour wasn't going to happen.

The apartment should've been chilly because of the rain, but I hardly felt it. A hot shower turned my skin bright red before I crawled naked under the tan sheets. The ceiling must have been more interesting than ever, because my brain could not shut off, no matter how much I stared straight ahead.

My phone chattered at midnight with a text. I grinned again when I read the name. Ethan put himself in my phone as *Sauceror* after we joked that his favorite thing to do when not running the store was cooking.

> If you ever tire of living in no-man's-land, my roommate left last month.

> Apartment's above the shop. Think about it. Rent reasonable.

The night kept getting better. I couldn't pass up the opportunity, especially since it was close to my work, and now I had people to rely on.

> That's amazing, actually.
>
> I'll chat with my guy here about when I can go.

Nice. I'll pull my ad.

Have a good night.

I nodded to no one and put my phone down for a moment. Ethan was a stand-up guy, somebody I got along with instantly, and living with him would be easy. Gavin and Hawk were funny and flirtatious, different from any gay couple I knew, not that I could claim many. Cordelia was creative and funny. Annie was, too, in a quirkier way that said she was happy being by herself. I imagined she was the type of girl who made things out of resin and glitter for an online store and didn't give a damn about anyone's opinion.

Reliving the humor of the evening, I went back through tonight's text chain. One by one, we said our names and added links to social media accounts—I did, too, even though I hadn't looked since the breakup. The only person who didn't share a link also had the most curt message:

Rob here

I huffed to myself, reliving our uncomfortable conversation when the game started. He didn't like me; that much was obvious. He was also unlike anyone I'd ever met. Bulky and strong, like a short football player, his dark hair was cut short, receding at his temples. If Ethan hadn't said he was trans, I wouldn't have guessed it. His deep voice and five o'clock shadow were striking. He certainly acted like someone who, in the past, would've picked on me for my nerdy status. The fact he challenged me about whether or not I belonged painted his name in red.

Only one person responded after Rob. I hadn't noticed it earlier.

Jaxson, I'm Tabby.

My heart jumped. I squinted and read it again and again. Of all the things I'd said to the group, I couldn't remember if I'd mentioned how my first name was spelled weird. Most people assumed the traditional way, but Tabby got it, no question. Like Rob, Tabby was stronger than me—not a feat since I hated the gym and always had—even if he was more than a few inches shorter. His pirate-like goatee fully outlined his chin, dragging up his jaw on both sides. I was jealous of it since my light hair was virtually pointless to grow out. Some of my favorite titles made up the graphics of his clever book shirt, and I wondered if we had more in common.

For a moment, I looked at my hand. When we shook earlier, he didn't hesitate. His firm grip was familiar. Like home. He said I didn't know him. But no harm in checking, right?

I clicked open his social link and searched for clues about where he'd lived and if we'd met in passing. Nothing. Not so much as a mutual friend. As I stared at a happy picture of Tabby and Rob snuggling together in a park, my pathetic heart longed to have someone, too. Tabby's gaze, washed out by the glare of the sun, still pierced through me even in photos.

My stomach rushed. I plugged in my phone, burying all the sensations that welled in my body. New friends or not, I wasn't ready to put that part of myself on the line, and I couldn't fall back into a routine of falling for someone so fast. The last thing I needed was another broken heart. Least of all from someone who was already taken.

sin of silence

· · ·

Tabby

I BRUSHED my teeth and crawled in bed, cozy with the thought that I wouldn't spend many more nights alone. Moving in together was a conversation Rob and I'd had—and paused—a few times over the past year, but Rob slammed on the brakes every time we fought about bullshit that shouldn't have mattered. I'd long since stopped counting how often that happened, but Annie chronicled them all.

To top off his long list of excuses, Rob feared alienating his current landlord and wouldn't drop his lease prematurely; he said if things with me didn't pan out, he needed an exit strategy. It burned me when he said it. Why couldn't we charge ahead as if there was no other future?

He argued it was foolish not to think like practical adults. He had little tolerance or room for romance. Guess I didn't really need it; after all, we loved each other, and that was enough.

Any doubts I had before tonight were stuffed deep in my sock drawer, which was now overfilled and consolidated with the drawer for my binders. He might bring in a dresser of his own, but why not at least try to make room in mine?

I let the lift of the future keep me awake for too long and scrolled through my phone while listening to the rain. Just when sleepiness was about to win out, a notification sang to me.

A new online follower. Jax.

I sighed, at first shutting my eyes tight to his name. *Don't look. You'll never rest if you do. And if you dream of him now, he'll never go away. He has to go away. You're a new man. Get over it.*

I tried counting sheep, not that it ever worked. Focused more on the rain. What a bore.

Think of Rob. Think of Annie. Think of your packed schedule tomorrow. Think of…oh, fuck it.

With a hunger for details, I went through his pictures and read every comment. Research, really; if he was going to encroach on my new life, he had to be vetted. Didn't we share our social links for this purpose anyway? Our lives were wrapped up in two planes of existence: real life and the virtual. What someone did or said online now counted toward everything else. One slip up could reveal his unknown biases. Poster beware.

If Annie had been there, she wouldn't approve. But she wasn't around, so my digging continued.

In the few pictures he posted that weren't of hiking trails, a pretty girl wrapped in his arms smiled through the screen. Either he still had hope for them, or he hadn't purged her yet. A click to her page showed a new man at her side—a douchebag by all accounts in a backwards cap and shorts even though it was snowing. The caption read:

I love this picture of us from last year. Chris and I were meant to be. We should've known when we first met that we couldn't resist one another. So get ready for our wedding at Red Rocks next spring! #Wedding #Engaged #RedRocks #Coloradogirl #Loveforever #ChrisAndHeather

I groaned aloud for Jax and wondered how long they'd been together before she cheated, especially if this picture was an old one. Since Jax hadn't posted anything in over a month, I figured he probably stayed off the app to avoid seeing them together.

Until tonight, when he followed my account.

His goofy smile, the one I always loved, was brighter and more like the one I once knew the further I searched back in time on his profile. Jax's deep chestnut eyes were rich and dynamic on film, though the pictures were nothing compared to him in real life. No—in person, he was more beautiful than could ever be captured with a lens. So much for his online self mirroring reality. His humor, his meekness, the way he never spoke above anyone at the gaming table, even when it was his turn and Hawk wouldn't stop fussing—it was all too complex to understand with one picture. Jax was tall. Jax was bold. He was gorgeous and his lips were soft, and if he whispered in my ear, I'd lose myself all over again…

I shut my eyes and traveled back in time, touching myself while reliving what it once felt like to have *his* hands on me. Surely now, he'd be well-versed with what to do. Instead of fumbling and guessing what felt good, my body looked different, making things more obvious. He'd kiss down my torso and find the happy trail which led straight to the prize, without causing me any bullshit embarrassment for having hair at all. Jax said he didn't care back then, but I did; it was easier to hide by overcompensating. But times had changed. Now I was myself, groomed but not bare.

As I quickened the motion of my hand, his voice echoed in my mind—*I can't wait to make love to you*—the same words he whispered on his seventeenth birthday when we lost ourselves and became one for the first time. Jax wasn't merely a horny, reckless teen. He truly feared hurting me, so we made out for hours while his hands explored, and when I felt ready, I invited him inside. Even though he was anxious, we felt right together, and Jax hit me deep with equipment much more substantial than the rest of his body would suggest.

Unlike those days, I now appreciated the magic of the hormones raging through him. Oh, holy testosterone, thy temple is the strength within the loins of a good man. Course through me and grant me your power. Mark me in ways my body was denied. Let me feel the pull of undeniable libido.

Yet Jax was always more than admirable flesh to me. When we were done, collapsed beside each other, his passion gave way to the same sentiments that nearly convinced me to tell him the truth. He pecked at my jawline and breathed in my ear, "Hwa, don't ever let me go."

The sentiment of "teenage love"—a term that brought me anger in those days—now made more sense than ever before. Teen love was far from illegitimate; it was intense. Enough to make young kids take their own lives to spite their families, as the melodramatic Shakespeare once taught. Teen love was everything. It was timeless. It imprinted on those lucky enough to find a connection that saw past puberty.

Now, as an adult, I understood: my teenage love would always burn. I was living proof that my sweet Romeo had never gone away.

The end was coming. I felt it build and finally released, yelling his name because no one could hear me, and only I would have to live with guilt the next day. With my eyes shut tight and my legs stiff, I imagined beautiful Jax beside me. Fucking me, fucking him, filling each other in more ways than I could describe.

But like the disappointment I felt for myself, the climax was weak, as if my own body inflicted punishment against what I was thinking. I rushed to the bathroom to hop in a cold shower and wash myself clean of my thoughts, as if none of it happened at all. With my future with Rob finally pushing forward, Jax couldn't change anything. Our past was that—the past—nothing more. My teenage love had been buried this long. It could stand to stay that way.

Justifying my silence was easy. *I'm protecting both of them. Nobody has to know.*

break down

. . .

Tabby

JAX TOOK residency in my brain where he wasn't welcome. It was a week, but it felt like an eternity. Left to my own devices at night, my fantasies often took over and I ended up repenting quietly any time he crossed my mind. The showers still left me feeling sticky and I was sour for lying to people I loved. Whatever punishment the universe was planning for me, I deserved it.

Rob brought over a few things to start moving in, but it wasn't official yet. We still had two days until move-in. He didn't feel comfortable taking furniture from his place until the last day and said he wanted to do it in one big load with the movers. Couldn't argue with him; if I pushed him to move in faster, he would've backed out and said I was nagging too much.

My list of prior relationships was short, to say the least. I never cheated on anyone and never had the desire to. But this one-sided, private unfaithfulness tainted me. I was horse shit mixed with spit and vomit, topped with a picture of my old self —dolled up with blonde curls and fake plastic glasses—covered in the uncomfortable film of fakeness that was my femininity. A hole in the middle, black as a matte and soul-sucking void of deep space, symbolically cut its way through the pile of refuse that was my existence. If Jax ever saw my real left eye, he'd know me for sure. After all, it still had the key to his heart.

I used to look forward to Thursday game nights. Today, I dreaded it. If Ethan really did have a crush on Jax, nothing could be said against it. How could I disapprove of wonderful Jax without oozing my own jealousy everywhere? And he was bi, too. Unreal. The mere possibility of seeing Ethan's shy smile against Jax's neck ran through my thoughts all day, because surely, he'd pull Jax into his chest and kiss up to his ear. They'd stare into one another, and Ethan would tickle Jax's cheeks with his rough beard on purpose.

After all, that's what *I* wanted to do. Charm the charmer.

I am so incredibly, undeniably, irreversibly fucked right now.

I flogged myself internally with curses and slapped my thighs hard to get back to reality. Rob's tangible commitment would have to conquer the lingering teenage hope that was Jax.

The day's patients at the eye center were more complex than normal, and I welcomed the distraction. I spent lunch scrolling through Insta blankly but couldn't resist going back through my notifications to find Jax's profile.

Since he'd followed me, the pictures of his former girlfriend were gone. *So, you've purged her. Glad to see you're ready to let go of someone who hurt you.* I ignored the fact that I was indirectly breaking my long-lost promise to him by being silent.

At quarter 'til five, the rest of the staff checked out for the day, leaving me alone with my growing dread for game night at six. My office phone rang while I debated going home early. I tapped my Bluetooth headset while scrolling through my unfinished charts.

"This is Dr. Ross."

Rob's voice was distant and scratchy on the phone, like he had almost no connection. "Hey, you're going to Ethan's after work, right?"

"That was the plan, but I'm thinking I might not go. Getting a migraine." My fingers were crossed that the lie wouldn't make one manifest.

"Aw, you should, though. You've been on edge all week, and I want you to get out. Time alone makes you sad."

I smirked. "I love that you know that about me."

"Yeah, well, I kinda love you a little." He chuckled. "Since I need to work late today, I don't know if I'll make it. Probably won't even get to leave until seven."

"That sucks. I'm sorry you have to stay late."

"I'll be alright."

"I promise I'll only have half as much fun without you. I'll tell you if Hawk has another name change this week."

His warm laughter soothed my rough edges. "You better. Love you, babe."

"Love you, too. Drive safe."

Once closer to game time, I hummed to myself and packed up my desk for the day, locking the office deadbolts before walking to my car. Once it came into view, I froze.

The passenger side door was ajar. *Fuck.*

While not the first time something like this happened, it was always frightening, nevertheless. I gingerly approached my silver Toyota, considering how I must've left it unlocked by mistake. My windows looked intact, at least. My coworkers had all left and I didn't know anyone who owned the other cars, so it had to have happened recently. The small lot between my office and the creepy alleyway discouraged random tourists from using the space over one of the parking structures under Union Square.

Once I was sure no one snuck inside the vehicle and accounted for everything tossed around from my torn-apart center console, save for a few bucks I kept around for random shit, I slammed the open door and sat inside to get things started.

Don't be dead. Don't be dead. My battery wasn't in the best shape, and Rob worried something like this would happen soon, especially since I was prone to accidentally leaving the lights on all night. He was certain one day the battery would be completely shot and not even a jump would revive it. To my chagrin, I twisted the key to a discouraging ticking noise, as if tiny creatures under the hood tapped away at two sticks to try and fire the engine.

"Come on...*come on*...it hasn't been that long," I growled, pausing for a moment before trying again. "Please start for me." Yet pleading meant nothing to the machine.

I stared at my phone. *This is a sign not to go to game night. Can't call Rob, he's working late and can't come get me. I'd get a tow, but what if all I need is a jump? Who's around here?* With all my coworkers gone for the day and the sunlight quickly fading, reaching out to my nearest buddy was the safest option.

I rarely called the game store itself, but Ethan wasn't the type to pull out his cell phone during business hours without cause. The ringing on the other end couldn't drown out my anxious heart. *Pick up, dude...*

"Dragon's Lair," he said quickly, which somehow brought me back to Earth.

"Ethan, hey. It's Tabby. You wouldn't happen to have twenty minutes to come give me a jump at work, would you?"

"Seriously?" He let out a long sigh. "I can't just leave the store. I haven't had help since Carlos moved out."

"Damn. Okay, well, thanks anyway, I guess."

"Wait, are you stranded at work? Can you call an Uber?"

"It's not the ride thing; it's more diagnostic. My car might not be shot, and if it needs a tow or a new battery, I'd rather know that now than wait until tomorrow. But I'll call triple-A, don't worry about it."

"No, hold on. Gimme a sec."

This is stupid. I shouldn't have bugged him at work. While I waited, too embarrassed to hang up, I put the phone in my drink holder and tried the key again. *Tick, tick, tick.* Nothing.

"Tabby, you there?"

"Yup."

"You park in that lot behind your office, right? Near Union Square?"

"Uh-huh. Same place you picked me up that one time."

"Awesome. Just texted some..."—the phone cut out for a few seconds, which made me curse again in frustration—"...give you a jump. He'll be there in ten."

"Wow, thank you." Weight lifted off my shoulders and I put my hands together in a thankful prayer to whoever was watching, even to Ethan for coming through.

"Your knight in shining armor's on his way. He's driving a little black Mazda. Says he's got cables, too, if you need them."

"As long as the guy who broke in earlier didn't take mine, it's all good. But that's great anyway."

"If your car needs a tow, he can bring you here after, so you get a break from thinking about it. Sound good?"

"I guess. I mean..." *He'd take me to game night?* "My phone cut out a minute ago. Who is this guy again?"

"You met him last week. Jax works around the corner from you. Look, I have to go, people waiting."

My heart gasped, painfully pausing in my chest. "Jax? What? Ethan, wait—"

"See you later, Tabby." *Click.*

I slammed my hands against the steering wheel and yelled, "Fuck," loud enough to scare the pigeons on the rail in front of me. *Jax is on his way. Too late to reverse my call for help.*

The internal hole of my self-image swallowed me, and I laid the seat back to sink down in my car, with vain hopes that Jax would arrive, not find me, and drive away. Ten minutes never lasted so long. I didn't scroll through my Insta or watch videos; the silence was self-inflicted punishment for the past week of runaway fantasies. As far as I was concerned, I was unworthy of everyone around me, and Jax's willingness to rescue a stranger amplified my guilt.

While I wallowed, a quiet tap on my driver's-side window startled me.

"Hey there," Jax said, waving with some cables in his hand. "Need some help?"

"Yup." I righted my seat and popped the trunk lever, avoiding his gaze at all costs.

He went to the front and opened everything, not even waiting for me. "Won't start?"

"Mm-hmm." I glanced inside his car—pristine, not so much as a coin visible in the cupholders. Smart, especially for someone new to the city. It was why, after so many years, I knew to only keep a couple bucks in mine and not have a detachable stereo. "I was a dumbass and left the door unlocked after lunch, and somebody went through looking for stuff. Left it open, which killed my battery, I think."

"Eh, shit happens, not your fault. Let's give it a try." He connected the cables effortlessly to my car and his. Even his engine was clean and dust-free.

"New car, huh?" I asked, admiring the leather interior.

"New to me, anyway. I miss my Subi, but you can't do a manual on these hills." He started his car and stayed inside, letting it run for what felt like an eternity before rolling down his passenger window. "Alright, Tabby, go for it."

Thank God, this will be over fast. I turned the key and my stomach dropped. *Tick, tick, tick.*

"Anything?" he asked.

"No. Dammit, the whole thing is fried."

Jax got out and rolled his hand for me to try again while he listened to the engine.

Tick, tick, tick.

He hissed. "Yeah, I don't think it's your battery. Might be

your alternator or your starter. Probably would've happened even if your door wasn't open, man."

I groaned and put my forehead to my steering wheel. *Seriously? Is my self-hatred not punishment enough? The universe had to take my car down with me?*

"Have a place to tow it?"

"Yeah." I stepped out and slammed the door.

"Don't fret. I'll hang out with you 'til the truck arrives."

"Thanks." Grumbling the whole time, I called AAA like I should've in the first place.

JAX MERCIFULLY LET me brew on my own while we waited. To pass the time, he sat in his car and talked on the phone with a smile on his face. I sat in mine and played a knockoff version of Super Mario. It was better than awkward silence between us, at least.

The tow truck came and went, and Jax rubbed his hands together when my car was out of sight. "Alright, you ready to head over to Ethan's?"

"Yeah." I ran my hand through my hair and resisted the urge to pull it all out. "I appreciate the ride. And the rescue. All of it."

"Not a problem, man. Sorry I couldn't fix it." He touched my shoulder. "You gonna be okay?"

"I just feel like an idiot. Let's go." My lie was so good, I almost believed it. *Sure, I'm okay. Not a single thing wrong with me. Nuh-uh.*

Jax whistled to himself as we cut through the thick evening traffic. He wasn't fazed by surprise pedestrians or the construction that closed off every other street. If he was annoyed, he didn't show it. The man was even more of a saint than I remembered.

Dammit.

We were stopped at the same light for two cycles because the traffic ahead wouldn't move, and it cracked his façade a little.

"You know, I always thought Californians drove like shit because they didn't know what they were doing. Now I think they escape to my state, so they don't have to deal with this shit anymore."

"I think you've got it, Jax," I said with a chuckle.

"I hate the cars that stop in the middle of the street the most. Like, 'Oops, here I am, making a delivery in the middle of the day, and there's nowhere to park. I'll just throw on my blinkers and hope you can get around me.' I don't like driving in the left lane, but you almost have to in this city."

We turned to each other at the same moment and smiled, breaking the invisible wall between us. Traffic moved again.

"Besides the shitty commute, how are you liking it?" I asked.

"Eh." He signaled *so-so* with his wrist side to side. "There are some nice things about it, but I miss home. The food here sucks. It's too crunchy."

I scoffed. "The food? You come from Denver, and you're complaining about the food? And what do you mean, *too crunchy*?"

"Crunchy's a word that means, like, modern hippie. It feels pretentious and unfamiliar. Everything's organic and super healthy, which generally means it doesn't actually taste good. I'm a dude, not a horse. Don't even get me started on how Californians are afraid of spice. Nobody's even heard of green chili here, and all the Mexican food is entirely different, too. I might be attached to my dad's favorite restaurant, but I figured I would be able to find *something* comparable." Jax eyed me from the side of his face. "People give Casa Bonita a lot of shit, but if you've never had a sopapilla drenched in honey, you haven't lived."

It never occurred to me how much food changed across the country when I moved around with Mom as a teen, but Jax talked about these simple comforts as if he lost an old friend. Maybe he did; after all, isn't that the most basic necessity when we're on our own? Finding anything that makes us feel at home?

"Scrubs, huh?" he asked, waving over my solid blues. "What do you do?"

"I'm an optometrist." Saying it made me smile, like it always did. "I love what I do."

"So does that mean you're a doctor?" Jax lit up. "That's really cool."

"Yes, and thanks. I hate the scrubs, though; I would rather wear one of my tacky shirts, but it's easier to pass this way. Blessing in disguise for a trans guy, I guess."

He laughed. "I get it. But the book shirt was certainly a winner last week."

You remember what I wore last week? I tried not to let the thought consume me, but I was flattered, if not a little fluttery. "I appreciate that. Rob's not so much of a fan."

Jax nodded and said nothing.

You don't like him. After last week, can't say I blame you.

"So, you know all about eyes, right? Weird diseases and stuff?"

"Mm-hmm. Everybody has two of them, you know." I thought my joke was pretty clever, and I let it calm my nerves as we reached our destination.

We passed the game shop on our way to the parking structure at the end of the street, and Jax rolled down his window to grab a ticket. He was quiet through the process of finding a good space but cleared his throat before turning the car off. "You know, I had an old friend with a weird eye thing. Maybe I could talk to you about it sometime."

I squinted. "Okay...?"

"A thing that makes the pupil look bigger than it should, like it's broken or has an extra piece. Coloboma, I think."

Shit. "What about it?"

"Oh, just wondering how rare that kinda thing is. I've never met anybody else who had one...not like *she* did, anyway."

My ears rang. *So, you do think about me.*

When I didn't answer, Jax pressed his lips in a line. "I'm sure Rob's waiting for you, right?"

The car suffocated me. The walls closed in. "Right." I jumped out and straightened my clothes, then texted Rob as we walked to the shop to alleviate some of my internal grief.

My car died.

I know you're tired, but please come tonight.

I need you.

confess

. . .

Tabby

WALK STRAIGHT AHEAD. *Don't engage. Don't —*

"Did I do something to upset you?" Jax asked before we got to the Dragon's Lair door. "You're like...hot and cold."

"No." I softened a little, ashamed of myself. "Shit, dude. I'm sorry. It's been a tough day. Rob's moving in and he might not come tonight, so I'm thinking about how I'll get home."

He nodded. "Makes sense. Congrats though. I figured you two already lived together."

"Not yet." *Hopefully the universe won't ruin that for me, too.*

"Well, where's your place? I don't mind giving you a ride." His raised brows and kind offer hid no obvious ulterior motive.

"Way far from here, really. Northwest, Outer Sunset."

"I don't know where that is. Near Golden Gate Park at all?"

I nodded.

"I live out there, too. At least, I do for a few more weeks. I'm moving in with Ethan next month." Jax stepped ahead and shook the door, which was already locked since we were just past closing. "Who knows? Maybe we'll see each other around now that I know your work's close by. Nice to have friends outside of my office."

"Yeah." I pocketed my hands and gave up my quest to be

cold to him. *Might as well proceed as if you're not going away.* Jax was becoming a part of my new life, whether I liked it or not. The least I could do was be nice. "I think I'd like that. Could do lunch or something. I'm sure I can find you more familiar cuisine."

Jax smiled at me like he meant what he said; he genuinely wanted to get to know me. No hesitation, in spite of my wishy-washy attitude. The gesture was familiar, and I knew it well. After all, the same approach worked on me at fifteen: find one thing in common and run with it.

My body flooded with heat, so much so I became itchy all over. I scratched my goatee as Ethan opened the door for us.

"You found him, nice. Come on, guys." Ethan patted us both on the back heartily. "Is Rob gonna make it, Tabby?"

"Don't know yet. Guess we'll find out."

AN HOUR into the game campaign, my text tone chirped for a message from Rob.

> Did you leave your lights on again?
>
> Sorry, going home to pack. Tell Ethan I'll be back next week.

His accusatory message set me off. *That's it? I tell you I need you, and that's all you have to say?* I balled my fists, too angry to respond, though I wanted to yell at the top of my lungs how he could've at least given me the benefit of the doubt that the car problem wasn't somehow my fault.

"Tabby, it's your turn," Cordelia said, snapping her fingers to get my attention.

"Whatever. I need to take a break. Hawk, roll for me."

He scoffed. "Um, it's *Cyan* this week, Tabby. Come on, you're usually good at this."

"Maybe I'm not in the mood right now, okay?" I stood for the soda machine and paced in front of it while tapping the aluminum lid of my can. I sucked in and counted to ten before releasing, then did it again—an old exercise I learned from my therapist years ago to keep myself in check.

Heavy boots squeaked toward me. I didn't open my eyes.

"Annie, not now."

"Enough of this," she said, getting a soda for herself and tapping along the same way I did. "Tell me what's going on."

"I can't."

"Bullshit."

"No, you don't get it." I opened my eyes and met hers. "I seriously can't tell anybody. If I say it out loud, it's too real."

She cocked a brow at me, then opened the bathroom door. "You. In."

"What?"

"You heard me. Get in. Now. Shoo." Waving her hands, Annie ushered me in and followed, locking the door behind us.

I put the unopened can in my scrubs pocket and folded my arms. "I don't know why you think being in here will be any different."

"Tabby, I'm not an idiot. You were moody as shit last week, and you're moody as shit now."

"Swear to God, if you're about to ask me if I'm on my fucking period, I'm gonna flip out on you." I kept my wide gaze fixed on hers, so she knew I was serious. "That isn't it, and what I'm going through right now is just...too strange to even put words to."

She went to the sink and turned the water on, letting it run to drown out our voices to anyone who might hear us outside. "Try."

Trapped. Why can't I chew off my leg? I turned around and talked to the corner. "Rob's moving in."

"Oh?" She stepped a little closer behind me. "That's a good thing, right?"

"Yeah. I mean, it's what I wanted six months ago. It's what I thought I wanted since we got together. But tonight…he worked late and isn't coming here. That's all fine and good, but my car broke down. Got a ride here from Jax, and now he'll have to take me home."

"Hmm." Her pause and otherwise lacking response said, *and you're bitching because…?*

"The thing is, I told Rob I needed him to be here, and he didn't care." I shook my head and looked down to my rainbow Crocs, which were comfortable but obnoxious, the same way Rob sometimes described me. "He isn't here to help me, but Jax is. It's not fair."

"Well, at least Jax is a nice guy, right? Can't be that bad if Ethan wants him to move in."

I kicked the wall. "Does Ethan want more than that?"

"More than what?"

"More with Jax. You know what I mean." I sniffed and wiped a runaway tear from my cheek. "Does Ethan, you know, *want* him?"

"Tabby?" She put her kind, soft hand on my shoulder. "Why would you care about something like that? Is Jax a bad guy?"

"No. Dammit, he's amazing." I buried my face.

Her firm tone was new to me. "Okay, I know you're not sneakin' around on Rob. What the hell is going on here?"

I took a few deep breaths and whispered, "I knew him."

"Knew…who?"

"Jax. I knew him in high school."

She cleared her throat. "Knew him, as in, had a class together and he doesn't remember you, or knew him, as in, he was a homophobe, and you don't want him near you?"

"Neither. Knew him, as in, he took me to prom." I leaned against the wall and openly cried. "Knew him, as in, he took my virginity. Knew him, as in, I broke his heart. Knew him—"

"Oh, my God. Tabby, are you serious?" Panic and surprise laced her voice.

I met her gaze again, this time through a film of tears. "He was my first love. I don't think I ever fell out of love with him." My hands shook and squeezed fists of nothingness. "What the fuck, right?"

Her mouth gaped. For an uncomfortable minute, her internal wheels spun on high gear. "You knew him before—"

"Yup."

"And now he doesn't—"

"Nope." I turned to look in the mirror and splashed my face in the running water. "So much for Rob thinking I'm not doing enough to transition. Add hormones and *voila*, I'm a new man. Even my high school sweetheart doesn't know me."

She looked at me in the mirror the same way Mom did when I gave her my new name. "I think *that's* the real issue here. Rob still tells you you're not doing enough?"

I shook my head. "What can I even say?"

"You tell him you're happy with who you are, and if he's not happy with who he is, that's his problem." She twisted my body to put both hands on my face. "You are a gorgeous man, Tabby. And I wouldn't lie."

I chuckled and wiped my eyes. "Thanks."

"You have to tell Jax the truth. Don't wait."

"And break his heart *again*? I'm not single. The Jax I knew wanted a future with me. I can't offer him that, so what's the point?" Fresh sadness crept up underneath all my frustration. "I don't know where to begin."

"Just begin with *you*. He likes you. I can see it on his face." Annie shrugged. "Who knows? Maybe he already suspects something and doesn't know how to ask, ya know?"

"Well, that would be a dream, wouldn't it? Some cheesy chick flick. Meet years later when one has amnesia and fall in love all over again." I smiled at the thought and nodded to myself. "*That* would be classic Jax. He's a hopeless romantic. He used to be, anyway."

"Ick." Annie snickered and stuck her tongue out at me, then

brushed back her long brown hair over the shoulders of her omnipresent black hoodie.

"I love Rob," I said, more to myself than to her. *Am I trying to convince myself of something?* The past week threw me into a veritable whirlwind of confusion. If the man I loved couldn't be depended on, what kind of future did we have ahead? And on the other hand, if I loved Jax but became someone else, did that make our promise null and void?

"I know you do." She never thought Rob was good for me, but dammit if she wasn't supportive of what I wanted. "Come on, let's get you cleaned up and finish the game. Oh, and little *Cyan* out there will throw a fit if you get his name wrong again."

"Can I call him Turquoise instead?"

We laughed, and Annie recovered all the bits that would turn me into a reasonable human, capable of interaction that wasn't topped with rage. While I had Mom and always would, my little found family with Annie at the head was all I'd ever need to get me through.

stirring

. . .

Jax

WITH ROB out for the night and me still gaining my bearings, our Battle Royale D&D night ended much like the last one did. Victorious Cyan hooted as he raised his arms above in celebration.

"Oh, yes. That's right, bitches." He flipped all of us off at the table, but did so with an effortless, beaming grin. "Tabby, that's what you get for not having your lucky ring."

I laughed along with everyone else, though his reference meant nothing to me.

"Shut up. I didn't get to go home before showing up here," Tabby said, flushing red and avoiding all eyes.

"Don't think I didn't notice that you didn't have it last week, either, and all your rolls sucked." Cyan kissed Gavin hard, then yelled over all of us once more, "Behold, I'm the new king of the castle, and Tabby can suck it."

Tabby stood and did a small bow in his direction. "Oh, Lord Cyan, great and awesome sorcerer supreme. I doth surrender my position to you until we meet again, sir."

The group dissipated in laughter, and I worked out a few logistics with Ethan for my move-in plans. Fortunately for both of us, my current roommate was pretty loaded on his own and wasn't upset that I'd be leaving, especially when I told him he could always send me a text if he was out of town, and I'd be happy to water the plants in his absence. No hard feelings and an easy change.

Annie stood by Tabby at the door when I was done with Ethan. She pushed him toward me.

"Still okay with giving me a ride home?" he asked, with a much less anxious disposition than he had when we arrived at the store.

"You bet. Annie, you need a ride, too?"

"Cordelia and I always share an Uber, but thanks, Jax." She opened her arms for a quick, barely there hug. "It's been nice getting to know you a little." Her high-pitched voice and the way she kept her hands hidden within her sleeves, close to her body, reminded me of a mouse. Adorable and kind, with a button nose that was hard to resist booping. She felt like a sister of sorts.

Having a girl around who couldn't make things complicated was exactly what I wanted in my life after what happened with Heather. "You, too," I said. I meant it.

Without rain this time, there was no rush in heading up the hill to the garage. Tabby walked at my side instead of behind me, though he still stared at his shoes instead of engaging. He was a mystery, like he wanted to talk but wasn't quite sure what to say.

"Do you feel it, too, dude?" I asked, taking a shot.

"Hmm?" He eyed me with the side of his face.

"I don't know. This, like, *weird* sense that we know each other. I feel like you're one of my people." We paused at the crosswalk just enough to look both ways. "Know what I mean by that? *People?*"

Tabby stammered, "I...well, Jax..."

"My dad believes in karmic connections that we can't explain. Do you buy that kinda thing?"

"I guess, I—" His exasperated, long sigh was an unvoiced

pause. Kept him from talking in circles. "I know what you're talking about. It's comfortable. Can I say that? Comfortable."

"Yeah. Good way to describe it." I smiled at him, though my head said more than I admitted aloud. *You fit with me somehow, and I don't know why. Why do I have an urge to reach for your hand?*

Tabby hid a shy smirk of his own as we approached the car. His hair, while not very long, shined with soft waves, and I wondered what it smelled like. What *he* smelled like. Was it a scent I couldn't detect that drew me to him? He wasn't even trying, and I couldn't stop staring.

Embarrassed with myself, I fumbled with my keys, trying to find the right button in the dark.

"Jax, you okay?"

"Mm-hmm. No problem." I was victorious with a random button press, though I also opened the trunk by accident and sheepishly slammed it closed as Tabby got in the passenger seat. Once we were out of the garage, he showed me a few shortcuts from east to west on the way back to his place.

It was quiet. Too quiet. Awkward, thick air, unspoken words quiet. I whistled just to cut the tension a little bit.

"Here," he said, pointing to a short building which thankfully wasn't too far from my own place. On the way, in fact.

I pulled up beside the front door, hugging the sidewalk. Even though it was late, he didn't get out right away. Tabby glanced up to his building, then stared at his hands, which he twisted in pretzels while he spoke. "So, your friend with the coloboma… did she tell you anything about it?"

His question was unexpected, not that I hoped for one thing or another. I welcomed some conversation. "No, actually. It made her unique, but she hated it. Tried to cover it with fake glasses. Personally, I thought it was fascinating, so I focus on eyes a lot when I meet people. Haven't seen another one yet."

He nodded for a moment. "They aren't something you see every day. Those who have them can be very self-conscious. But when it comes to looking at people's eyes first, we definitely have that in common."

Finally, something real about you. "Probably 'cause you're an eye doctor, right?"

Tabby's genuine smile departed from the tight-lipped expression he kept most of the night. "Part of it, yeah. But I've always liked eyes. Eyes can tell you a lot about a person. Look into people's eyes enough, it'll make you psychic."

"Ooh," I said, waving my fingers. "Tabby can see the future. No wonder you're so mysterious."

He laughed with his whole face and let his deep voice bounce around the car. It lifted my heart like the swell of a song. Joy. Ease. Comfortable, like he said. Only more than that. Wanted. Needed. Missing from my life.

I turned the car off and relaxed a little, settling in for conversation since the only thing waiting for me at home was a silent row of plants. "Tell me about yourself."

"Me?" He pointed to his chest like he was surprised.

"No, I was talking to myself." I cocked a brow. "Yes, *you,* Tabby." I flicked his nametag. "I mean, Dr. Ross. Tell me something stupid. Something you might say at work when doing icebreakers."

"Shit." He sighed and folded his arms. "Um...I don't know. My favorite animal at the zoo is a peacock."

Chuckling, I remembered the big ones at the Denver Zoo that always hung out behind the giraffe house. "Why, you like to chase them?"

"Hell yeah. I have a collection of peacock feathers. Everything else at the zoo is a bonus. Except for the bug house. I *love* the bug house."

"Wow. Too bad we're not in Denver. You'd probably go apeshit for the Butterfly Pavilion." I hissed in a breath through my teeth. "Your answer's too good. Nothing I say will beat that."

"Oh, come on. You're new to the city. What did you tell your coworkers when you first came here?" He settled even more, unbuckling his seatbelt, giving no indication that he itched to leave.

"Uh, 'Hi, my name's Jaxson Grady, and I'm superstitious.' That's always a good conversation starter." I lifted the lid to my center console and displayed its organized contents with an open hand. "Behold, my small collection of lucky pennies."

Tabby burst with laughter. "My God. Are they organized by year?"

"No, 'cause if I did *that*, I'd become obsessed with finding a valuable one. Talk about a complete waste of time."

While watching him poke through the clutter of my private car stash, another burning question came to mind.

"Hey, how'd you know how my name was spelled, anyway?"

"Hmm?" He didn't fully lift his head, too distracted by putting the coins in order.

"When we met last week, and you texted me. You spelled my name right, with an X. How'd you know that?"

Tabby looked up and didn't blink, like he was caught in a trap. More stammers at first, but his reason made sense enough. "I just...happen to know someone who spells it that way. Guess it was stuck in my head."

"Ah. I forgot, we're in California. I bet you see all sorts of bullshit names out here."

He nodded, then went back to investigating the coin collection.

Five minutes became ten. Ten became twenty. A half hour. More. By 11 o'clock, a light drizzle made the windows fog inside. We discussed the college years. Our passions. Plans for the future. The state of modern politics, and what country we'd escape to if right-wingers went too rogue.

Rob must've been a sore spot. Tabby didn't mention him much, and even cringed when I asked about him. Odd, since when I met the pair, they played footsie the whole night and I saw nothing amiss on Tabby's socials. On the other hand, he didn't ask me about Heather even though I'd mentioned her before, so I chalked it up to him not wanting to make me feel bad for my failed relationship. It was a relief in a way to keep that subject private.

"What about your folks?" I asked, relaxing my seat all the way back so I could look out through the roof at the moon.

Tabby did the same on the passenger side, getting flat. "Well, my dad's gone. Died in an accident when I was ten."

My heart hurt for him, the same way it did whenever one of friends said they lost a parent. Jamie was the first one I knew, and it was getting more common. Losing his dad so young, too? Brutal. "I can't even imagine that, Tabby. I'm so sorry."

The moonlight above streaked across his right cheek, high-lighting him, which enhanced the empathetic tug inside me that said he didn't deserve to know that kind of pain. He shrugged. "It feels unreal now. It's been almost twenty years. Mom's still not over it. For that reason, she panics if I'm ever late to our Friday night dinners."

"That's sweet you see her so often. So, she's local?"

"Yeah. She's just north of the city in Marin—a real hoity-toity place. Her real-estate business boomed after we moved." He repositioned like he didn't want to talk about her anymore. "Anyway, what about your parents? They still together?"

"Afraid not."

"Seriously?" He raised up a little on his left shoulder. "They're divorced?"

"You seem shocked, like it couldn't be true." I stretched, cracking my back a little, which helped me not focus on the sting of talking about my parents. "Funny thing is, it came as a surprise to Dad and me. Mom went off the deep end five years ago—she wasn't always the most stable person to begin with, but something inside her head snapped. She met this young guy, barely older than me, and ran off with him."

"Mid-life crisis in cougar town?"

I snorted. "I'm stealing that. Dad will love it."

With more concern in his voice, Tabby whispered as if Mom could hear. "How'd he take it? Your dad?"

"Awful. Completely devastated." I covered my eyes and saw Dad in my mind, begging me to try and talk some sense into Mom before she married Brian. The tears he shed were acid to me, burning deep, and I'd never forget them. "I love my dad. He worships Mom. Asks me about her all the time. I talked to him on the phone earlier while we were waiting for the tow. He's handling things fine now, but I miss him a lot. Miss spending time with him, shooting the shit, drinking beer, going to his regular burrito spot."

Tabby hummed a quiet note. "If I had to guess, I'd say your dad was the kind of guy who would sneak treats to you and your friends growing up. Drive you anywhere and always be willing to come get you, no matter how late it was or where you were."

I grinned as far as I could stretch my lips, remembering times in my teen years when those exact scenarios played out more than once. "You nailed it for sure. And Dad's always been really passionate about teaching me how to be a good guy. He's completely hopeless when it comes to love. Everything I know about being a charmer comes from him. Probably my tendency to dive headfirst without thinking, too."

"Oh, so you're the romantic type, eh?"

"Completely. I'm not as bad as Dad, but I give him a run for his money sometimes. I like to think I'm a little more practical, but his fantasies are appealing."

Tabby bumped my shoulder. "What do you mean?"

I looked at him with my brows up, waiting for him to tell me he was joking. Why would he care about my fantasies? Did I trust him enough to tell him these things, or was he about to tease me for it later?

But something about his gaze, even in the dark, was soft and inviting. Trustworthy. Honest. Meant me no harm.

I sighed. "Dad believes in love at first sight. The power of first loves. He and my mom got together when they were teenagers. Sure, she's living this weird life with Brian right now, but Dad is one hundred percent convinced she'll come back to him." I looked away to keep from appearing too wistful myself. "He believes my first love will come back to me, too."

Tabby left a pause on purpose, as if digesting what I said before responding, "What?"

"I believe in some of the things my dad says. But that?" I shrugged. "It's a little too crazy for me."

Tabby pressed the button on the side of his seat, lifting the back so he'd be upright again. I took his signal and did the same, figuring it was time to head out anyway.

He didn't budge. Tabby stared at me, an intense stare that said *pay attention* and *Be brave* to me and to himself, respectively. His lips moved, but not clearly. "Wha...wh-wh—"

I tipped my right ear toward him. "I'm sorry, I can't quite hear you."

His mouth hung open for a moment, then he cleared his throat. "Wh-when do you need to be at work tomorrow? It's getting super late."

"Shit, I think you're right." I turned on the car and saw the clock—11:53 p.m. "Oh, man. I need to be in by nine."

"Work starts at eight thirty for me."

I nodded. "Wait, do you need a ride again?"

He froze. The wheels in his mind might as well have made his ears smoke. "Fuck."

"Don't panic, I've gotcha covered." I shook his shoulder. "What do you think, seven thirty, same place?"

"Jax, are you sure? I don't want you to—"

"Come on, we're both going the same direction. Might as well go together. I figure after I drop you off, it'll take me a little bit to get to my office, so the time between works out fine."

He took a deep breath and released it, reluctantly accepting my offer with a bob of his head. "Okay. Rob will get me after work when I hear about my car. Honestly, it's *him* who should be taking me to work, not you. But that's his fault for not even bothering to make sure I was okay after my car died."

The new mention of Rob halted everything. *What the hell kinda guy wouldn't step up to the plate here?* It was none of my business, so I carried on as if Tabby hadn't mentioned him. "Sounds like a plan." I presented a closed fist for him to bump against in our deal.

As his surprisingly soft skin met mine, I couldn't focus on anything around me. No sound. Dense haze. *Am I tired?* My head was heavy, and I forced it to look up and straight ahead.

Tabby's dark lashes curled upward. They could've been fake, but I saw no obvious line the way Heather's stuck out in the corners. His were too perfect. His goatee was full, but it looked soft, not scratchy or wiry, like he took care of it. I wanted to test my hypothesis and brush against it.

"You okay?" he asked when I stopped moving.

The late hour brought a punch-drunk attitude to my brain. "You have great eyes, Tabby."

He blinked in quick succession—not like a flirting girl, but in surprise. "What did you just say?"

"No, I mean it." I chuckled and smiled to play it off as a normal compliment, but it wasn't. Told myself it meant nothing, but it didn't. *What the hell am I doing?* I couldn't stop. Words spilled from my lips without control. "I can't tell if it's the shape, the color, or what. Something about 'em—"

Tabby rushed his interruption, like he was hoping to capture the mood in my next answer. "What do you see in me? When you look in my eyes, what do you think you know?"

"Like, that psychic thing you were talkin' about?" I tipped my head side to side. My gaze danced over his face, which was still illuminated by the moon above in a blue cast that put us in an underwater cave. I was suddenly aware of my quick breath, half the pace of my racing heartbeat. His scent wafted over me in a way I hadn't noticed before: sweet, musky, and sandalwood, maybe? Unfamiliar familiarity. Like the bridge. Like New York.

I feel like I know you. Like you've been missing all my life, and I finally found you.

But I couldn't say that. That would've been crazy. "In your eyes, I see...a man who wants to be seen beyond the surface. Someone who doesn't have hidden motives. An honest guy. Somebody who should be more secure than he is." I caught myself chewing my lower lip before I finished. "I see somebody I wanna get to know."

"Wow." He sniffed a couple times.

Are you teary? Or is it late for you, too?

Tabby reached. His thumb barely stroked the side of my right cheek as he investigated, reading my mind in the dark. "Jax, I see a guy who hopes to make connections. Couldn't be mean if he tried. A guy who loves his family and wears aviator sunglasses. His favorite color is light ashy blue. Simple taste, simple wants, simple man. Somebody I can see getting close to."

Heat washed out from the center of my chest in all directions until I felt it in my fingertips and toes. "Impressive."

"What can I say? I pay attention."

"One thing, how did you know about the aviators? I'm guessing the color of my shirt—"

"Jax?" he said, leaning over the empty cup holders and center console toward me, curling his finger for me to listen.

I wanted him near me and hoped his signal was an invitation. The jump in my chest was familiar and terrifying. Tipping my ear, I closed the gap between us, hoping for more than a quiet secret.

Tabby whispered at the same moment I closed my eyes, "You have a pair in your console."

I snorted, killing whatever mood had been building. "Christ, you had me goin' there."

He laughed along with me, clapping as he backed away. "You thought I was really psychic there for a minute. Some kinda trans superpower."

Psychic? No, pretty sure— I stopped myself from even considering it and tried to make a joke instead. "Hey, how would I know? All this is new to me."

We filled the car with more hot breath, which fogged the insides completely. Tabby wrote his name on the passenger window, then made a small footprint with the side of his fist and five dots for toes—just like the ones my friends did on the school bus windows long ago.

"Please don't tell your boyfriend I stared into your eyes until midnight," I said, half-teasing and half concerned that Rob would come after me if he thought anything happened between us. "I have no doubt he could kick my ass if he wanted to."

Tabby shook his head. "I won't. I really should get going, though."

"Yeah. Get to bed. I'll be here bright and early."

He got out of the car and jogged to the door of the building through the cold humidity, and I waited until he disappeared inside before driving straight to my apartment ten blocks west.

I went in silence, soaking in the warmth his presence left behind, and the sandalwood that marked him in my memory.

trouble

. . .

Tabby

MY COLD AND empty apartment was such a drag. Rob didn't show up to game night, and he didn't even bother bringing over a load of stuff while I was out. Annoyance boosted the confusion bubbling to the surface over Jax's reappearance.

I pulled my phone out, which remained in my pocket on silent the whole time I sat in Jax's car, not so much catching up as we were getting to know each other all over again. The fact his parents were divorced shocked me; I had many fond memories of his dad especially and mourned for the loss of their tight family unit. He wasn't tipped off by the mention of my dad's passing and thankfully didn't ask for a picture of my mom. If he couldn't figure *me* out, surely he would still recognize her—how could he not? It wasn't in his nature to forget.

The sweet flattery he offered me *was* in his nature, even as a friend. That part of him hadn't changed.

I shook my head and focused on the phone. No messages from Rob; instead, a frantic one from Annie:

> What happened when you told him? When are you going to tell Rob? Please keep me posted.

For someone who hated the mushy love stuff, she sure was curious about the drama surrounding mine. I had even more shame than earlier when I wrote back.

> Couldn't do it.

> I called him by his old nickname and he didn't recognize it.

> Might be best to just let it go.

Only an instant before she responded.

> It took you two hours to write that? What have you been doing since you got home?

> ...sitting in Jax's car chatting

> WTF Tabby? Two HOURS and you couldn't tell him?

> Look, I know what I'm doing. I will handle it. Rob doesn't have to know.

> Right. Not like Jax is your first love or anything and you just hung out in his car for two hours.

> Rob didn't even care what I went through tonight.

> At least I got home safe and somebody listened.

> Number one: I would listen

> Number two: look me in the eye and tell me you don't think this is dangerous. Or just plain stupid.

I begrudgingly took a selfie for her, taking care to capture my contacts since they were the only thing saving my ass after Jax stared into my eyes—a fact I would *not* be sharing with Annie.

> Here. I see him again in the morning. I'll be upfront when the moment's right, I promise.

> Don't tell anyone, okay?

I'm not the idiot here. Of course I won't.

Sleep tight.

She'd tease me tomorrow, that much was obvious, but her care wasn't entirely unappreciated. It was nice to know that I had someone in my corner, especially if the situation blew up in my face.

After I brushed my teeth, I stared at Rob's insensitive texts for a while. I knew I should leave it alone, but he hurt me. He should've given me the benefit of the doubt. I refused to let him get away with his failure.

> I made it home fine, thanks for checking in on me.

> And I didn't leave my lights on. Somebody broke in and left my door open. You'd know that if you asked me without assuming I fucked up.

It was petty, sure, and I was prepared for a snarky response. It was predictable enough. He'd tell me I overreacted and didn't care about his own stresses of the day, and I'd say he didn't give a shit that I needed him. He'd answer with, "But you always need me," and I'd shoot back, "And you *never* need me. Isn't that all a guy wants? To feel needed?" We'd bitch long into the night, sacrificing sleep for the sake of the argument, and both of us would end up feeling like shit for hours until one of us caved and said they were wrong.

But I wasn't wrong here. With Jax in my life, Rob's faults were more obvious.

To keep from going crazy, I plugged in the phone and shut off the light, hoping my body would understand that I needed to sleep. I counted backward from fifty by fours to clear my mind. *Please don't dream about Jax. Please.*

My phone buzzed at my side. Like an addict, I turned to it, muttering, "Here we go."

But it wasn't Rob. It was Jax. A steady stream of messages came in—so fast, my phone didn't even chime after the first.

> ::tap tap tap::

> I forgot to ask for your coffee order. I bet you're already asleep, so send it to me when you wake up.

> On that note, Good Morning!

My heart jumped. Past midnight, and Jax was checking on me. He wanted to know who I was and what I liked. He thought my work was interesting. Asked about my family, my plans for the future. Jax still loved D&D, adding role play to his messages in an effortless, non-cringey fashion. Maybe my brain was still stuck at sixteen and I saw him through rose-tinted lenses, but the rush of adrenaline keeping me awake felt so good, I didn't want it to stop.

> ::opens window::

> I'm easy. Whatever it is, put more sugar in it. Bonus if the name on the cup is spelled right.

> Tabi? Tabster? Tabs? Tabberoo?

> Shit. They don't have a chance.

> ::waves goodnight::

::waves goodnight::

This was the cherry on top of the evening. Even though I still prayed I wouldn't dream of him, deep down, I wanted to see the fantasy played out in any medium. "Goodnight, Wah. I'm sorry you didn't hear me."

I TOSSED and turned all night, unable to get comfortable. Jax did fill my dreams, but not how I hoped. He appeared in a nightmare that answered my worst fears.

"What the fuck did you do to yourself?" Jax screamed, shaking my shoulders and frightening me. "Look at you, Jamie. You're ruined!"

"No," I begged, trying to get away, desperate to talk some sense into him. "This is still me. It's always been who I am. You said you'd love me no matter what."

"Not like *this*. How could I?" He turned around and walked into an ever-darkening void. The imaginary argument was everywhere and nowhere all at once. No escape, no prediction, the possibility of it becoming reality all too palpable.

The scene that replayed every time I shut my eyes only drove my stubborn plan to stay silent into certainty. Even the thought of him deadnaming me was bad enough, but fully rejecting me? We had no future, so the mere prospect of telling him was moot. Rob and I were together, despite all his flaws and mine. I couldn't risk losing what I had for a pipe dream, even if that dream filled me with electricity.

Eventually I relaxed enough to sleep hard for an hour. I woke up as a familiar, warm hand squeezed my calf.

"Babe? It's time to wake up."

I groaned. *Rob?*

He leaned down and kissed my temple. "I have coffee for you."

"Huh?" Slowly waking, I rubbed my eyes and tried to focus though my lingering fatigue. "I'm confused."

Rob sighed and trailed his hands through my hair, being more tender than normal. "I'm so sorry I didn't come get you. You said you needed me, and I didn't listen."

"What? Where's this coming from?"

He gave me puppy eyes and pointed at my phone on the nightstand. "Got your text last night. I knew better than to try and argue; had to come here in person and apologize. I was wrong. Besides, you'll need a ride to work if your car's dead."

Shit. My pulse quickened and I was no longer tired. "Um. Yeah, I do—"

"I can't believe I didn't pick up on what you were telling me last night. And your car got broken into? Babe, you should've told me that earlier. Annie told me you were super upset."

"*Annie.*" My stomach rolled and I grumbled. *You said you'd stay out of this.* "That girl has got to learn to mind her own business."

Rob chuckled, "Yeah, you might be right. But she reminded me that you're one of a kind, Tabby. If I lost you, I'd never meet anyone else who could even come close." He sat me up and caressed my cheek, gazing at me like the first time we kissed. "I'd never forgive myself if I fucked this up for good."

I echoed his movement and brushed against his left eyebrow, admiring his strong jaw. "You really think so?"

"Don't be ridiculous. I know how much you're worth, babe." Rob kissed me long and soft and hummed against me as he finished. "You're my everything. And today I'm moving in officially, so I don't have to sleep away from you ever again." He pointed to a large trash bag on the floor with hanger hooks coming out of the top. "My furniture's coming tomorrow, but I brought my closet today."

"Wow." I smiled, wishing I could call out from work and take the day with him to dream. "This is one hell of a wake-up call."

"So, you forgive me?"

I moved in for another kiss. "Yeah, I forgive you. Even if I want to strangle Annie a little bit for butting in."

"You know what? Don't even mention it to her. I don't want her to be embarrassed." Rob brought over a steaming takeout cup. "Drink up, sleepyhead."

Whatever made him repent, I liked it. So refreshing. "You haven't treated me to takeout coffee since you bought that Keurig. I *am* a special boy today." Before taking a sip, I breathed in the steam coming from the small hole in the lid. Sweeter than the standard drip coffee he used to buy me, I made yummy noises and brought it to my lips.

Another surprise. Rob never bought sugar-filled things. "What is this? It's delicious," I asked.

He beamed. "It's Friday. A good cheat day was in order. Got you something sweet, 'cause I think *you're* sweet. White chocolate mocha. You really like it?"

"Mmhmm." I nodded and kept drinking, but now my eyes went to the floor.

Seriously, what on earth's gotten into you? This is some Twilight Zone-level weirdness.

My phone alarm went off, later than usual since I didn't need to shower. Seven. My expected chauffeur would be here in half an hour if I didn't warn him to stay away. Keeping my cool without telling Rob the existing plans, I shot off a few quick texts to Jax before getting ready for the day.

> Rob came over and is taking me to work.
> You're off the hook. Thanks for the offer, and I
> hope you get to sleep in a little.

He didn't write back, and I considered it a blessing.

While I brushed my teeth, Rob packed me a sandwich and some treats for lunch. He held the small brown bag daintily by the front door as I put on my shoes. "Alright, Dr. Ross. Are you ready for Friday?"

I didn't question whatever switch had flipped within him or

what Annie said to transform Rob into a version of himself I'd always hoped was deep inside. It was too nice to waste. "Sure am."

"You know, every morning can be like this now. Wouldn't that be great?"

Nodding, I ushered him out toward the car.

To an all-new beginning.

intervention

. . .

Jax

STILL DRIVING BACK from Tabby's place, halfway between his apartment and mine, intense guilt replaced the fuzzy feeling in my stomach as midnight inched ever closer. The wafts of his scent reminded me how long we sat talking, and if anyone found out, it wouldn't look innocent from the outside.

Shit, it didn't look innocent from the inside. The adrenaline rush when I thought he might kiss me—that was *my* fault, not his.

I considered how I wanted to be in good graces with everyone surrounding Ethan, especially if a fight could result in my being kicked out of his place. Chris's betrayal acted as a benchmark of what I wanted to avoid. Even if Tabby only saw our long conversation as a nice gesture, the privacy and atmosphere of it crossed an invisible line. I gripped the steering wheel to white-knuckle status and sped home, keeping a keen eye out for cops on the way. Once parked, I went through the text chain from a week ago, calling someone I never thought I would.

"Hello?" the groggy voice growled on the other end.

"Yeah, Rob?" I asked, all too anxious to make up for my

stupidity. "You might not remember me. This is Jax Grady from the D&D group."

He yawned loudly. "Okay?"

"Look, I know it's really late. I'm sorry to bother you. But I think you should know Tabby was way upset tonight after his car broke down."

"Huh?" Rob became more alert, angry even. "What the hell's going on with him now?"

You don't even sound like you care. Jesus, are you always like this? "Well, I couldn't get it to jump, so he called a tow. I brought him home and he was really anxious about it. He needs a ride to work in the morning. I don't live far, so I'm happy to do it, but I figured I'd give you a chance to, like, come save the day."

He groaned. "Oh, man."

"Hey, like I said, I'll do it if you can't. And—"

"Why is this any of your business, dude? No offense, but I don't know you. I don't like people calling me at midnight. I especially don't like people calling me at midnight about my boyfriend. This is the sorta thing Annie used to do. If Tabby has a problem, he needs to man up and tell me himself. No more of these bullshit games."

The hair on the back of my neck stood on end. "You wanna push him away? That's your business."

"Excuse me?" Rob scoffed. "What the fuck would you know about it, punk?"

"I know enough to say you're on thin ice. Why the hell would I have to drive *your* boyfriend home? Aren't you moving in together soon?"

"Jesus, you're annoying. I don't have to tell you anything, Jack."

"It's *Jax*. But fine. Sorry I bugged you. I'll get Tabby in the morning and take him to work. Buh-bye." *Click.*

The whole exchange made me want to pull my hair out. "What a fuckin' asshole. Who would wanna be with that tool?" I stormed from the car to the empty apartment, slamming the door behind me. The neighbor's dog upstairs went crazy. The plants on the kitchen windowsill mocked me with their peppy greenery. What was once the odd euphoria of feeling like I belonged here was replaced with a sense of disappointment and disgust.

No—not quite. The emotion had another name. One that dripped deep green.

I can't believe I actually called Rob. What did I think he'd say? "Thanks for helping"?

The bathroom mirror cast its own judgment upon me after I aggressively scrubbed my teeth. Two hours spent bonding with Tabby, and now I was alone. My bed was icy from late night humidity. So was the air. It wasn't my place to get between them; I only wanted to do something good.

My motives were pure, at least. I could be nice, even if Rob couldn't be. If he refused to see Tabby's worth, that was his problem.

Texting Tabby about morning coffee was innocent enough. I prepared not to get a response. But to my surprise and delight, Tabby answered, giving me banter and an answer to my role play note. We *got* each other. While I moved to San Francisco alone—no girlfriend, no best friend, no one I could trust beyond Dad—my circle was growing thanks to this little game group, and Tabby was top of that list.

I took a deep breath of the cool air around me, happy I'd messaged him. But the ringing chirp of my phone sank my stomach to a new low. Not a text.

Oh, great.

"Yeah?" I answered, playing up my fatigue.

Rob spoke with a quiet, uncertain tone. "Hey, uh, Jax? Right, Jax?"

"What do you want?"

He hemmed and hawed a bit before spitting it out. "I got a text from Tabby. He really is angry. If I write him back now, I'll just make it worse." He exhaled on the other end too long, the same way Dad did when he picked his words wisely. "You were right, okay? We're moving in together. It's time. But I had a real shit day, and now I've fucked it up again. I don't know how to fix it."

Are you fucking serious? Now I have to coach you on how to be a good guy?

"So, I guess, I wanted to thank you for calling me," he said. "If you hadn't, I wouldn't have seen his text until the morning. Did he say anything else to you?"

It was my turn to groan. "Like what?"

"What I should say so he won't hate me?"

"You shouldn't *say* anything. Words mean shit without action. You hafta *do* something." My father's words spilled from my lips, which made them easier to give. "I already told you earlier. You should drive him to work tomorrow."

Rob protested with an even longer sigh than before.

"You have two choices here—step up, or step aside. Where I come from, somebody like him is pretty damn special. Tabby's smart, he listens, he does fun shit outside of his job, he's driven enough to have a real career, and he's not even thirty yet. Anybody like that has a wider pool to pull from than they think they do. But despite all his strength, he still needed you, and you didn't come through."

"But he always needs me, dude. That's the problem. I'm constantly running around trying to fix—"

"So the fuck what? Don't you wanna be needed?"

Rob was silent for a moment. "He says that all the time. Did he tell you to call me?"

Great. Yet another thing we have in common. "No. Tabby doesn't know I called, and I would like it to stay that way. You have to do something. Prove you know he's worth your time."

More silence. "What time is he expecting you?"

"Seven-thirty. Show up early and bring coffee."

"Come on, I don't need to—"

I spoke slowly so he'd hear me. "Make an effort, Rob. What would he normally get?"

"Just a plain coffee."

Probably because that was all the prick was willing to spring for. "Get him something sweet. Caramel latte, something chocolate, or vanilla with a pump of raspberry. Like that."

"I don't think he'd want it. With my diet, we've talked about how bad sugar—"

"Trust me, alright? He'll like this. It's a treat. Say something about how you think he's sweet, too."

We stayed on the phone for an awkward minute, not sure how to end our mistake of a phone call. But Rob cracked in a final attempt to prove he wasn't a complete douchebag.

"I really love him, you know. I'm just not good at this."

I felt for him. Genuinely. If Heather went to Chris because I wasn't doing enough, I would hope he would try to help me first before giving up on our potential. "That's fine, 'cause I'm great at this. I'm happy to help, okay?"

"Thanks, Jax. Um. Welcome to the family." *Click.*

Family. Huh. I resisted the urge to repeat the word in a heavy Italian accent, and chose to fall asleep instead, putting my phone on *Do Not Disturb* so I could get some real sleep.

An unspoken part of me didn't want Rob to succeed. But if my interference could help make my new friend happy, that was enough. After all, he was only a friend. My comfortable, familiar, beautiful new friend, who happened to fill the lonely space in my soul where love was missing.

acknowledgment

. . .

Tabby

I RESISTED the urge to write to Jax all day Friday. Rob's move into the apartment took all my attention over the weekend. It was stressful and tiring but satisfying to complete, even though the place was filled with boxes.

Rob and I took Monday off to finish unpacking; at least, to the point that we were both satisfied. We made love when it was over. He took care of me unlike ever before, and I was never more grateful to have given him so many extra chances in the past.

This is it. My forever.

Tuesday morning was a blur. Rob was stressed about making it to work on time because he woke up late. We fought over who had time to shower. The bathroom sink, always big enough for me, felt cramped with our respective medications lining each side. Our electric toothbrushes each demanded their own outlet, and there weren't enough to go around. We'd have to share a base, which Rob didn't want to do, because he felt it would be too easy to mix up the brush heads.

Grumble, grumble, grumble. Fuss, fuss, fuss. I swear, you're all bitch and no solution.

I barely had enough time to put in a simple pair of blue

contacts with the little bit of time he left for me by the mirror. He didn't even say goodbye when he rushed out the door and slammed it behind him. Fortunately, my car was working again, so I was thankful to get a little bit of space to myself before seeing patients.

Catching up from a missed day was always somewhat of a slog—orders to fill and questions to answer. Emails that couldn't be left alone any longer. But work energized me. Eye tests and glasses alone might've been boring to some optometrists, yet I saw every person as a challenge. They weren't just eyes—my clients were great people, some of whom I'd known since I first graduated. The most repetitive days still weren't boring. It was a luxury most of my friends didn't have, least of all Rob, who worked in warehousing. Even though his blue-collar job didn't bother me, when we'd fight, he'd bring up my career as if I secretly felt I was fundamentally better than him.

At noon, I checked my phone for any messages and found only a text from Mom making sure I wouldn't skip our dinner this Friday; I'd missed the last. After answering her with an enthusiastic gif of a thumbs-up, I left the office to forage for lunch on my own.

People bustled all over Union Square as they normally did. Even on cold mornings, live bands played outside. Tourists excitedly ran through on old trolleys. Shops came and went like the road construction, which was inconvenient at any time of day. A few doors down from some swanky art galleries—which recently carried somewhat salacious pieces by Dr. Seuss himself —my favorite sandwich shop beckoned with salty fresh bread in the air. Simple and family-owned, it was the only food place I frequented enough to be seen as a regular.

The redheaded girl at the counter smiled and gave her usual greeting. "Good morning, Dr. Ross. Number four today?

"You know me too well." I was embarrassed not to remember her name off the top of my head the way she did mine.

"Extra mayo, no tomatoes?" she asked, tapping away at the screen.

"Yup. That's me."

"What'll you be drinking today, sir?"

I still got a jump of euphoria any time that happened, even after all these years passing in public. "Eh, let's just do water today." My wallet barely left my back pocket when a warm presence behind me interjected.

"His lunch is on me."

No way. I did a double take when I turned to him. "Jax?"

"Hey, Tabby," he said with a smile, nodding to the checkout girl. Jax crossed his arms and stared at the menu above her. "Let's see…I think I'll do the number two again today."

"Nuh-uh," I said. "Give him the same thing I ordered."

He cocked a brow. "I don't know if I should trust you and your crunchy tastes."

"This place isn't *crunchy* at all, no matter what you order. I was going to recommend it to you, actually."

"Well, surprise, surprise. I've been in here at least twice a week for the past month. Right?" He pointed to Miss Redhead. "You can vouch for me, can't you?"

She blushed and played along, eyeing me. "He's been here a lot."

"See?" His genuine, warm grin lit the whole room. "I guess you don't leave me much choice. Whatever he ordered, I'm game." Jax ordered a Sprite for himself and directed me to find a place to sit while he paid.

With nothing else to do but concede that we'd be having a quiet lunch together—not that I protested one bit—I picked one of the only open tables by the window so I could make a quick escape when the time came. As much as I was shocked to see him, it was exactly the kind of rendezvous I'd always dreamed of: casual friends who run into each other, anywhere, any time, and the chemistry doesn't fade or falter.

Friends. Just friends, though, Tabby.

Jax flicked through his phone by the order window until his name was called. His body proportions were so unlike how they were in our youth. With full shoulders, a long torso, and a filled-out neck, Jax wasn't scrawny and barely past puberty the way I remembered. It seemed every time I laid eyes on him these days, he became some new version of an impossible ideal.

Aware I was staring, I shook my head and turned to look outside, just as an inconvenience of tourists on Segways buzzed past. They looked silly in their oversized helmets. Many had wide, panicked expressions from overstimulation.

But on the far side of the sidewalk behind them, dangerously close to the trolley rail line, an elderly couple embraced with complete ignorance of their busy surroundings. He looked down at her with a dreamy expression that superseded their advanced ages. She glanced up at him with the bright eyes of a wistful girl who wanted nothing but him. Watching them filled me with undefined longing.

"How do people drive those things?" Jax asked as the last of the Segways moved out of sight. He handed me my cup of ice water first before putting the lunch trays side by side. Jax effortlessly slid into the opposite side of the booth, suave in a way that would've made his teen self jealous.

I silently smirked at him, careful not to give myself away. *Age suits you, Jax.*

"Now, what's this thing you ordered for me, hm?" He peeled back the thinly sliced sourdough bread on top of the sandwich and poked at the contents with a long toothpick. "I see...turkey, mayo, a little lettuce, and—ah! You said this wasn't crunchy!"

"What?" I chuckled, taking a bite and talking with my mouth full. "Scared of a little avocado? It's good for you. Good for your eyes, actually."

He glared at me playfully. "Avocado alone, I will forgive. There better not be hummus on this thing."

"No hummus, I promise."

We enjoyed our basic sandwiches for a few minutes, not

needing to fill the silence between us. Like we'd said before, our time together was comfortable. This was no exception. Rob and I couldn't do this with ease until we'd dated for a month and a half, and that was because he had a dentist appointment that day and couldn't talk much.

Was it Novocain or laughing gas that day? I thought, staring at the passersby again.

Jax cracked open his Sprite and relaxed into his seat, following my lead. "They really don't know how lucky they are," he said, gesturing to the tourists outside. "Ocean's right here, redwoods are close, too. There's a city pulse that never stops. Sometimes I miss the quiet of being at home, but I think I'm finally starting to see why people pay a fortune to sleep in a hallway just to live here."

"It's the most exciting place to be these days. Have you noticed that all the action movies have been destroying *us* lately instead of New York?"

He tittered. "Yeah, I have noticed that. Though now that I'm here, it's hard to believe that anything could take down the Golden Gate. It's massive. The height of the spires gives me vertigo." Jax shifted his attention to me again and leaned into the table, taking the last bite of his sandwich. "Look at that—your choice wasn't bad after all."

"Told you I wouldn't steer you wrong."

"Nah, guess you haven't yet."

The burn in my chest to confess our connection was almost too great to ignore, but I didn't want to rip the newfound ease between us. He made the most mundane things exciting. His present made me want to stay in our booth catching up like we did in his car, even though I usually grabbed lunch to-go.

So Annie's words to fess up had merit. I buried them deep, just in time for Jax to shift the subject.

"How'd the whole move-in thing go, by the way?"

Oh, shit—Rob. Emotional whiplash forced me back into

reality along with a fresh dose of guilt. "It went great. The place is a total mess, but Rob's all moved in."

"Domestic bliss, eh?" Jax smiled, but it was tainted—not the same bright grin he had at the counter when we first saw each other. This one was forced, as if the corners of his lips were pulled like a marionette. A brave face, at best. "That's great. And your car came back okay?"

"Yeah, it was fine. Alternator, like you said. What'd you end up doing this weekend?"

"Packing, mostly. Ethan's giving me a key on Thursday at game night so I can start bringing stuff in."

It hurt to ask, but I had to hope he would meet someone else so he could get over the pain of the girl he left behind. "So, no hot dates, I take it?"

Jax snorted into his drink. "Would have to know somebody hot for that."

I was grateful he didn't take the opportunity to hit on me because it would've stopped my heart, but an immature part of me wished he had. The nearly empty restaurant became oppressive with a desire to hear him confess that he'd never find love again, just so I wouldn't have to risk the pain of watching him fall for someone else.

Pointing to the redheaded checkout girl, I put away my selfishness in favor of trying to help his loneliness. "Why not ask her? She's into you."

"Huh?" Jax did an exaggerated stretch to hide when he glanced at her. "Oh, Megan?"

Of course, you're friendly enough to know her name already...

He paused for a moment, then scrunched his nose and shook his head.

Now that he'd rejected the notion, I had to double down. "Seriously? Come on, what's wrong with her?"

"I-I don't know, I just..." Jax stared at his Sprite and flushed a shade of pink I hadn't seen on him since we were teenagers. "I don't *feel* anything with her. If we dated, she would just be a rebound from Heather. Megan's too sweet for that, and I'm too much of a softie to ask her out just to get my rocks off."

Gulping, my humble eyes magnetized to the bag of sea salt chips below as if they held a secret code. *Can't argue with that.*

"Hey—thanks for trying," he said, tapping on the table to get my attention again.

"Sure, of course. I know you just went through a pretty tough breakup, so I get it. Take all the time you need."

His phone buzzed, and as he looked at it, something changed in his face. He stiffened, as if biting his tongue or holding in a grimace. After quickly typing a text, he put the phone in his back pocket and looked out the window again. His strong jaw was more than just squared. It was clenched tight.

"Everything okay?" I asked, worried he was hiding something.

Jax nodded. "You know, I really enjoyed getting to talk with you last week. But let's agree not to do that again."

"What? Why?" *Too abrupt. Too defensive. Retreat. Retreat!* "I mean, *sure*, but—"

"The car was…well, it felt a little *too* intimate, didn't it? I guess if Rob's fine with it, I don't care, but I know if Heather had been meeting with somebody late at night—"

"Oh. Yeah. Sure, I get that. Yeah." My heart thumped away, but I needed him to stop. He was right. The guilt I still harbored proved spending time with him was a risk. It wasn't innocent. "We're just friends. Friends don't do that. I understand."

Jax let out a long breath. "Right." He tipped his Sprite my way. "To friendship, Tabby."

I met his can with my ice water cup. "To friendship, Jax."

Boundaries were good. It would keep him at a distance and help me with Rob. The less I saw of Jax, the better—and the less Rob knew about my past, the more stable our future could be.

The lunch get-together was spontaneous and all too easy, but I vowed then and there to call my orders in from now on.

changes

. . .

Tabby

ROB GREETED me at the door with a bottle of wine and music whispering in the background.

What's all this? You were such a crank this morning...

"Been thinkin' about you all day, babe," he said, snuggling his scruffy chin against the back of my neck. Since we were the same height, he could wrap his arms around me from behind and trail kisses to my ear without trying. "I got a present for us."

"What kind of present?"

"Something that will make both our lives easier. Come on." Rob tugged at my hand and led me through the hall, into the bedroom, and past the closet to the bathroom. He opened his arm to display the new sink setup. "Ta-da."

I blinked a few times, trying to figure out the riddle, when my eyes finally fell on the new toothbrush station. Instead of sharing a single handle as we'd talked about that morning, he bought a whole new set that came with two.

"See? It's great. It's the brand I like, *and* we don't have to worry about them getting mixed up. Everybody wins." Rob pointed out a new organizer for his meds, and a matching one for my side of the sink by the plug. It was more put-together than it had been before and still left room in the middle to keep things from crowding.

The gesture left me speechless simply because this sort of spontaneous action was so unlike Rob, I wondered if he bought a book on how to be better. I wasn't about to pull the threads of his kindness apart. "Wow, I...Rob, this is great. Thank you."

He turned to face me head-on. "I really want this to work for us, babe. You're worth every little thing to me. That's the *tooth*."

I snorted. "Shame on you for that one." It was cute but left me racking my brain to figure out what he was secretly asking for. *Did I miss something?*

"Now, come have dinner with me in our kitchen. I got a new recipe book. Maybe we'll finally help you get rid of those last few pounds, eh?"

There it was. It stung. Even while trying to be sweet, he nagged. Nitpicked. Found my insecurity and went for it. I couldn't really ask for better, could I? Not when I had such a complex mess of a psyche and body on the table.

If Rob can change some habits for me, I can bury my judgment over his control. "Can't wait," I said. "Let's eat."

patience

. . .

Jax

ETHAN WAS everything I ever wanted in a roommate. He was
tidy and left me alone for the most part, but he also invited me to
come hang out whenever he left the apartment. Even let me go
through things in the store downstairs if he needed help. Though
I declined his offer to officially work there so I could get paid, I
was happy to help him set up a better tracking system for his
inventory. We spent late nights unpacking all the little kitschy
items he kept in the display cases and laughed at old George
Carlin stand-ups. Since I got first dibs on any great dice sets, he
eventually stopped asking to pay me and accepted my assistance
for the kindness that it was.

Because of some late trainings at work that just happened to
occur on Thursdays, I missed three game nights in a row. Ethan
said the group asked after me each time—confirmed when
Annie found me coming home just as the third week's session
was ending.

"Jax, where have you been? Are you ever coming back? We
start a new campaign next week, so it would be a great time for
you to jump in." Her bouncy, excited tone juxtaposed her dark
clothes and unkempt hair, which was shorter than the last time
I'd seen her. It made her already petite face even more mouse-

like and adorable. "I know I'm not the only person who's wondered where you went."

Her light pleads made me smile, and my stomach flooded with warmth, though I silenced my heart's insistence to guess who she meant. Besides Ethan, who folded the tables and chairs in the back, everyone else seemed to have left already. "I should be back next week. We had a few new employees come on board, and we're piloting a new database system. It's taken a while to work out the kinks."

"Have you talked to anyone else besides Ethan since you last gamed with us?" she asked in an expectant tone that said she anticipated the answer.

The truth was, the person I'd spoken to the most besides my new roommate was the one guy I had no interest in getting to know. Since I didn't think Rob mentioned our bi-weekly text exchanges to Annie, I decided to keep it private. "Not really. I ran into Tabby not far from my work a few weeks ago, but that's it."

She nodded and hummed. Her knowing grin said it all.

Cordelia came out of the bathroom and opened her arms to hug me. Her undercut changed since I last saw her and was dyed bright orange. It peeked out beneath her bouncing, tight curls. "Hey there, you. Thought you disappeared."

"Not yet. I'm like a fungus. I just kinda grow on you."

She snickered and put her light jacket on. "You missed a big win tonight. Gavin rolled so well, I think his D20's loaded. Tabby normally kicks ass with that, but since he lost his lucky ring, he's had to put his trusty die in the dunce cap chair."

"Yeah...Cyan mentioned that last time we played," I said.

Cordelia curled her lip in confusion. "Cyan? Oh, right. He changed it again tonight. But continue."

I shook my head and sighed in understandable annoyance at his flip-flopping moniker, though at least I was making an effort. "Anyway, yeah. What's this lucky ring about?"

She eyed Annie, who opened her hand to let Cordy tell the

story. "Well, ever since I met Tabby three years ago, he swore his D20 rolls were better whenever he wore this ring. It's old and made of pewter, I think, 'cause it's pretty beat up. He had it every time he played until the first time he brought Rob to our group. All his turns were shit. He almost had to burn one of his oldest characters because of it, but I bailed him out. Since then, until that first time you came anyway, he's never been without it." She shook her head and laughed again. "I once told him he was full of it for being so superstitious—guess he was right."

I felt for Tabby, especially because I did believe in things like that, and his suspicions were proven true with every bad week. "Where'd it come from?"

Annie chimed in. "That's the thing—nobody knows. He's never told us."

I scratched my temple to release the anxious energy built up from curiosity. *Mysterious Tabby, once again.*

"Uber's here," Annie said, pointing to the street. "See you next week, Jax."

"Bye, girls," I said, joining Ethan in the back to finish putting the chairs up.

The shop was his pride and joy, and he lived behind the counter more than he did in our apartment. The joyful, circus-like tune he whistled every night while closing proved how much he loved every second of maintaining it. While it wasn't the *Friends*-like atmosphere of Chris's house, the life inside was its own fantasy where anything was possible, and everyone was welcome. It charmed me how he opened the place up on week-ends for families to come in with small kids to paint figures or learn how to play basic games. Unlike the many people I knew back home who claimed to be all about social inclusion, Ethan put his money down and made it happen. Associating with him made me proud.

With the last of the tables and chairs put away, we shut off the lights and locked up to go upstairs. The apartment was small, but enough, and neither of us complained about feeling cramped into what was essentially dorm space living. It reminded me of the first apartment I lived in with Chris at college, only we couldn't leave the door perpetually unlocked.

Once I was settled and ready for bed, my phone went off, heralding yet another call for rescue I didn't want to answer.

> What kinda gift should I get Tabby for our anniversary next month?

I grumbled and took a deep breath, grateful I wasn't as close to Tabby as I thought I would be after we met, though Rob's constant nagging for tips was exhausting. *I've given you enough material for weeks. Haven't you actually learned anything?*

Swallowing my pride and irritation because Dad's voice protested too strongly inside, I gave him a curt response.

> He lost his lucky ring, didn't he? Replace it.

He wrote back quickly, but I could practically feel his icy resistance through the words.

> If I get him a ring he'll think it's too serious.

> Let me know if you think of something else

I rolled my eyes. *Grow up.* "Yeah. Sure. I'll get right on it, Rob. Sheezus." Fuming, I put both hands over my eyes and rubbed my temples with my thumbs, hoping to squeeze the undefined jealousy out of my brain when my phone chimed again.

"Christ. What do you want now?" I said, squinting at the screen in the dark.

> Missed you at game night tonight.

> Hope you come back soon.

Tabby's message was short and kind. It echoed the attitude Annie had earlier. And like earlier, I floated with heat.

"Fuck," I whispered, putting the phone down without giving a response, because if we got to chatting, we'd both be up all night. That couldn't happen. It was torture enough knowing Rob reaped the benefits of my good ideas.

Despite my resistance, I stayed up anyway—every time I dozed, his technicolor eyes got closer—so close I forced myself to wake before dreaming of something I'd regret...

excuses

· · ·

Jax

TABBY'S TEXT still dominated the screen when I got up, which helped start my Friday on a happy note. Ethan noticed my grin, even through the extreme sleepiness from a restless night.

"What's up with you?" he asked, downing his usual morning protein shake as I sat down.

"Nothing worth mentioning." I tried to play it off but was so bad at lying that I cracked and started laughing.

"Come on, roomie. What is it?"

My thoughts spiraled as I ran my hands through my hair, one after the other. *I'm totally fucked. But I really can't tell you. You're too close to Rob.*

"I know that look." He egged me by shaking my shoulder. "Spill it."

Sighing, I rolled my eyes. "Just a dream I had. No big deal. I think I really just need to get laid."

"Ah, I hear that." Ethan curled the edges of his thick mustache. "Anyways, gotta hit the gym. See you later." He patted my shoulder one last time before he left, and I stayed at the table, alone.

Without another witness, I pulled out my phone to look at the message again and let myself daydream a little.

Yeah. I missed you, too. It was enough positivity fuel to charge the day.

I had a few emails from Dad, all bullshit forwards except for one: a reminder for Mom's upcoming birthday. It killed the fuzzy mood. He insisted I find something fancy for her that he could never hope to get back home. I'd try my best, like always, though I had no idea where to go. Something would pop up.

He ended his emails the same way he did his phone calls: *Extra hot, extra cheese, extra crispy relleno, kid. Love, Dad.* The sentiment sent a wave of homesickness over me.

As if the universe wanted to amplify my hodge-podge of emotions, Rob texted again while I put on my shoes.

Any other ideas

"Seriously, man? It's not even eight in the morning yet." I debated ignoring him but didn't have it in me.

> I've got nothing. Why don't you ask HIM what he wants?
>
> Amazing how people tend to know that information.

Was it petty and a little passive-aggressive? Sure. But I didn't owe him anything, and my only motivation to help him at all came from my muddy connection to Tabby. It was time to tell him the answers were right in front of him anyway.

But he snapped right back.

He likes surprises

Don't be a prick

Why don't you ask him for me?

I snorted. "Yeah, sure. *I'll* go fishing for the answer because you're too chicken shit. What are we, fifteen?"

> You work by him. Meet him for lunch or something

> Then ask about me and bring it up

His last text made my stomach twist. He didn't know what he was asking of me.

> Seriously?

> Yeah do it today. He didn't take a lunch from home

> I told him to but he didn't

> Please

My heart rushed. *An excuse.* Maybe the only excuse I'd have for a while, if ever again, and Rob already knew.

He didn't need to ask me twice.

> Fine.

> No promises for information, though.

I was officially a regular at the sandwich place since I went at least two days a week. To be fair, it was the closest spot for something remotely edible by my office, but the prospect of seeing Tabby again made it the highlight every time I went. Today, time couldn't move fast enough. Nervous energy bounced in my skin like a spring from my feet to the top of my head.

The girl at the counter, Megan, beamed when I came in the door. Tabby was right—she gave me the kind of smile that couldn't be misinterpreted—but I still couldn't bring myself to take her out when I had someone else on my mind. It wouldn't be fair to her.

"What can I get started for you today?" she asked, bubbly and bright as ever. Her round, thin-rimmed glasses were too wide for her face, but it softened the severity of her red hair.

I leaned close to her, not wanting the customer waiting by the close soda machine to overhear. "Actually, I need a favor. Do you happen to remember when I came in here a few weeks ago and ran into my friend? That other guy?" Even though my chin was bare, I mimed stroking a goatee in hopes she'd understand my hint.

"You mean Dr. Ross? Yeah, he's in here *all* the time."

"Great. That's great. Do you know what he likes? I want to bring him lunch today but don't have much time before he'll probably come here himself."

"Aw, that's so sweet. Of course I do." She rang up the order and bounced as she did, proud to be my secret accomplice.

"Thanks, Meg. I owe you one." We settled the bill, and I left her with a smile.

Tabby's office was north of the sandwich shop, and I prayed while I hustled my way through the tourists that I wouldn't somehow miss him. It was going to be a surprise—after all, Rob said he liked surprises, didn't he?—so taking lunch to him became a mission.

The eyecare center's front entrance was like any other glasses place, covered in posters of models who could make any ridiculous frames look good. It made me grateful to have my mom's eyes instead of Dad's so I wouldn't need lenses anytime in the near future. The office bustled with people, decently busy for the noon hour, and I anxiously waited in line behind a few legitimate customers before ending up at the front desk.

"Name?" the receptionist asked, barely looking up from her computer screen.

"Um. Delivery for Dr. Ross," I said, holding up the white paper bag with our sandwiches.

She squinted and looked me up and down, then tapped on

her keyboard again. "Have a seat and I'll let him know you're here."

"Thanks." I felt like a reprimanded child for bothering him at work when he could've been busy with a patient. *Dumbass. This is why work gifts are never a good idea.* But I sat in the corner, careful not to get in the way of anyone taking a gander at the wall of frames on either side of me.

Tabby came out from around the corner with a puzzled expression, squinting and searching the room. His blue scrubs were crisp and tidy like last time I saw him, though I paid more attention to things I might not have noticed before; the sharp curl of his shiny dark hair behind his ears was a touch shorter than before, meaning he got a new haircut. When he stood straight and turned away, the distinct outline over his back, beneath the scrubs, reminded me of a sports bra.

For the first time, the reality of Tabby's *transness* occurred to me, and I resisted the urge to wonder what he looked like naked and how he had sex. It was none of my business, despite my curiosity. I'd never ask. Whatever was beneath the surface didn't matter, regardless of how little my ignorant ass understood about his journey.

Nevertheless, he impressed me just as much now as the last time I saw him, and my heart fluttered when he first glanced in my direction. I sheepishly stood so he wouldn't pass me by when he looked again.

His eyes met mine from across the room, and he froze. A smile flashed on his lips, though it was held back, either from myself or the eagle eyes of his coworkers.

I waved, then pointed to the white bag in my other hand and shrugged.

Tabby gave me a real grin this time and waved me over. Whatever he was doing when I came in, he could drop it now.

"Hey," I said, still feeling sheepish for interrupting him in the middle of the day. "Sorry if I'm bothering—"

"It's fine. Really." He scratched the back of his neck and

looked up at me through his thick lashes. "Beth says you have something for me?"

I choked for a moment, almost forgetting why I was there. "Yeah. Y-yes. I brought you lunch." The bag crinkled in my hand as I held it out toward him. "We could eat together if you want to?"

Tabby chuckled at first, then gave me a nod and led us through the doors behind reception. The woman at the desk, who I assumed was the aforementioned Beth, cocked a brow at me when I followed him.

I know what you're thinking. Rob should be here, not me.

The place was much quieter once we were out of the main room. He pulled in a second chair for the small office at the end of the hall and closed the door behind us.

"Thanks for coming in. It's great to see you." He settled in the rolling seat and dove into his sandwich without even commenting if I'd gotten his order right. The surety in which he unwrapped the complicated fold said he was familiar enough with how his favorite place worked, and he had no doubt what it was.

My stomach kept flipping, preventing me from having much of an appetite, so I only went for my bag of sea salt chips. "Any major updates since I saw you last, besides your haircut?"

He smiled and talked with his mouth full. "Not really. Things are good at home, good at work, nothing to report."

"Nice." I searched his office for evidence of anything I could use to learn more about him, but the walls were bare. "Friday... you're going to see your mom tonight, right?"

"That's the plan." Tabby searched the lunch bag for something else. "You got me a soda?"

"Is that not okay? Shit, I'm sorry if—"

"No, no, it's fine. Just don't get to do that a lot." He took the can of blood orange San Pellegrino out and tapped the lid. "I've been trying to lose some weight, to be honest, but I'll make an exception for my favorite stuff any day."

Duly noted. I wanted to get my task over with so we could talk about something that made me less edgy. "So, how's Rob?"

Tabby paused for a moment or two, taking a few sips. "He's fine. He's, uh...been *great*, actually." The way he stared at his desk as if studying it, furrowing his brow, said more than his words did.

"Yeah? Word through the grapevine is you've got an anniversary coming up, right?"

"Ethan told you that?" His face shot up to meet mine. "I'm surprised he remembered, though I guess I can't be shocked." He averted his eyes again, and a softer smile took over his cheeks, revealing small dimples I hadn't seen before.

Dammit. He had to be thinking about Rob. *Why couldn't I make them appear?*

"But yes," he said, "Rob's and my anniversary is coming up. Two years at the end of this month. Really crazy."

"Two years, wow. Congrats, man. Any big plans?"

Tabby shrugged. "Now that he's moved in, not really. That's what I wanted for us the last time we celebrated, but it took him this long to do it."

You're giving me nothing. Maybe that's for the best. Either because of my stubbornness or the awkwardness, I opted to change the subject. "Hey, you know, my mom's birthday is coming up around then, too. Dad says I need to find her some kinda fancy-schmancy gift, but I'm not sure where to go. Any ideas?"

He lit up again as if he was just as grateful to talk about something else. "In San Francisco? Pick a street corner."

I rolled my eyes. "I'm not gonna buy her a knockoff Chanel wallet. Sorry, excuse me, I mean '*Channel*'," I said with sloppy air quotes. "Union Square has to have something legit, right? All these tourists hang around here for a reason."

Tabby pursed his lips and sighed before the lightbulb went off. "Have you ever gone to Neiman Marcus? Headquarters of fancy-schmancy."

"You think so?"

"Oh, man. You'll be in for a treat. It's the kinda place that's so overpriced, you're afraid to breathe on stuff."

A memory from long ago sprung to the forefront of my mind —nights spent on the internet with Jamie, trading links from random luxury stores for the most ridiculously expensive things. We found solid gold paperclips, chinchilla fur rugs, even a forty-thousand dollar enlarged photo of a scarf. It was a game we played to challenge each other to guess the price of what we found. To us, there was no greater way to burn the stars until we could see each other again.

But going into the store was like leveling up. And Tabby had that same sensibility...right? Couldn't we do the same thing to kill time?

"Any chance I could get you to come with me?" I asked, half expecting him to immediately shoot me down. "Could use a chaperone to make sure I don't have any errant exhales on the merchandise, you know."

He did what he did last time we were together and investigated my face before answering. The seconds dragged.

Come on. Gimme another excuse.

Tabby relented. "Guess it wouldn't hurt to find something nice for my mom, too. Meet me here at five and we'll walk together?"

Suddenly I had an appetite again, and I tore open my sandwich to hide my excitement. "You're on."

playing with fire

. . .

Tabby

THE CLOCK in my office was slow. It had to be. There was no way it had only been five minutes since I last checked it.

Come on, five o'clock. Come on.

Rob had no interest in coming with me to mom's place for dinner, so he didn't care when I said I was running an errand after work. I justified seeing Jax again because, in broad daylight, it was harmless to do so. After all, he visited me out of the kindness of his heart. Jax had no ulterior motives.

The clock continued to mock me. *Tick, tick, tick.*

Once the day finally ended and the last patient left, I stood in the back parking lot by my car until Jax pulled up. He hopped out and untucked his blue polo shirt, which hung over his slim hips to be more casual.

"Might want to tuck that back in," I said, pointing down the alley toward our destination as I walked. "Not sure they'd let you past the doors if you're not already dressed to the nines."

He cocked a brow. "Next to your scrubs, I look like the King of England."

"Hey, my scrubs are more than appropriate, thank you very much."

"Just in case, our first stop should be to buy a couple of ties.

You know, to make sure we're appropriate." He winked, the kind of halfway-smooth move he never quite mastered because winking was far from sexy.

"Wait, wait—" I left all my guilt behind and embraced the fluid energy between us. "There's a giant Macy's next to it. Let's go get a couple to start with and walk in as we are, but with ties on. No collars or anything. No tucking it into your polo, that's cheating."

He laughed and put his hands in his pockets, sidling up to me. "I'm game for that."

We did as I said and wound through the huge Macy's to the men's department on the fifth floor. I teased him by holding up floral velvet sport coats and he did the same, daring me to try on hot pink shoes. Somehow we ended up dressing each other in whole new ensembles that served no purpose except to make each other laugh. To the registers we went, him buying my stuff, and me buying his. We looked ridiculous. People around us were visibly annoyed, rolling their eyes at our juvenile laughter. Meanwhile, I hadn't had so much fun in so long, I couldn't remember if I'd ever laughed with Rob the same way.

Instead of settling on ties alone, we had a veritable collection of mismatched items and our original outfits in large paper bags, carried wistfully over our shoulders. The Neiman Marcus was on the next street corner, and we stopped outside the doors to triple-check our tie knots.

"Why'd you do the double Windsor? Now the knot's too fat at your neck," Jax said, undoing my purple- and blue-floral skinny tie and adjusting the length. "You have a short torso, so don't start so high."

I tittered as if drunk while he breathed down on me. "I have a confession—I never really learned how to do this. Not like my dad was around to teach me, and nobody ever wanted me to look so formal on dates."

He pursed his lips in concentration as he straightened everything and tucked the tail in. "Have no fear, young *grasshoppa*. I'll show you the way."

"You should talk in an accent. After all, you said you were the King of England…"

"Oh, I'm way ahead of you," he said, straightening his back and clearing his throat. The affected tone in which he spoke was somewhat of a mixture between posh Shakespeare and high fantasy formal. "It is I, Jaxson of House Grady, coming forth to claim prizes for my mother. Forsooth, I have laid claim across the land and ended *here*, before this very vault of treasures before me."

I bowed, then mimicked him as I held the door open. "After you, good sir."

"With great thanks, Sir Tabby."

We poorly hid our infectious laughter and were immediately glared at by people on the ground floor. I pointed to the escalator, wanting to usher us upstairs so we wouldn't make too much of a scene.

As we ascended, he stared at the gilded, domed ceiling, which was still wondrous to me even though I'd been here a few times to look.

"It's cool, huh?" I asked.

"Definitely a big shiny cave. So, *this* is where George of the Jungle went."

"My God, I cannot believe you're here and thinking about *that* movie." I closed my eyes. "Now I am, too. Mmm… Brendan Fraser."

Jax prodded my side. "He gives you dimples."

"Shut up," I grumbled and bowed my head in embarrassment.

Each floor up was like another world. Different clothing designers set up dioramas and displays for things in outrageous colors and cuts, none of which were suitable as gifts. Like we did in the Macy's, we held things up for each other and scoffed at the prices of everything, though we were a bit more surreptitious in our disdain for the merchandise. Still needing to actually complete his goal, though, we opted to search ladies' accessories.

"Summer, summer, summer. It's, like, actually a season here," Jax said, gently lifting the brim on nearly every hat within reach. "If I got mom one of these hats, she'd probably like it, but she could only wear it for about four days at the beginning of next month before she'd have to put it away."

"Oh, come on. Summer doesn't end in August."

"It might as well, considering where she lives now. Brian moved them into the mountains past Leadville—too high of an altitude for a warm climate without wind." He moseyed through the tables and stands of belts and purses to find a small table marked *Clearance*. "Help me find some good gloves."

I did as he asked and picked out a few pairs, then remembered a game—one my teenage self invented with him on late nights when Mom was out too late working to patrol our conversations. "Hey Jax?"

He barely looked up from the pile. "Hmm?"

"Guess how much these are?" I held up a pair of bright red, fur-lined gloves and dangled them by the fingertips.

Jax paused and squinted at me. "No way."

"What?" I looked over my shoulder since his bewildered expression didn't fit what I asked.

"I was literally thinking we should play a game like that earlier. No joke. Used to do it online with a friend."

Shit. It terrified me to think he was on such a similar wavelength that I'd be caught in my lie without thinking.

But he didn't dwell on it. As if waking up from the boredom of gift searching, Jax rubbed his hands together and pursed his lips. "Okay, I guess…hundred bucks?"

"Higher. *Way* higher."

"Okay. Three hundred."

"Still higher."

"Bullshit." He lurched toward me and snatched the gloves.

"Holy hell, over five hundred? And they're on sale for that? No way, man. Nuh-uh. Totally ridiculous."

"Lucky for you, *these* ones are more reasonable." I handed him a pair of leopard-print, cashmere-lined gloves. "I mean, if she's living in cougar town…"

Jax burst with such loud laughter, the woman at the counter behind us actually made a shushing noise.

I put my hand on his tall shoulder. "Shh, you'll get us kicked out. I haven't even—"

Just then, my phone rang. Mom's tone. *Oh, great. I'm late.*

"I have to get this, Jax." I moved as close to the wall as possible. "Hey Mom. Sorry I haven't updated you yet."

"You can't do that to me, sweetheart," she said, letting out a relieved sigh. "Are you still coming tonight?"

"Well…" I glanced behind me at Jax, who fiddled with more gloves on the table so as not to bother me. While our weekly dinner was important to me, this time with him was precious. I didn't want to let it go.

"Tabby?"

"Sorry. You know what, don't count on me tonight. If I change my mind and want to get out of the city, I'll give you a call. I'm out with a friend right now."

"Really?" Mom's voice went into sing-song mode. "Anybody I know?"

Jax heard me say it, too, and a distinct smirk laced the corner of his lips.

I felt caught between the truth and my mother. The worst combination. "Let's just say I have no doubt you'd love him."

She snickered. "Okay, my love. Have fun. Don't leave me out of the loop, alright? And give Robby my love."

"I will. Love you, Mom."

"Love you, son."

Warmth flushed through me. *Thanks, Mom.*

Jax hummed quietly until I came back to his side. "That your mom?"

"Mm-hmm. I'm not sure if I'm going up to see her tonight. It's getting late."

"You really think she'd like me?" He swept an imaginary long lock of hair off his shoulder. "Aren't I special."

"Yeah, maybe you are, a little." My tone softened from the humor into a more honest place.

"Think I'd like her?" he asked, arching his brows.

I sighed, but slight pain took over where I should've felt comfort. *Rob doesn't like Mom. Thinks she's too clingy. He's jealous my mother still talks to me.* No matter how long we were together, Rob didn't feel comfortable letting her dote on him the way she wanted to. If she could've, Mom would have adopted every one of my trans friends.

Since I was too distracted to answer, Jax picked up our large paper bags and the gloves for his mother and headed for the small checkout counter where the cashier glared at us before. He charmed her with his usual kind smile, and he led back toward the escalator with a spring in his step.

It happened so fast. He got on first, but I tripped on my over-sized pants. While the stairs headed down, so did I, and Jax caught me.

"Whoa, there," he said, holding me up without faltering. "Haven't you ever been on one of these before?"

I felt feverish from shame. "Shit, I'm so sorry."

He let me right myself on another step and kept his hands on my shoulders. "It's okay. I've gotcha, Tabby."

There it was again. A perfect moment. A moment like when we sat in his car, and I stared into his eyes. Here was my Wah, so close, yet the ocean of a secret stood between us.

I pushed off the railing to catch my balance and refused to look him in the face while we awkwardly meandered our way to my office parking lot. Even with daylight savings, the city's tall buildings shadowed the sky. At eight o'clock, it felt oppressively dark.

Jax still took a risk I hadn't considered. "You know…if you're not sure about driving to Marin, I'm happy to take you."

I stared at him with wide eyes. *Oh, God. Don't even suggest meeting Mom.*

His tone was muted, like he knew it was a risk. "I mean, you and I get along so well. Maybe—"

"No," I blurted, regretting my panicked tone but couldn't rein it in. If I brought him, he'd know her instantly, and so would she. "Sorry. No. That's not something friends do."

Jax's attitude immediately chilled. He looked at me like I shot down a very public proposal—embarrassed and broken for trying.

But he had to know that would cross a line, right?

"'Kay." He threw his bag in the back of his car. The proverbial wound drew a scar on his face.

"Jax, wait." I held my hands up before he got in. "I didn't say that right. It's too early, that's all. Mom gets stressed easily. Please…I'm not trying to keep you out."

Jax paused as I hoped he would. "No, I get it. Really. Strange guy you barely know, but not your boyfriend, asks to meet your mom? How weird is that?"

While I wanted to say it wasn't weird at all, he was right, and I had nothing at the forefront of my mind that I could say.

Without meeting my eyeline, Jax shut his front door, looked out the back window and reversed with a jump. Speeding off through the alley, Jax left me in his trail of dust.

mother knows best

· · ·

Tabby

ALL THE TEARS made driving incredibly dangerous, but I risked it to get to Mom's house. I sobbed like I hadn't in years. The look of betrayal on Jax's face would haunt me until I spoke to him again. Calling him wouldn't have helped, because I couldn't give him the answers he really wanted.

But I *could* tell Mom.

Keeping the secret from her for a month was hard enough; now that he'd spent even more time with me, he would become even harder to hide. The fact Annie knew still scared me, too, and telling Rob was out of the question. If he knew my first love was living with Ethan, he would explode with irrational jealousy. Like we needed more reasons to fight.

Mom's bungalow in the bay was petite and appropriate for one. She had a great view of the green hills behind Sausalito and wasn't so close to the marina that it smelled like pond scum at low tide. In "the sweet spot," as she called it. Fortunately, there was space on the street out front for my small car, and I ran up to her door without texting that I was on my way.

The porch light flashed on, and she peered through the window, yelping in surprise. "Sweetheart, what's going on?"

"Mom?" I sniffled and wiped my face with both hands,

careful not to rub my eyes since I still had contacts in. "I need to tell you something."

"Okay...come in." She held me close and draped careful hands on my strange clothing when we sat down. "What is all this?"

"I went out. You know, with that friend." I took a few tissues from the box on her side table.

"Oh, no. Did something happen with your friend?" She cupped my face. "Tabby, what did he do to you?"

"No, it's nothing like that. He's fine. He's sweet. He's charming. He's generous." I hiccupped, unable to control it. "He's gorgeous. He's—"

"*Not* Robby," Mom said, squinting. She had her issues with him like everybody but helped ground me when I felt like giving up on us.

"Nope. He's not Rob." I shrugged and barely squeaked, "He's Jax."

She squinted even harder. "What do you mean, like Jax?"

"No, not *like* Jax. He *is* Jax." I felt like my age reversed by ten years. Nobody but Mom could see my panic. "He found me."

Mom was stunned. She offered nothing else.

"Guess now you know why I said I was sure you'd love him." Burying my face, I broke down in more bitter tears. "I still love him, too."

She dragged her fingers up and down my spine, still not saying anything at all. We marinated in our respective shock over his reappearance.

"He doesn't know it's me. Doesn't recognize me. It's a dream and a nightmare together. He's here, he's grown up, and he's just as wonderful now as he was when our lives were nothing more than potential plans. Now reality's here." I wiped my face again and righted my spine, staring at the ceiling as if that would help the downward flow of tears. "Tonight, we spent hours together, laughing and bonding like no time went by. But he asked to come meet you, and I shot him down. I'm so terrified of him finding out who I really am that I'm pushing him away."

"Oh, Tabby," she said, in a judgmental tone that screamed disapproval. "If that boy is anything like the one I remember, I'm sure it'll be fine if he knows. His father raised him right, that's for sure."

I frowned at her. "What would his dad have to do with it?"

Mom paused for a moment, halting the movement of her hand, then spoke with slow, careful words the way she did whenever she talked about *me* from the past. Helped her not use the wrong pronouns, so I was used to it. "Dale taught Jax how to be…respectful, I think, is the best word for it. Traditional. Jax came to our door when he got his driver's license and asked for my blessing to tell you he loved you. You two had been together for a while by that point, but it was very sweet to see a young man, dressed in a smart shirt and tie, nervously confessing his plans with my kid. It's the kind of thing your father would've wanted to see."

Like it did many times over the past few hours, my heart rushed. "He asked for your blessing just for that?" Even years in the future, his actions caught me by surprise. I recalled every moment of the first time he said it, the anxious tremble of his hands and the awkwardness afterward. But in retrospect, it wasn't spontaneous—Jax recited a well-practiced script.

"Of course not. He asked me not to tell you so it would be a surprise. I laughed about it with Dale later."

I tried to let her lightness set the mood and wiped my tears. "I can't believe you remember his dad's name."

She cocked a brow. "You didn't think I'd let you two go places without checking in on his end, did you? Parents talk, as they should. Especially when their teenagers might be sleeping together."

"Jesus, Mom." I turned away, not wanting to discuss it any more now than I did at sixteen.

Mercifully, she changed the subject back to the existing issue. "How long has Jax been in San Francisco?"

"Over a month. Now it feels too late to say anything." Shame forced me to surrender to her shoulder. I played with my tie, not wanting to remove it since his hands put it on me. "And I *shouldn't* say anything anyway. We have no future. I'm with Rob. I *love* Rob. He's been doing so much better lately, and I can't risk screwing that up over Jax."

Mom ran through my hair and relaxed, letting us both fall into the soft cushions of her oversized, green couch. "What does Rob think about all this?"

I scoffed. "Are you kidding me? He doesn't know. Jax moved in with Ethan, so if Rob found out our connection, he'd go ballistic. Can't risk it."

"So, your plan is to live happily ever after with Rob, never tell Jax who you are, and hope you can keep your feelings for both of them separate?" Mom tipped my chin up to her. "Sorry, son. I know you too well."

My eyes fell and focused on nothing just to escape her mind-reading glance.

"I don't have an answer for the next right thing to do. It's your choice. But remember what your therapist said all those years ago? You can't expect people to respect and accept you for who you are if you never show them. If you don't give Jax a chance to see who you've become, that's such a shame. I bet he would be proud of you."

This only made me cry harder. The truth was red-hot and cut through me. *Of course he would. He'd say it, too, and would ask me what I wanted to be called. Would whisper that I was a handsome man, and yield to my want to charm him in return.*

Yet I owed someone else the same chance to prove himself. "If I tell Jax the truth, and he fully accepts me, I'd be giving up on what Rob and I have. I can't risk what we've built for a chance with my teenage dream. Rob's better than that. God, how selfish can I—"

"Stop that," she said, attempting to halt my downward spiral of thought. "You deserve to have what you want in your life, Tabby. Telling Jax the truth won't change what you have unless *you* want that to change. Don't conflate telling him with having to be with him. One does not equal the other."

I sniffed and tried to focus on her through my waterlogged eyes. "But what if I do want to be with him? What then?"

She sighed. "Then you need to tell Rob."

"Ugh...Rob...why did Jax have to show up right when Rob seems to be getting his shit together?" My upset turned to frustration, and I stood to pace in front of the couch. "Seriously. Since he moved in, he's an entirely different person—except it's not perfectly consistent. One day, he'll bring me flowers or write me a cheesy note. The next day, he'll harp on me for not losing enough weight, or he'll ask if I'm considering surgery again. I keep tellin' him that I'm fine the way I am, and for a little while he'll act like he heard me, but then the cycle repeats."

"Have you actually talked to Rob about the good things, or are they just happening for no reason?"

"That's the thing—it's spontaneous. Like he stumbled on a blog post of ideas for charming your boyfriend. It's *weird*. And I think it's weird because the things he does..." I stopped myself, not wanting to say it out loud.

"What?" Mom leaned forward again. "Come on, say it."

I deflated my lungs and folded my arms. "He does things the way Jax would. It's like...Jax showed up, and now Rob is more like him than ever." There were no more words to help me pinpoint how to feel about Rob's change. Only one sufficed, and I said it while holding up both my hands. *"Bizarre."*

She stood and hugged me, pecking my cheek as she did. "I don't have an answer for you, sweetheart. But I trust that you'll do the right thing."

I groaned. *Sure. Except I can't be trusted with anything right now.*

. . .

IN TOO DEEP. *In too deep. In too deep.*

I couldn't very well Google, *How late is too late to tell someone the truth?* Without doubt, somewhere between *he asks if he knows you from somewhere* and *you could jump into the past without missing a beat.*

Guilt was a suffocating weed, and I'd spread the seeds all by myself.

As if keeping my secret from Jax wasn't enough, keeping it from Rob felt even worse. If I couldn't tell my boyfriend about my past, how could we ever move forward? My sideways betrayal of his trust had little to no justification. I debated the right way to tell my partner that my first love had emerged in our lives, and my heart hurt. Rob's volatile nature meant he could easily break up with me for keeping it from him or punish me by sticking around to rub the secret in my face for years. It really could go either way.

I drove home straight from Mom's place after changing back into my scrubs, determined to sit down with Rob as soon as I saw him, baring my soul and the minutiae of my life that he didn't already know. Even rehearsed certain phrases out loud in my car, all the way down to comebacks for all the hard questions I could imagine.

"Yes, Jax was my boyfriend a long time ago. No, he doesn't know who I am. No, I'm not still in love with him. How could I still be in love with him? I love *you*, Rob. Nobody else. You know better than to ask me that. Well, if you paid a little more attention, you might've noticed how my ring disappeared the night he came to D&D. This might come as a shock to you, but that ring? It came from Jax. If I wore it, he'd know, alright? It's too much. Too big. If anything, it proves how well he knew me then. Now? Yeah…yeah, he knows me pretty well. Understands me. No, I swear it isn't because I…I don't know if there will ever be a right time. But that's why I wanted to tell *you*, okay? You're supposed to love me back in this scenario. Our anniversary is coming up. If you don't want to stick around, guess I have a good choice for backup, don't I?"

The fake argument in my car felt too real, so I had to stop before it made my blood boil. My confession needed a delicate touch—not a rush of misplaced, defensive anger.

Here we go. Come on. I let out a long exhale and hopped from my car. Every step toward the front door of our building grew by another three feet for how long it took me to get up the stairs. The door was unlocked, and I said a silent prayer that Rob would be his newfound, patient self.

"Hello? Rob?" I called to the rest of the place, surprised he wasn't in the living room watching TV. Instead, from the back of the hall, I heard moaning.

Not just any moaning. Rob crying. A heart wrenching noise that made my stomach flip.

Dear lord. What happened?

I took ginger steps to the bedroom, finding him face-down in the black cotton pillowcases. A complete mess. It had been a long time.

"Rob?" I whispered, sitting at his side and rubbing his back. "Tell me what happened."

He choked into the fabric and pounded the mattress with heavy, strong fists that were powerful weapons. I was sure to stay clear of his rage. "My cousin Serena called me. Found me and called me. Wanted to let me know our grandma died."

"Oh, my God," I said, deflating to comfort him. "Rob, I'm so sorry. When is her service?"

"They already had it," he screamed, curling into himself even more. "Serena noticed I was missing and wanted to reach out so I would at least know. They didn't invite me. Didn't even fucking tell me. It's like I don't exist."

What came out of him was more than just tears. He wailed. Alone. A whole family out there who didn't want him, all because he'd rather be Rob and not Rachel.

"My mom told me I killed her baby. But her baby's right here.

I'm *right here,* and I need her. Fuck my dad. Fuck my brother. All the assholes who judged me. But Tabby, I need my mom." He coughed and stopped talking, drained of all feeling, having poured every last drop into the bedspread.

I spooned him tight against my chest and cried right alongside him, unable to pretend his words didn't hurt me, too. For all Jax might struggle to get over me, Rob was here, and his struggles were ten times as large. He understood me in ways Jax never could.

Our lives, no matter how joyful or good, were always tinged with a large dose of fear. Fear for our loved ones, our family, our friends. Fear for our jobs, our doctors, our care. It was fear that drove Rob and I into each other, and fear that made sure neither of us would leave.

So I kept Jax to myself and my lover by my side. "I'm here, Rob. I love you. I love you, I swear…"

autumn

. . .

Jax

TO PRESERVE MY SANITY, I avoided him for a week. Then that week became two. Three. August came and September buzzed by. At game nights, we barely made eye contact. Tabby sent me no texts, so I sent no replies. I deleted my socials and spent time building a computer with every customizable gadget I could get my hands on just to waste evenings away.

Rob's messages overran my phone at every turn. What I'd suggested over the past few months would've been regular gestures from someone like me—late night massages, small notes, affirmative gifts of time and attention. Rob fished for ideas as if I were a damned Hallmark catalog, but he never asked me to meet with Tabby in person again. Without an excuse, I took that—and Tabby's harsh rebuff the last time we were alone—as a sign to keep my distance. Instead, I poured my undefined, unrequited feelings into suggestions I would've wanted to perform myself.

My favorite time of year was transformed to the worst. With no one at my side, I'd never survive autumn.

Dad was the only person I told about my torn existence. While the fact I was hung up on a man caught him by surprise, he said my life was mine to live and I should love whoever I wanted. In his infinite wisdom, he gave one piece of advice:

"Kid, have you at least told him what you're feeling? Or are you hoping he'll figure it out on his own? Hate to break it to ya, but men aren't any better at mind-reading than women. That's why I taught you that playing games is a stupid thing to do."

"Staying quiet might be stupid, but trying to woo someone who's not single is an *asshole* thing to do, Dad." I put him on speaker phone while I installed a cooling fan at the back of my computer tower. "I'm struggling 'cause it's not going away, and I only see him once a week. Any tricks for that in your wheelhouse?"

Dad let out a quick sarcastic laugh. "Sure. Pick somebody else."

"God…easier said than done." A few people flashed in my mind as potentials—Megan from the sandwich place, my old friend Kelsey from back home, even Ethan. But a block in my head and my heart kept me from moving forward. "Maybe I picked Tabby 'cause I already know there isn't a shot. Makes it easier than being outright rejected."

A long sigh on the other end told me Dad was losing patience with me. "What's that ridiculous thing people say about basketball? If you take no shots, you'll make no baskets, or whatever the hell?"

"Something like that."

"Right, well, this is the same thing, isn't it? For cryin' out loud, Jax. Make a move already."

Whether it was his encouragement or admonition that hit my psyche hardest, I couldn't tell. But his counsel was clear. *I have to stop stalling.*

"I'll figure out something," I said, wanting so badly to mean it.

"Sounds good, kid. It's time to move on for you. World's still spinnin'."

"Right. Extra hot, extra—"

"Cheese, crispy relleno, give it a shot-o." Dad chuckled at his own clever half-rhyme, then sighed again. "Love you, Jax."

"Bye, Dad."

His words were somewhat hypocritical—after all, he hadn't done anything to get over his hang-up on Mom. But that was the point of his pushing me, wasn't it? He didn't want to see me stay stuck. I needed to make solid connections in my new home sooner rather than later, or loneliness would drive me insane.

MID-OCTOBER, and as things turned orange and gold, I missed home. Missed the snow. Missed what it felt like to have someone want me. Missed snuggling on the couch next to someone I loved.

Ethan knocked on my bedroom door frame soon after closing the shop downstairs. Thursday night, and I'd opted to skip D&D. "Hey, why didn't you join us?" he asked, peering over the many empty cardboard boxes for components I'd unpacked and installed through the evening.

"Not in the mood." I didn't take my eyes off the minuscule screw I was working on. The machine was always in need of improvement. Or maybe it was the fifth time I took it apart just to put it together again like Lego.

"You okay?" He sat on my bed and consolidated a few of the smaller boxes on my floor into a large one. "What's eating you?"

I finished putting the tower upright and sighed. "It's hard to explain."

"Our apartment's like Vegas. Talk to me." Ethan moved to the bottom edge of my mattress and patted the empty space next to him. His hair was no longer bright green on top; instead, he dyed it a shocking red for the season, which made his black beard all the more prominent. The tattoo of an anchor on his tanned forearm stood out, too. For all we had in common, we were nearly polar opposites—my conservative, unaltered appearance hid my inner nerd. He wore his personality proudly.

Taking his invitation, I plopped down beside him, leaving a solid foot between us. While I couldn't tell him the truth about my feelings for Tabby, I could still sidestep and discuss my frustrations.

"It's just...when I came out here, I thought moving on from my shitty ex would be easy. Turns out, that isn't so simple. I'm tired of trying to find someone new. Every new person has to get the life story over again. Makes early days feel like therapy. Wouldn't it be great if you could date like an online job interview and upload the same history for every contender, so you could skip past the 'let's see if we're compatible' shit and get right to the 'can this be the end of the line' stuff instead?"

"Pretty sure you just described online dating..."

"Come on, you know what I really mean. It's not about meeting someone for the first time; it's about finding someone who makes the hard work worth it."

Ethan's exaggerated smile was cartoonish in a way, though that might've been a side effect of his sculpted mustache. "I understand that. I take it you still haven't gotten laid since you've been here? I mean, you haven't brought anybody home with you, but I figured you at least found a hookup somewhere else. You're a decent-lookin' dude, Jax."

"Thanks." I scoffed and aimed my face at the floor. "I'm... hung up on somebody, but they're not interested. I'm not sure I'm built for one-night stands, and everything else feels too exhausting."

He shifted beside me and put his elbows on his knees, leaning his chin against his put-together knuckles to relax. "The occasional stranger never bothered me. But since Carlos left, it's been pretty quiet on my end, too."

"Were you two...you know...*more* than roommates?" I asked, pretty sure of the answer.

He nodded without meeting my eyes.

"Is that why he moved out? You broke up?"

Ethan sighed, saying enough by saying nothing at all.

"Damn." I wasn't sure how to comfort him. Rubbing his firm shoulder, I stayed quiet.

He broke through after an uncomfortable minute. "I think you're right. It *is* tiring to get to know someone else. It's so much easier to find a release that's not tied to somebody's feelings."

I nodded. "Guess you're right. I've just never tried it."

"Why not?"

As I glanced at him, I asked myself the same question. There wasn't a good answer.

His mischievous grin sent a shockwave through me. "Like, wouldn't it be great if you found a friend with benefits?"

Never in my life had I ever considered it, but talking to Ethan, it made too much sense. "I don't know if I believe that can really exist. But in theory? Yeah. I'd take it in a heartbeat."

"Oh, it can. Friends care, but not *too* much. They make sure you're safe and comfortable." He righted his spine to sit straight on the bed. "It's somebody to take your mind off things without an expectation. Even if it's only once, you know you aren't alone."

Thumping in my ears radiated to the tips of my body in unfettered pounding. It wasn't love, but it was what I needed. His confidence passed over to me. "That would be nice."

"And...it's not like it would be weird if we were both cool with it," he whispered.

For a moment, I forgot about Tabby. About Heather and Chris. About Dad. About Rob. Anything. Months of bottled-up energy boiled my blood.

"Honestly?" I said, staring into his face, "I'm cool with anything that helps me move on from the shit in my head."

"I'm happy to help." Ethan made the first move and scooted closer to me.

I'm doing this. Gazing over my mattress, I answered his invitation. "Right here okay?"

"Oh, hell yeah." Ethan yanked me in by my neck. His lips were soft beyond the forest of his facial hair. I hadn't kissed anyone in so long, my insides responded the same way it would while drinking a tall glass of water on a hot day—even without being ice cold and perfect, every drop felt good. Necessary. Sustaining. Welcome, and I needed more, to the point that I wouldn't dare stop. Didn't want to stop. Contact unlocked my bonds.

We pulled at our clothes until they were no more. He was gentle and didn't push my limits too much, letting me set the pace as I dropped to my knees.

Looking up at him, I focused on his handlebar mustache as it twitched with his breath. I was eager but unpracticed, so each puff was an insight to my performance. He stroked over my head and watched with a familiar longing—like he pined for contact the same way I did, even if it wasn't necessarily from each other.

There weren't many words between us at all, only nods and an unspoken signal for more. My nightstand supplied all the things that we needed. Ethan knew how to touch and the best ways to move, helping me learn as he helped me forget. He prepped well and fucked me to turn off my brain. As the night passed, we traded, one after the other, until both of us finished and said our goodnights.

I fell asleep hard and dreamed about nothing. The next day, I asked Megan for her number, without fear that I'd treat her like a rebound. I had a clean slate.

And that's how my roommate helped me survive autumn.

zoo day

· · ·

Tabby

EVERYONE in the city knew the best time to visit the zoo was
October. The warm weather, early burn off of the marine layer,
and the lack of tourists always made for a better experience. Rob
and I were on good terms—getting better all the time, thanks to
his extra effort and newfound penchant for acts of kindness
toward me. So even though it was my special day, I woke up
before noon on Saturday, made a smart breakfast of egg whites
and turkey bacon, and waited for Rob to join me at the table.

He grumbled, as usual, never a morning person either, but no
one could resist the delicious crackling from our stove. With a
wide yawn, he sank into his preferred chair. "What's this for?"

"Well, I figured since you've been so great to me lately, I can
make breakfast. Nothing on the no-no list, I promise." I pushed
his plate forward. "You'll need energy for what I have planned
today."

"Hmm?" He took a bite and, quite unceremoniously, talked
with his mouth full. "Whatcha wanna do?"

I tried not to be bothered by the fact he didn't remember. He
made no comment on the taste or even a thankful nod. He dove
in without thinking. Classic Rob, so I couldn't expect anything
different. Making him feel guilty wasn't the goal, so I left out the

big thing. "It's a zoo day," I said, showing him a wide grin. "I haven't been in years. That's the big plan today."

Rob cocked a brow. "The zoo? Are you twelve?"

"Everybody likes the zoo. Even *you*. Come on, you knew I was a nerd when you met me."

He groaned, then stared at his plate, which was quickly empty. "Whatever."

My stomach rolled over. I wanted Rob to keep up the same attitude he had whenever he surprised me. His sudden appreciation for my interests and my plans made his typical grouchiness more tolerable. Right now, I wanted Rob to act like Jax and find my excitement endearing; instead, Rob was embarrassed by me, and we were alone.

"Do you not want to go? Because I can call Annie. Bet she'd love to come. In fact, the whole group would. You're the only one who'd be a stick in the mud."

Rob dropped his fork with a loud clank on the plate, and I startled. "Is that all you want from me today? To go to the zoo?" He was annoyed, but that was the worst of it.

While my nerves were still harried, I recited inner comebacks. *It would be a damn start. And a thanks for making breakfast would be nice, too. Oh, how about, how did you sleep? Anything on your mind? How's your mom? Sorry I didn't do dinner again yesterday.* I let my mind tear around with unexpressed frustrations before answering, "It's the least you could do for your boyfriend on his birthday."

"Holy *fuck*. It's your birthday, babe?" Rob snapped into action and took my hands, going back to the sweetheart he'd been as of late. "I am so sorry. I didn't know it was the tenth already."

"Right. I didn't make a big deal out of it on purpose. But yeah. Today's my birthday. Big three-oh."

At least his remorse meant he'd try a little harder. "Do you want the group to come to the zoo? I can do that. I can get everybody together. Is that what you want, babe?"

Babe. Today it irritated me. The term didn't flow well some-how, and I never said it back. It felt cheap. So unspecial. Couldn't change it now. "Actually, yeah. Let's all go."

"Who all do you want there? Whole group, or..."

"Everybody. Invites all around."

"You got it." Rob pecked my cheek, put his plate in the sink, and tapped away on his phone for a while. "Noon okay for you?"

"Perfect. I'm taking a long shower first."

"Enjoy yourself," he said, then went back to focusing on his phone.

Ready to start my thirtieth year with a squeaky-clean slate, I reveled in the hot water flowing down my body. Steam filled our whole bathroom like a sauna even after I was done. Gifted with time to clean myself up, I used a straight-edge razor to carve the straight jawline of my goatee, then put sleek oil in my hair so my natural wave would show after it dried.

My chest wasn't sculpted like Rob's was, but it made me happy. As a teen, I thought about top surgery many times, but opted out. Gender fluidity complicated how I felt about my body, and I decided long ago that hormones were enough for me. I didn't focus on the dysphoria anymore; instead, I made a conscious effort to appreciate what made me feel whole. Black boxer briefs. Being called "Sir". Rob used a packer, and I had a modest one, but I didn't wear it every day. It was another thing to think about, and it didn't make me feel any more like a man.

I'd hurt myself and bruised my ribs by accident in the early days of my transition, flattening my chest; since then, I'd learned how to wrap myself with tape correctly, and disciplined myself to take it off so I could breathe. In front of the mirror after putting on my favorite skin-toned binder, I fluffed my tease of upper chest hair so it would show regardless of whatever I wore for the day.

It's good to have layers. The breeze off Ocean Beach...

Rob spoke loudly in the other room. Phone call; he didn't

have my bad habit of talking to himself. "You gonna carpool? I figure we can all take him for dinner after. Did you know it was his birthday today?" He paused, and his volume dropped. "Oh. Oh, you did. Yeah. What? No, of course I did. I'm not that much of an asshole."

You completely forgot. Why save face now? Who is that?

"Anyway, *you* were the one who almost killed Carlos when you bought him that strawberry thing for his birthday. We all knew he was allergic."

Ethan. Gotcha. They'd been friends long before I met either of them, though Ethan fit in better with my clan than Rob did, and now I thought of him as an essential part of the group. Nevertheless, I was glad they had each other, and Rob had someone else to talk to besides me.

I pulled out a loose pair of jeans and a black T-shirt, complete with my favorite button-down. It was covered in various-sized mushrooms. Totally tacky, perfect, and me.

"Um, yeah. I don't see why not. The more the merrier, I think. As long as she's cool with...oh yeah? Right on."

With the little bit I could overhear, I guessed Ethan had a new girlfriend. Someone who was probably just as eccentric, but still too new to warrant mentioning on Thursday.

Rob gasped. "No. You're kidding." Another long pause. "Uh-huh. Oh, I'm sure. Shit, man. When are you gonna learn?"

I shook my head. *What did he get into now?*

Once I finished getting dressed, I came out to the living room and picked my phone off the coffee table. Almost everyone in the group responded to Rob's first message, but two were missing. Ethan and Jax. That's why Rob called.

"Alright, well, we'll see you three at noon, okay?" Rob smiled at me and held up one finger, almost done with his call. "Right. I won't, I promise. Scout's honor. I just can't believe it happened again." He laughed—truly genuine, not like the chuckles he gave when he didn't get the joke or he wanted me to stop talking. "Well, you didn't *have* to tell me."

Ooh, a secret? I pouted and gave puppy eyes.

Rob gave me a thumbs up and nodded.

Sorry, Ethan. I'll still get to know.

He sighed and turned on his judgmental tone. "Call it whatever you want, dude. You still slept with your roommate."

The instant Rob said it, my mind went blank. Numb. My stomach fell ten stories in a small space.

It can't be. Not Jax. He's not like that at all. He doesn't want to rebound. He told me so. That's why he stayed single...it's why...oh, God. I tried to shake my jealousy out of my limbs with a full-body shudder, all too aware that the moment Rob hung up, I'd have to hear details I didn't want. *Ethan did this before when he slept with Carlos. They ended in disaster. That can't happen to Jax. It's not fair to him. He's too sweet. He's too perfect. He's my Wah. Wah deserves better.*

Goddammit, this is what I was afraid of. Jax shouldn't be with Ethan. He should be with—

"Wow, babe. You are not gonna believe this." Rob continued to shake his head when he sat at my side with a drawn-out sigh. "Ethan did it again."

I unglued my lips to respond, though my jaw was still tight. My only comfort was knowing that reading between the lines of what Rob said meant I didn't have to hear him say it out loud. "Are they...um...together now, you think?"

"Nah. Just a one-time thing." He joined me on the couch and put his phone down, relaxing with his arms behind his head.

"One-time thing, huh?" I didn't want to know, but I wanted to know everything. "Why would they do that?"

Rob shrugged, not sensing my urgency. That was probably for the best.

"Like, why would Ethan want to sleep with Jax in the first place? What good would that do?" I asked, speeding up with every passing word.

"I think of it like this—it means Jax wasn't full of shit when he said he was bi."

"Of course not. Why would somebody lie about that?" I stood from the couch and lost my internal filter. "Bi, pan, whatever. Maybe it's great for you to have proof, but I always believed it. Jax doesn't lie. Even if he were gay, it wouldn't make sense. Ethan's such a goddamn man whore. Why couldn't he pick somebody else?"

Rob grimaced.

I was in a corner with my foot in my mouth. *Shit. I said too much, didn't I?*

"It was one time for Christ's sake. I don't know why they fucked, Tabby, but who cares?"

"But how do you know it was really one time?" Out of my control, I yelled in my panic. "How do you know he's not going to turn Jax into another Carlos?"

"'Cause Jax is bringing a date," he screamed, matching my volume and then some.

This news wasn't any better. I still had the same twisting yank in my belly. To avoid another fight, I softened my voice. "A…a date?"

"Yeah. Ethan says you know her, apparently. Some chick named Megan."

Megan. The sandwich place.

"Jesus. Whatever happened between them, it happened, and it doesn't mean anything. I shouldn't have let you eavesdrop." Rob stood and muttered something nasty under his breath that I couldn't quite hear, and I didn't ask. He put on his shoes and waited outside while I tied up mine and locked everything.

It was my birthday, dammit. And I was determined to have a good time—Jax or no Jax, Rob or no Rob, confusing pulled heartstrings or comfortable love.

I just needed to figure out which one was which.

THE CAR RIDE was short but silent. Our raised voices were enough to spoil the mood even though our exchange at home barely counted as a fight. I directed as Rob drove, trying to stay meek so he'd remember why we were doing this at all.

Once we parked, I put my hand on his thigh. "Rob, I want you to have a good time. I'm sorry I overreacted. Guess I'm just a little bit moody today."

He didn't stay to talk with me and slapped my hand away, then jumped out of the car with a slam. His patented "I need to blow off steam" move.

Like this morning with the fork on the plate, I had a flashback but quickly dashed it. Rob's bullshit would have to wait until later. I took a deep breath and suppressed every urge to scream until the windows shook.

Annie, Cordelia, Gavin and his boyfriend stood together by the front gates. Gavin made a new introduction for all of us so we were on the same page with his beau's moniker for the day.

"My lover has decided to go by Memo for the weekend," he said, holding him tightly against his chest, flexing his biceps. Nearly monstrous next to Memo, but it was endearing.

"Memo?" Rob rolled his eyes.

"Knock it off, Rob," Memo said, squeezing up against Gavin's thick, tattooed arm. He flipped Rob off and displayed a professional rainbow of pristine nail polish. "Annie likes it."

"Of course I do, sweetie," she said without a hint of sarcasm. "Who are we waiting on? Ethan and Jax?"

"And Megan," I said, eyeing her carefully. "Jax has a date." *Please read my mind today and stay by my side.*

She nodded, giving me a knowing tip of her head. "Good to know."

Cordelia hopped in place from one foot to the other, echoing my own giddiness. Seeing her normally dark self get excited was a treat. We'd bonded over a mutual love of Anne Rice at a time when she wondered if she might be like me, but she conceded a cisgender lesbian life filled with masculine hobbies was just as valid. *No Shame Train* was her motto.

"Happy birthday, Tabby," Cordy said. "This is so awesome. I

can't remember the last time I did this. I hope they let us feed the giraffes."

"Oh, me too," I said, doing my best to ignore Rob's pout.

"There they are," Gavin said, pointing behind me.

"Jax! Ethan!" Annie raised her hand high and bounced twice to be seen. Shortest of all of us, she had springs in her heels, peeping for attention.

Reluctantly, I twisted to watch them, forcing the lump in my throat to stay low. I didn't wear contacts, but my sunglasses were sufficiently dark to hide my eyes.

They meandered through the parking lot. Megan, with her bright red hair, looked distinctly different and more carefree than she ever did at work. She chose a knee-length dress covered in sunflowers—clearly a choice that she wanted to use before the year's weather turned. Jax's decidedly casual dusty blue shirt, emblazoned with the Colorado flag, matched his navy baseball cap. Not trying too hard in the slightest.

But nothing he had on could distract from the most magnetic aspect of his outfit: his blinding, carefree, look-at-me, no-tension, confident and irrepressible smile.

God-fucking-dammit. That's an "I just got laid" face if I ever saw one.

Ethan walked on the opposite side of Megan, dressed in a black and red T-shirt covered in anime characters I didn't recognize. His black jeans and red shoes completed his head-to-toe color scheme. It matched how badly I felt he burned me, even though he had no clue.

I turned to Rob and grabbed his hand. He raised his face just long enough for me to move in for a kiss.

"Whoa," he said, releasing in surprise. "What's that for?"

"It's my birthday." I moved my glasses down enough to meet his eyes with mine. "You're all I want, okay?"

I swear, if you push me away now, I might implode.

He softened, then pushed my glasses back up. "So are you, babe."

. . .

ONCE WE PAID our way in, the troupe debated which exhibits to see first. Like she normally did at D&D, Annie stood in the center of us, taking control of the map.

"If we go down this way, there's a petting zoo and a bug house. Giraffes are the other direction, winding through this big island of lemurs."

"Yuck. We can skip the bug house," Rob said.

My face fell. Didn't he know me at all?

"No, we can't miss that," Jax said, speaking loudly enough for me to hear his voice for the first time today. He remembered what Rob didn't even know.

Megan, virtually a complete stranger, spoke with a grating high tone. Like her oversized earrings, she almost wore it as an accessory. Something to get Jax's attention. "Uck, a bug house? Don't they keep tarantulas in there? Somebody save me," she said while leaning backward against him.

Behind my sunglasses, I hoped he wouldn't see my jealous eyes when he flashed a glance my way. He didn't respond to Megan fast enough, and she clutched his clothes after tipping too far.

"Whoa—"

Ethan stepped in front of him, catching her before she fell completely. "Be careful there, you."

"I can't believe I almost fell," she said, nodding in thanks to Ethan, but planting her feet next to Jax once she righted herself.

I didn't want her to fall on her face, but I secretly rejoiced that he didn't catch her.

"Tabby, it's up to you. Where do you want to go?" Annie asked.

Too flustered to pay attention to my surroundings, I caved to Rob's suggestion. "Giraffes are fine with me."

back in it

. . .

Jax

TABBY CHARGED AHEAD with Rob and Annie at the front. Megan, Ethan and I made the other bookend far behind everyone else. Gavin, Memo, and Cordelia made up the center, spreading out so far, I could barely see Tabby anymore. We might as well have been three separate tour groups.

Why did I even agree to come? Moving forward with Megan wasn't a bad idea, but bringing her to a place where I wanted Tabby's attention only meant I was too distracted to give any to her. She hung off my arm, but it felt like nothing. I had no butterflies or secret plans for Megan. She might as well have been my sister for all that I wanted to turn on the charm. If meaningless sex with Ethan taught me anything, it was what meaningless really felt like. It proved my unsettled stirring for Tabby was something I couldn't ignore.

Still, I tried to enjoy the atmosphere, the weather, and the chance to find something about the city that wasn't work or the game shop. The date on the calendar marked an anniversary for me that I didn't want to acknowledge; I had every intent to snooze the day away and invite Megan for drinks later, but a sun-filled date to the zoo? That was right up my alley. I jumped at the opportunity.

The chance to see Tabby had nothing to do with my eager acceptance to go. Nothing at all. Except everything.

"Jax?" Megan asked with a grind in her tone, like she'd already said it three times. "Yoo-hoo, are you in there?"

"Huh?" I snapped into reality as everyone moved off from the mandrill exhibit and on toward the tigers and other large felines. My thoughts took me down memory lane of the layout I was used to from home. "Sorry about that. I feel disoriented here. I've only ever been to two zoos in my life, and this one's nothing like either of them."

"Tell me about that," she asked, letting Ethan go ahead of us by a few feet.

Part of me wanted to stop everything early, since I wasn't going to talk to Tabby at this rate, and Megan wanted me to be a chatterbox. But Dad would've said I was being rude, so I obliged her, doing my best not to sound too disinterested. "Denver and Cheyenne Mountain. You can only go to the zoo back home on days when the weather's just perfect—out here, every day fits the bill. It's odd to me that we're here in the sunshine and Dad sent me a text that said they were gonna get snow this week. But that's Colorado for ya."

She absorbed my every word. "So, are you close with your dad?"

Already, I was exhausted with giving my life story, and I hadn't even scratched the surface. "I am, yeah." I pointed ahead to the group. "Let's catch up. I don't wanna fall too far behind and get lost."

Megan deflated a little, obviously hoping to do just that, but she played along, and we skipped ahead.

By the big cat house, a parade of small kids swarmed around the tigers, since two of them were awake and walking by the glass. It was a cool sight, but it made me homesick for the exhibits I knew so well. Wistfulness was already on my mind.

The largest tiger hypnotically paced back and forth. It might've been the stripes, or his sheer size, but he didn't have the expression of a ferocious beast. Instead, he looked like an oversized housecat with an unmistakable long-whiskered grin.

Like a tabby cat, I thought, shaking my head. *Shit, this has to stop.*

Megan and Ethan chattered behind me. He said something that made her laugh, and unlike the giggles she'd given me all morning, it was genuine and heartfelt—nothing like the high-pitched cackling she did for my benefit. I didn't bother trying to win her attention and quietly celebrated that I might not have to.

We circled the cat house until the path ended by the penguins; their stench made everyone grimace. Disgusting, but cute. An ice cream cart was just upwind enough to be tolerable, and Tabby flagged the whole group down to stop at a nearby bench.

"Snack, anybody?" he asked, scanning all of us before taking a few steps toward the snack cart.

Gavin and Memo jumped in line along with Cordelia. Ethan and Megan lagged before ultimately joining them. Annie ran to the water fountain, and I opted to hold down the empty bench.

Now alone together, Rob got too close and spoke like a hurricane. "Okay, birthday ideas. Quick."

"What?" I narrowed my gaze. Face to face, I couldn't hide my disdain for his lack of foresight. "I have an excuse because I didn't know until today. Did you seriously not get him anything yet?"

"I lost track of the date. Come on, gimme something." He scoped toward the cart to make sure we still had a little time.

Only the tiniest shred of mercy motivated me to speak at all. "Peacocks. He likes peacocks. Find something like that here."

Rob groaned. "Are you kidding me? That's the best you can do?"

My blood boiled. "Well, normally I would have more time and some other resources, wouldn't I?"

"I thought you were 'Mr. Romance'," he said with wagging air quotes.

"I thought *you* were Tabby's boyfriend."

He checked back to the cart again. "If I mess up his birthday again, he'll never forget it. I already shit the bed last year when I had to work late, and he ended up going to dinner alone. Please."

Rob's remorse was genuine, and he wanted so badly to be the good guy. Why he hadn't picked up anything on his own, I didn't understand, but I could still be kind.

Sighing, I caved. "I already gave you a good idea. Peacocks. Seriously—find a big feather at the gift shop and...I don't know...tell him to chase you."

He glared.

"I'm serious. He'll love it. Just use it to your advantage and ask him to name anything else that he wants. You don't want me to guess. Let him tell you."

"I can't fucking believe—"

"Hey." I put my hands on his shoulders to hold him still. "Have any of my ideas failed yet?"

Rob rolled his eyes. "No."

"Then you have to trust that I know what I'm doing."

Annie trotted up to us sooner than expected, mercifully interrupting. "You guys okay?"

"Yeah," Rob and I said in unison. He walked away without another word.

She sat at the bench and stretched her back. Even in the sun, she wore all black, but her earrings were seafoam green glitter fluffballs and her bracelet was some kind of amateur chainmail. I would've bet money she made everything. Like she showed with her D&D maps, Annie's creative side covered her, too. "It's so wonderful out, don't cha think?"

"Mm-hmm." I kicked at the ground, wishing I could go home.

"So, uh..." Annie moved a little closer toward me. "Meg's pretty sweet. Where'd you find her?"

"She works the register at my favorite lunch place."

"I see. And you work downtown, right? Union Square?"

"Yup. Tabby's not far from me."

As soon as I said it, I felt like a fool. *I can't keep his name outta my mouth for five minutes, can I?*

"Oh, so *that's* why she looks familiar. He's taken me there a couple times when I'm in the area." Annie inched closer still. "But Jax?"

Raising my face to see hers, I was all too aware of my blushing.

"I think Ethan's going to take your girl home if you don't wake up," she whispered.

"Ugh." I leaned my head against the tree behind me. "Whatever, man. She likes him better anyway. Can't blame her."

Before we could keep talking, the group swarmed with their cones and oversized cotton candy, fully embracing the childlike whimsy that Tabby encouraged everyone to explore.

"They didn't have plain chocolate. I hate this sherbet stuff," Memo said, fussing in his usual manner and pouting at Gavin.

"Aw, I'm sorry, *Legal Pad*," Cordelia said, taking an innocent jibe at his moniker.

"Hey—"

"No, no," Annie chimed in, "*Stationary* has a point. Tart isn't for everyone."

Tabby cracked up. "That's my favorite thing ever. Oh, my God."

I couldn't resist when I saw him enjoying it. "Really? Sherbet's my favorite. Jot that down, *Notebook*. Or would you prefer *Journal?*"

Ethan and Megan were too busy feeding each other small spoonfuls to join in, but they did snicker at Memo's beet-red face.

"You assholes can't appreciate a little bit of creativity," he said, only half-angry, too eager for the attention.

"If you were really creative, you would've chosen *Disserta-*

tion." Tabby could barely choke it out through his snorting laughter, which lit me up inside.

"Honey," Memo whined, pawing at Gavin, "They're making fun of me again."

Gavin sighed and kissed him on the cheek. "You'll be okay, my little *Post-It.*"

Memo melted a little and grinned. "I like that one."

"Aww," Annie said, putting her hands over her heart. "That's so sweet, I might get sick."

As we laughed, Rob came back from the bathroom and stood behind Tabby, wrapping him with strong arms.

My heart jumped, but not as far as it did when Tabby turned and kissed him openly.

I turned to watch the penguins and their acrobatic leaps from the top of the fake rock island to the water. Over and over, like the tiger before, I shut my brain down to temper my jealousy.

Happy birthday, Tabby. I wish you nothing but the best.

bonds so tight

. . .

Tabby

ONCE EVERYONE FINISHED with their ice cream, we moseyed through the bears and wolves, stopping to take a few pictures as a group. I stood in the center next to Rob and tried to make sure no one felt left out. That was a challenge since I hadn't so much as spoken to Jax all day—I didn't even try to make eye contact long enough to nod at him. He might as well have been absent.

Megan continued to rasp on my mind every time she spoke, and so did Ethan. But by the time we made it to the kangaroo exhibit, they bothered me because they spoke to one another, not to Jax. His voice wasn't anywhere in the mix. In fact, he fell behind, reading every info sheet like he was taking a field trip quiz when we were done.

I couldn't focus on him. This was *my* day. When Rob squeezed my hand and said, "Let's look for peacocks," I was with the right guy once again. He didn't tell me how he knew, but he did. That's what mattered. Like always, his wins made up for all the losses, each one a new tally in the *pro* column.

Cordelia insisted on stopping again at the main cafeteria on our way out, in front of the flamingos. We all crowded inside to find something more filling than ice cream. People bustled all around us; their voices echoed off every hard surface, making conversation next to impossible. A wave of fatigue from my early morning caught up with me. I wanted to sit down, sleep, rest my eyes; the dark sunglasses made it worse. Even if I avoided Jax inside, I couldn't take the glasses off because Annie wouldn't stop snapping pictures that she shared on the group text chain.

Overstimulated and needing some air, I patted Rob on the shoulder. "I need some air. It's stuffy in here."

"Alright. Don't go too far." He didn't offer to come with me, which I expected, so I took it as a win for privacy when he chose to pay more attention to his cheeseburger than to me.

Beyond the flamingos, I stopped at a bench outside the antique carousel. Dissonant tones of the old-fashioned music leaked from inside the turntable of horses, reminding me of almost forgotten days with Dad. It had been so many years, I could barely remember what he looked like. But he loved the carousel. *This* carousel. A truth I didn't even tell Rob: San Francisco was where I was born, and as such, this zoo was my childhood comfort. He thought I was being immature to want to be here. I was simply nostalgic. I missed my dad.

My phone buzzed in my pocket. I expected to see a snarky message from Rob about how long I'd been gone, but it was a surprise relief instead.

Psst. Meet me at the bug house.

I smirked, then looked both ways on the path and snuck past the carousel to the kid's section. A playground and petting zoo paved the way to a small research building covered in acrylic, colorful insects. Unchanged by time.

The doors opened wide to a quiet space, no larger than a typical classroom. To my delight, it was how I remembered it, lined with terrariums and fascinating creatures. My first stop was a small box that allegedly housed a black widow spider.

When I couldn't find it, I moved on to the next, which was filled with stick bugs clinging to a black netting.

Jax, having turned his baseball cap backward, looked at me from the other side of the enclosure. "Well, well, well. Fancy seeing you here," he said, smirking with his whole face.

I poorly fought back a smile. "Yeah, what a coincidence."

We didn't break eye contact, though through my glasses, I wasn't sure what he could actually see. It didn't matter, though. The pull between us was magnetic, out of our control. He stepped to the right, and I stepped to the left, until we were face to face with no barriers.

"Happy birthday," he said, with a drop in his tone that was almost a whisper.

"Thanks."

Awkwardly, he tipped his whole body to the side, then opened his arms to invite me in.

For a split second, I was paralyzed, wishing for more, but I chuckled to break the tension. "Come here." I hugged him tight against my chest and breathed in the scent of his skin.

Clean. Tide. Maybe a little cologne? For Megan. Right. I released faster than I wanted to.

He put his hands in his pockets and rocked on his heels. "Well, it's not The Butterfly Pavilion. But it will have to do. What's your favorite thing in here?"

You. Resisting the urge to flirt with him outright, I glanced over the walls. "Is it too much if I say I like watching the caterpillars?"

Jax cocked a brow. "Could you *be* any more gay?"

I burst out laughing. "Damn right. What can I say? Turning into something beautiful is kinda the whole point of my life."

"Butterflies are so fuckin' cliche. Let's find something better." He moved to the many dioramas by the walls that held pinned insects instead of live ones. Pointing to a black, horned monster no smaller than his hand, he hummed a victorious tune. "Look at this guy. You're not a butterfly. You're a rhinoceros beetle. I mean, I don't know what you used to be like, but I know you now. So, I say, you went in a horrific, grubby creature, and came out something *way* more badass."

Jax's description was funny and beautiful, exactly the kind of thing he always excelled at. I'd take it. "Horrific, grubby creature, huh?"

He chuckled. "How about you focus on the badass part instead. Relax. You haven't even taken your sunnies off."

"Right." We moved along to make room for a group of young kids who wanted to see the beetle board. I stopped again in front of the largest tarantulas, fascinated and terrified by their size.

"I can't believe you almost skipped this place," Jax said, half under his breath.

"Not everybody gets why it's so important to me. Especially not—" I stopped myself, suddenly aware I was about to blame him by mentioning Megan.

No need. He already knew where I was going. "That's on me. I brought a squirmy girl. Didn't know she was squirmy until today."

"Not your fault. I can sacrifice to make people comfortable. Got a whole life of practice for that." I forced myself to say anything supportive, despite the way I had to mine my heart for it. "You better not screw that up, by the way. She knows we hang out. If you hurt her, I'll have spit in my sandwiches for the rest of my life."

Jax hissed in through his teeth. "Then I guess it's a good thing I basically set her up with my roommate. They really hit it off today." He shook his head.

"Are you, um…disappointed?" I asked.

"Not really. I said the first time we had lunch there that I didn't feel anything for her. Don't know why I tried to force it."

It was a risk to mention what I knew, but I couldn't escape it. "Not Megan. What about Ethan?"

Jax stopped cold and frowned.

"He told Rob…Rob told me." I pressed my lips in a knowing line. "Are you sure you're okay?"

"Jeez. Yes, I'm fine. It was nothing. Ethan was just…trying to make me feel better. It's not a big deal."

For all he said, there was so much he didn't—like what he needed to feel better for. But I let it go. If I had any hope to restore the great bond we had the last time we were alone together, I couldn't do it by invading his privacy. Instead, I tried offering up some of mine.

"Can I tell you something, Jax?"

He shuddered like the last topic needed to be brushed away. "Of course. Go ahead."

I didn't pause my exploring and walked from terrarium to terrarium. "I know coming to the zoo for your birthday as an adult is somewhat childish. But this was the last place I remember going with my dad before he died. He taught me to love this stupid little place." Tears threatened, yet they didn't manifest. My voice shook just shy of the breaking point. I rode the line of danger like I had every day since Jax appeared.

He stroked my arm with the back of his fingers. "Oh, Tabby…"

"Nobody knows that." I faced him, glad again that my eyes were covered. "Nobody but you."

He hardened his face. "Thank you. I'm honored."

"I know things have been weird between us since…well—"

"It was stupid. You're entitled to your life. I'm not a part of it."

"No, Jax." I took his hand with gentle touch. "I *want* you to be part of it. That's the point."

This time, Jax inhaled with a stagger. He squeezed my hand, then released it. "Can I tell you something, too?"

"Yes." I gulped, praying he saw through my lies so I wouldn't have to correct them out loud. *Please know me, Wah. Kiss me right now.*

"This day..."—he started, then stared at the floor—"...you're the second person in my life with this birthday."

"I am?" *Yes. Get closer. Come on.*

"October tenth was my first love's birthday. The girl I told you about with the eye thing?" He bit his lip and turned his cap the right way around, probably to try and keep his cool. "Every year on this day, I look for her."

Look for me? I blinked a few times. "I don't understand."

"Online. This is the day I spend searching the web for her name. Where she went to school. Mutual friends. Clues." He shrugged. "I never find anything."

That's not an accident. "Lots of people don't do social—"

"Yeah, but nothing? I mean *nothing.* No trace. No family. No pictures. She could've changed her name. Could've changed her look." His crestfallen cheeks and lips all screamed defeat. "This morning, I finally figured it out."

I couldn't imagine where he was going with it. If he solved the riddle, he didn't sound happy. "Okay..."

"Tabby, she and I made a promise. A promise we would give our love a chance someday and would search for each other. It's why my dad was always certain she'd find her way back to me." A tear fell down his cheek, which he quickly wiped away, trying to hide it from the kids in the room.

"I don't get it. If you've looked, that's all you can do, isn't it?" Fear and guilt spoke for me, trying to justify my own broken false promise.

"That's just it. Even if she wanted to stay hidden, I didn't. I'm easy to find on purpose." He folded his arms and looked at the ceiling. "I have a profile on every site possible. A single search will take you right to me, especially since I have a funny name." Redness stained Jax's eyes, obvious despite the dark cast from my glasses. "If she was out there, she would've found me. Would've wanted to, like she said. So now, on her thirtieth birthday, I have to accept that my Hwa is gone. Dead."

No. Oh God, what have I done? My heart caught in my throat.

He didn't forget our special words; he really just didn't hear me the time that I said it in the car when I had a burst of courage. I couldn't pretend to ask him what it meant—now I stammered and sputtered, trying to backtrack. "Jax, no. N-no, you don't know that. You *can't* know that."

"But I do. If she hasn't found me, that means two things: either she's gone, or she didn't love me. And the latter...that's just too hard to take." He sniffed hard, then turned his cap backward again, trying to be strong. "If she found happiness somewhere else, she would've told me. That's the kind of love we had." Jax gently took my hand again. "So, while I'm heartbroken over her loss, today I'm grateful for something new."

"What?" I whispered, still praying he'd figure me out.

"You live in the city where she used to live. It's like you can read my mind sometimes. All my lucky pennies and stupid beliefs—none of it compares to this." He ran his thumb over my knuckles. "We're comfortable and have so much in common. I mean, look at you. You're such a *fun guy*." Jax smirked and nodded with his chin at my shirt; until that moment, I forgot it was covered in mushrooms.

I chuckled even though my mind spun in circles. So close, so far, so tragic and painful.

"I'm too superstitious to think this is an accident. Call me crazy or say what you will. When I learned this morning that you share her birthday...Tabby, maybe she brought me you."

Jamie was dead—once to me, now to him. She perished in some stupid game I played to hide my teenage fear, which resurfaced at thirty years old as if it never faded. "Jax, I—"

"It's a hell of a replacement, Tabby. I'm so glad you're my friend." He released my hand. Let me go. Gave me up.

Friend. Suddenly, I hated that word. All it implied. Nothing more than that.

"I have to get going. I told Ethan to take Megan for a drink, and I'd get a ride home. Your sandwiches are safe as long as he calls her again." He patted my shoulder and turned.

"Wait, you're not coming to dinner with us?" I grabbed his arm before he could get too far away.

He twisted to me and shook his head.

"Why?" My tone was more frantic than I intended, but with my low voice, nobody could tell.

His gaze drifted away, not focused on anything. "Tell you what. You do dinner with the crowd. Maybe sometime this week we can do lunch again. Just us."

It wasn't the door I wanted it to be. A window was enough. "Sure. But you have to promise me you won't flake."

"I won't." He pulled away and left. The bright light outside surrounded his body in a halo when he passed through the doors.

There I stood. Alone. Lost and broken in the bug house, the last place my father would want me to be.

what i want

. . .

Tabby

> Where the hell are you

ROB'S TEXT brought me out of the funk and the clouds to reality. Terrible, darkened pit, ugly reality.

> Sorry, got sidetracked. Meet you guys at the gift shop.

I hustled to get there before anyone else so I could pretend I'd been touring the place. Fortunately, I beat them as planned. Gavin and Memo found me perusing sweaters.

"Hey," I said, finally lifting my glasses. "See anything you think I *must* have?"

Memo bounced in surprise when he saw my face. "Are you okay?" He squinted. "Have you been crying?"

"What? No." I couldn't put my sunglasses back on fast enough. "I'm allergic to something here. All the dander or weird plants or something. Anyway, shirts. What do you think?"

"Nobody needs another sweater for sixty bucks. But you do you," Gavin said, leading Memo away by their pinkie fingers.

I found a mirror and, to my horror, I was undeniably puffy behind my lenses. *Shit.*

Rob threw his hands up when he saw me next. "Babe, I thought you fell off the planet for a minute there. Where were you?"

"Sorry, I got caught up reading about some conservation stuff. Any idea where we're headed next?"

"Cheesecake. Your favorite." Rob knew that much about me, at least. Jax's absence was now a blessing in disguise. It would've been too on-the-nose after our last conversation if I took him to the last place I saw him as my former self.

"So, anything you want in here?" he asked, blindly gesturing at the hangers. "It's all overpriced crap, but whatever."

Despite his incredibly romantic offer, I shook my head.

"Go find Annie, then. She said she wanted you to see the pics she took today. I wanna look around."

"Will do." I smiled, burying everything else. *Refocus. It's your day. Nothing can ruin it.*

By the front gates, Ethan and Megan chatted through some giggles, touching each other in that cautious way that showed how interested both of them were. Cordelia muttered on the phone with her girlfriend, Nadine, who lived in Chicago not far from my aunt. Gavin and Memo held each other and made moony faces, still just as in love as when they first got together four years ago, and Gavin had barely discovered the gym. And Annie, ever the one to be lost in a world of her own, flipped through her phone on a bench by herself.

I joined her and sighed. "This has been one of the best birthdays I can remember."

"I'm glad." Annie's soft voice was even more quiet than normal. Even her pacing was sluggish, like her words fought against an invisible wall. She patted the hand I rested on my thigh. "You deserve to have the best birthday every year. I'm so glad you were born, Tabby."

"Aww." Her mushy words were another level of love I couldn't describe if I tried. "Thanks."

Her delicate fingers worked their way between mine and squeezed. "You know how much I love you, right?"

Her sad undertone bothered me. "Of course I do."

"Good." She shifted a little to face me more without taking her hand away. "I want to know what you want for your birthday."

"Come on, you don't have to get me anything."

"No, I know that. But that's not what I'm asking. What do you *really* want?"

I chewed on the inside of my lip. "Like, anything?"

"Yeah, anything. If you could have anything in the world, what would it be?" She tipped her head like a puppy, searching behind my glasses for more answers. "Don't think. Just say it. First thing in your mind."

Her words were like a witch's spell. They cut through the bullshit of my secrets and pierced me in a tender spot. What I wanted was simple, but I couldn't say it out loud without pain. Exposed and raw, I stared at the ground. "I don't know what to say."

"Yes, you do. You just don't want to."

"How are you always reading my mind?" I kicked at the earth and ran my free hand through my hair.

"I pay attention," she said. A line she uttered many times and one I stole as an excuse when getting to know Jax. She released my fingers and handed me her phone. "Look at this."

A photo album titled *Tabby B-Day* lit up her screen, and the thumbnails were detailed enough without enlarging them. Still, I pressed every one and swiped through, reliving the day even though it was fresh.

Ditzy selfies from Annie by herself. Cordelia flipping off the lens with a smirk. Gavin and Memo snuggling sweetly, and even a few shots of Ethan and Megan. Jax lagged in the background, only otherwise present in the few group shots Annie took by the bears.

"You have a good eye," I said, still flicking through,

purposely passing most of myself because I wasn't terribly photogenic. "Is there one in particular, or…?"

"Yeah. This one." She brought up the best of the group shots. "Look at you and Rob."

I stood in the center with Rob wrapped around me. While I had a big smile, he looked…downright bored. No life in his eyes and a flat affect. By instinct, I flicked through the photos again. As long as he appeared, his face remained unchanged, except for one which caught him mid-eyeroll.

"Wow." Classic Rob, nothing more.

"Now find Jax in it," she said, pointing at the screen again. "Same one I tapped before."

I sighed, then did as she asked. *Why does this feel difficult? It's just a picture.*

In the group shot, Jax was almost hidden. He stood at Ethan's side in back, ready to step out of frame. But unlike Rob, or anyone else, his eyes weren't focused forward—they shifted to the side.

Is he…is he looking at me?

Again, I swiped through and found him in the background. It wasn't my imagination. With heart-eyes fit for cheesy anime, if we were in the shot together, Jax fixated on me.

Not in a creepy, stalkerish way—his boyish half-smile and pink cheeks turned the clock back on his age. Innocent. Not once did Annie capture a shot of him so much as glancing at Megan.

Cutting into the buzzing of my ears, Annie said, "Rob *never* looks at you like that." She took her phone back and stared clear past my soul.

I gulped. "He's not good at mushy things. He's getting better lately. This isn't proof of anything."

"Yes, it is, because you never look at Rob that way, either. But what you do is your business." She stood from the bench and put her phone away, then stretched her back while looking at the cerulean sky. "You're my best friend, Tabby. I just want you to have everything you deserve." Annie turned toward me and sounded more matronly than ever before. "All of us who really love you? That's our wish for your birthday."

I squinted behind my sunglasses and fought back the itching under my eyes. "Thank you. I...I do. Because I have people like you."

She curtly nodded. "I'll meet you at the restaurant."

While Annie walked away, I felt an invisible spotlight on me. One by one, I met the gazes of my closest friends. Gavin and Memo shrugged at me. Cordelia pouted and pointed at Annie. Ethan was busy talking to Megan; if I had to guess, he knew more than anyone.

I was the reason Jax needed help feeling better. His Hwa wasn't dead; I was here the whole time.

As if I wasn't confused enough, Rob jogged to me from the gift shop with one hand behind his back. "Hey, babe. I finally found the perfect thing for you."

"Yeah?" I couldn't keep flip-flopping my train of thought. Something would give, bend, or tear. "Can't wait to see what you came up with."

"Look what I found." Other than hiding it behind his back, Rob wasn't playful at all when he revealed a full-sized peacock feather.

"Oh, beautiful," I said, touching it gently and being careful not to mar the eye, likely why I was so fond of them in the first place. "You've been all about peacocks today. How'd you know I liked them?"

He shrugged, then made a poor attempt at a flirtatious tone. "Maybe later you can chase me."

I arched my brows. "Seriously? Come on, you've never asked me about peacocks before. Who'd you talk to?"

For an instant, he reminded me of a trapped animal, wide-eyed, quiet, and frozen in place. The color returned to his countenance as he answered, "Annie, of course. She knows everything about you. Don't bust me though, or she'll be pissed."

With what she'd just shown and said, I couldn't disagree. "I won't mention it, don't worry. Let's go eat."

The group left as one to meet at the restaurant, and I waved my feather back and forth in the car like a dancer along with our radio. Despite what she said, Annie had to believe what I really wanted in this world was Rob. After all, if she didn't, why would she even attempt to help him change?

reconnected

. . .

Jax

HIS BIRTHDAY CONFIRMED IT. I was smitten with Tabby and totally fucked.

Still, I believed what I said about fate bringing us together and used that to soften the edges of my mind when thinking of him. Sure, he was funny and got all my jokes. He lived the way he wanted without apology or fear. Tabby's fierce sense of self made me jealous over the fact I had also just turned thirty yet hadn't figured myself out yet. All those qualities made for a beautiful platonic foundation as much as they did a romantic one, so when planning to meet with him again the following Wednesday, I kept the former at the forefront of my mind.

Rob sent me a text to thank me and mercifully hadn't asked for any more advice thus far. The fact he was so unprepared for Tabby's birthday helped prove my theory that he had no instinct for charm while mine was otherworldly; I shouldn't have been so spot-on with my suggestions, but by Rob's report, I was.

Tabby sent a couple of short texts over the weekend, and we agreed he'd call me Tuesday night to make arrangements for the next day. I assigned him a new ringtone so I wouldn't miss it and chose the theme to *Hitchhiker's Guide to the Galaxy*, a classic in my mind that he would undoubtedly appreciate.

The familiar twang of the song I knew well called through my apartment at nine o'clock. Before answering, I took a deep breath and let it out over five seconds so I wouldn't stammer my way through the call.

"'Sup. This is Jax."

"Hey, you. It's Tabby. This a good time?"

The mere sound of his voice made the lights in my apartment look as if the dimmer switch was turned on high. "Of course. We still on for lunch tomorrow?"

He hissed. "That's the thing. Yes, but I can't join you with takeout. I, uh, promised I'd try not to cheat on our diet this week."

"That sucks. It's a little hard to meet for lunch if you can't eat with me."

"No, it'll be fine. Just come to my office again, and I'll pack something."

"Nice. I can do that, too. You'll really get to see how simple my taste is that way. Do you have any allergies?"

Tabby paused, then let out a single chuckle. "Why, do you?"

"No. I just don't want to accidentally kill you with my peanut butter sandwich. Could be dangerous if you get too close."

"Or it could be the perfect crime."

"Would be if nobody knew you were allergic. But if you carry an Epi Pen…"

Real laughter this time. "Nah, I have no allergies that I know of. And call me crazy, but a peanut butter sandwich sounds amazing. Crunchy or smooth?"

"Smooth. *Obviously*. And strawberry jam, not grape. Soft bread. Man, I'm getting excited just thinkin' about how awesome my sack lunch will be. Might stock it with a few Oreos."

"That sounds…surprisingly awesome. Pretty sure my salad will feel pretty lame by comparison."

"Eh—we can rate them side by side tomorrow." The more we spoke, the warmer I became. Time to get off the phone. "Noon okay? Or twelve thirty?"

"Noon. I'll text if I have a late patient."

"Sounds like a plan. See you tomorrow, Tabby."

"Same to you. Night." *Click.*

A lightbulb went off in my mind, and I traded the phone between my hands. He was only my friend. What harm could it do to be friendly?

MY WORK UNIFORM of a blue button-down and tan slacks made me feel like an idiot, so I put on a tie to elevate it a bit. The front of my hair fell into my eyes with the wind on my way to Tabby's office. Overdue for a haircut. I'd ask where he got his done. Yeah. Small talk that wouldn't feel too intimate was the plan.

Like last time at his office, I was anxious to see him, but it changed from an unsure worry that I'd bother him to a hopeful wish that he'd notice my extra effort. The advertisements on the side of the building changed to a seasonal flare and were decorated with fall colors and window-stick leaves, obvious additions from the staff. Without snow on the ground to help orient me to the changing seasons, it reminded me that the year would be over soon. Getting faster all the time.

The receptionist at the desk was the same one I saw months before. She cocked a brow at me when it was my turn.

I dug through my memory to find her name. "I'm here to see Tabby. You're Beth, right?"

"That's right." She smirked. "And who should I say is calling?"

"My name's Jax. Whenever he's free, just—"

"I've got a note here to expect you. Go on back to his office; he'll be there in a few." Beth waved her hand to the door at her right.

Fortunately, I remembered my way around. "Thanks." I did as I was asked and found his office at the end of the hall again.

It was neater than last time. The desk was cleared off and a standard chair waited for me, opposite his rolling one. Before I sat down, I admired his large diplomas on the wall. None of the pictures I saw from a distance last time were still up, but I didn't question why they might've been moved or changed.

After only a minute, he tapped on the doorframe, interrupting my private tour of the space. "Hey, you."

I shifted to see him and stepped back in awe. *Wow.*

Instead of scrubs, Tabby wore an outfit that looked something like mine. His black button down and gray slacks showed off his physique. While he didn't have a tie, a peek of chest hair made itself known in the gap below his collarbone. The ensemble suited him well, much better than his scrubs. It sent shivers up my spine.

"Something special happening at work today?" I asked, gesturing blindly over him with my open hand.

"Trying something new lately. Scrubs aren't mandatory; they're just easy." He closed the door behind him and sat, inviting me to do the same. "Thanks for coming down here. It's great to see you."

"My pleasure." I put my brown bag on his desk while he peeled the lid off his salad with a frown. The downright sadness in his pinched brows said enough.

"You look *so* excited for that," I joked.

He grumbled.

"Good thing I had a plan." I pulled out my sandwich, as well as an extra one for him. "Ta-dah!"

"You made lunch for me?" His smile grew more intense by the second. Even his sweet dimples appeared. "Thank you. Really. I've kinda been dreading the arugula all day."

"Least I could do for missing your birthday dinner. Where'd you all go?"

"Cheesecake Factory. One of my favorites. Hence the need to be better this week." He gingerly opened the sandwich bag so he wouldn't get excess sticky jam on his fingers. "You didn't miss much."

"Did you get everything you wanted, at least?"

Tabby tipped his head side to side. "Yes and no."

"What's left on the list?" I took a bite and leaned back in the chair, giving him space to breathe and open up.

For a moment, he merely tapped his fingers on the table and took a strong bite of his own. When his internal walls fell, he shrugged. "I'm not really sure. I thought when I reached this age, it would mean something, you know? Like I'd wake up and feel more like an adult or something."

"I completely understand. I turned thirty in September and was so pissed that all I have to show for it are some gray hairs."

"Liar."

"I'm serious, check it out." I leaned across his desk and pointed above my ears, where a few wiry strands stood proud.

"My God. You *are* getting old. I remember—" Tabby stopped himself with a choking gulp.

I stared at him for a moment. "Hey, you okay?"

"Yeah. Sorry about that." He shook his head quickly. "I meant to say, you remind me of someone I knew. Guess I wonder if he's also turning into a silver fox."

I snorted. "Silver fox. *Sure.* More like silver squirrel."

Tabby smiled, but it was reserved. Held back. Disjointed. He took another bite of his sandwich. The energy in the room changed, like a cloud swirled above us.

"You know, sometimes memory lane is a good way to get to know somebody." Relaxing into the chair again, I cracked open my Sprite and took a few sips. "Tell me about this guy. Was he special?"

He closed his eyes and took a few deep breaths, chewing more than he probably needed to before answering. "My first crush, actually. He was wonderful."

"Mm-hmm. To get *your* attention, he'd have to be, right? Go on."

Tabby flashed his eyes at me. "You're trying to flatter me, and I just want you to know, I'm here for it." He took another breath and hummed. "My crush…he was kind. The sort of person who put others first, no matter what. Did his best not to judge. I imagine he's the kind of person who would accept me for who I am now instead of who I was then."

"Ah. So this happened before you were Mr. Tabby Tabs, I presume?" I worried I would offend him with my casual reference to his status and immediately wished to take it back. "Shit —I'm so sorry if that crossed a line. I really don't know what's allowed or not."

He smirked. "It's allowed, with me anyway. Rob, not so much."

"Why is that? Is it tied to why he's kind of a prick sometimes?"

With a sigh, Tabby rolled his eyes. "He isn't a prick, he's just…defensive. Rob didn't have the same experience I did. I told my mom, we moved here, and I started life over. Within a year, I started taking T, and—"

"T? What is that?"

"Oh, sorry. Testosterone. I also had my name legally changed. Mom was supportive and helped me with every step. She never once gave me shit for it. It was a hard year even with how great she was, because of course, all the pictures I had of myself were of this person I didn't recognize. When my voice dropped and my beard came in, it was a second puberty, but I loved every squeaky, pimply second of it. My really wonderful therapist taught me to focus on the things that made me feel good as affirmations, instead of using the things that made me feel bad as proof that I didn't belong as a girl."

My mind buzzed with more questions. The concept of not belonging to oneself fascinated me. "I hafta be honest. I consider myself to be a pretty empathetic person, but I can't even imagine that."

He shrugged. "Cis people tend not to think about their gender the same way trans people do. My therapist would say most people have the fleeting thought, *what would it be like to wake up in another body?* Not the same thing as gender dysphoria. I've met people who can't decide what they are, so they spend years asking themselves, 'Is this normal, or am I trans?' Now there are new categories and labels, which helps a lot. But in our community, there are still exceptions, and the trauma that so many people face gets thrown around to those on the outskirts who are seen as 'less committed.'" Tabby said the last piece in sharp air quotes.

"Less committed? What does that mean?"

Tabby bit the inside of his lip trying to find a good way to explain it. "Well, if somebody in the media comes out as trans, what's usually the first thing people ask them?"

"The first thing? I guess...people wanna know what they look like naked."

"There. That. Right there." He clapped once, like I got the answer right. "That's such a bullshit cliche, and it's nobody's damn business anyway. Trans people just want to be who they are, which could be anything. Some are happy just making a few changes, and some people go for the full enchilada."

"Mm. Enchiladas. Sorry. Continue."

He smiled at my joke but kept going. "I'll be frank. I—"

"No, you're Tabby. Be Tabby." I laughed.

"Shut up, I'm trying to be serious." He huffed through a few chuckles and dropped his shoulders. "For me, I didn't want surgery for anything. The idea of going under really scares me. My T does enough; I mean, it's kind of miraculous what a change in hormones will do to your body shape, sensation, appetite...everything. I don't think it's common to settle for T, but it's what I wanted. Rob's different. His top surgery was done by a complete miracle worker with a knife, and you can't even register that he has scars at all because of the approach they did. From the waist up, Rob is all man. You'd never be able to know he was AFAB—assigned female at birth. Don't repeat that, though. Not all trans people like medical labels, and every one of us is entitled to how we want to be referred to and discussed.

Word to the wise, if you want to know what somebody wants, ask."

"Okay, but why does that make him defensive if he could fool anybody?"

"He doesn't want to *fool* anyone. Nobody who is trans wants to do that, even if they aren't out publicly…and we hate the idea, just so you know. To say we're fooling others perpetuates the idea that trans people are liars and sneaks who aren't upfront about what we're packin'." He wasn't angry or irritated, yet the way he recited the words so well told me he'd said it many times. A common argument. "We say *pass* instead. Like, Rob passes as a cis guy really well."

"Duly noted. Thank you."

"Anyway, Rob's family did basically the opposite of what my mom did. They kicked him out. When he left, he fought hard to find a doctor who would treat him and get him started with T as soon as he could. Found his top surgeon through a program helping trans youth, and had it done before he turned twenty. Even got a hysterectomy. If he had his way, he'd get more done tomorrow." Tabby picked his fingernails and swallowed hard, enough for me to hear it. "The problem is, Rob isn't great at communicating, and he still figures everyone in his life is about to drop him. He puts up walls, so he doesn't get hurt. Hasn't learned that it pushes people out."

"I…wow." My stomach rolled like it did over the weekend when I saw Tabby kissing Rob and looking so happy. Rob lived a life I couldn't possibly relate to, and I had no right to give him shit for how he did it. "Okay. Now I feel like a complete ass for calling him a prick. Please don't tell him I said that."

"I won't, but you're not really wrong. In his effort to keep people at arms-length, he ignores what happens in between. Being rude to you when you first came to D&D is part of his issue. He worries the community is filled with people who don't really mean it and won't ever understand the kind of hardship he went through. We trust each other, and I brought him close

165

when everyone else thought he was too tough to handle. That's why we started dating in the first place—I was the only person who gave him a chance besides Ethan."

For all that I hated how Rob couldn't get past the easy stuff, the way Tabby cared about him anyway only reinforced that first night I called to give Rob advice. Don't we all deserve a chance to be happy?

Tabby continued, "There are people in the trans world who think being trans means you *have* to cut up your body, or you're illegitimate. They think people who come in without hating themselves to the point of suicide are impostors—dysphoria and self-hatred aren't the same, and those of us who focus on what feels good aren't lying to anyone. There's enough confusion around what trans really means, and enough kids kill themselves every year trying to figure it out. I don't know why our society thinks people who are gay or trans or bi or whatever are trying to recruit, but that's such a bullshit notion." He finished his sandwich and slapped his hands together to get rid of the crumbs. "So, when thinking about my first crush...you're right, it was before I transitioned. But I believe, even now, he'd be the kind of person who would ask questions to try and understand instead of guessing. He was just that great of a guy."

"Amen to that. Jax approves. To wherever he is." I lifted my can of Sprite to Tabby and took another sip. *Hopefully I can live up to that kind of review, too.*

"Ugh. I can't believe I've gone on and on about this." He eyed me with a sideways glance. After a moment of un-comfortable silence, he pursed his lips. "So, it's your turn. Tell me about *your* first love, Jax. What did you love about her?"

"Oof. Tough question." I sighed and picked a few loose fibers off my slacks, purposely avoiding his gaze so I wouldn't accidentally imprint my feelings for Jamie on him. "What *didn't* I love about her? Like your guy, she was also kind. Unique. She loved my puns, stupid jokes, all my cheesy gestures. Other girls told me it would be creepy if I did role-play in instant messages online—man, that's a blast from the past, isn't it? I-M instead of texting?—but she liked it and did it back to me. She taught me about D&D. She spoke Pig Latin fluently and knew every answer in *The Lord of the Rings: Trivial Pursuit.* I can't imagine, if she were still around, that she'd be anything but magnificent."

When I twisted to see him again, he faced away from me. "Did you think she was beautiful?" he asked.

"Of course I did. But not how you might think."

"And that means?"

I cracked my knuckles, more than ready to spread the gospel of my father and the risk of too much weight being put on appearances. "Dad taught me that beauty fades, so don't count on it. She was cute, but that wasn't why I liked her in the first place. I mean, consider how you talk about your pre-transition self; did you transition and become a whole different person? Or were you the *same* person, with the same favorite color, favorite hobby, favorite movies? Sure, your style could change, but style doesn't have to be one thing or another, does it? The things that make up who we are aren't really completely dependent on that physical shit. It's just a body. What if she were in an accident? What if she had surgery? What if she and I really did get to live happily ever after and grow old together? The way she looked wouldn't stay the same forever. It was our *love* that I had long-term faith in." I hummed and imagined Jamie's face, which was now only a blurry image in my mind, surrounding the only thing that wouldn't waver. "Tabby, do you know there is one thing about our bodies that never changes?"

He turned to me again. "No. What?"

I pointed to my face. "The eyes. Eyes don't really change. Her coloboma would always be there. So now, all these years later, I can barely tell you what she looked like; not the shape of her nose, if she had lots of moles, if her smile was crooked, et cetera. But her ash-blue eyes with that keyhole lock, holding the very key to my heart…that's how I'll remember her."

"Is there a reason you haven't told me her name? Why you

don't say it?" He squinted as if searching for the answer on my forehead.

"Honestly? I feel like saying her name out loud will make her absence all too real. So, I keep it to myself. We had nicknames for each other, and I think of her that way instead. That love can't disappear for me. She'll always be my Hwa."

After I said it, I ran out of words. A flood of uncomfortable, impossible tingles rushed through my limbs, like she watched over me. A haze settled in Tabby's office again, and the light changed. Clouds outside parted, letting a beam of sun highlight the room. It meant our lunch hour was nearly over, though I swore I felt Jamie's presence around me.

Her ghost pushed me toward Tabby. Inch by inch, the space between us closed.

"Hey." I reached for his hands, though I wasn't sure why. His fingers in mine were just as comfortable as his whole body the last time we hugged. "Thank you for being someone I can trust."

A buzzer on Tabby's desk cut everything short. *"Dr. Ross, your first patient is here."*

"Thanks, Beth," he said, and the intercom clicked. "That's my cue."

"Yeah. I know." I released him and grabbed my noisy bag on the desk, crumpling it in my hands.

"Get outta here," he said with a bad Jersey accent, gifting me with those dimples again. "But promise me this time you won't stay away so long."

"You got it." Strolling down the hall to leave, I couldn't help myself and turned to see him one last time before going through the double doors.

Yup. Totally fucked.

home

. . .

Tabby

I LINGERED at work after Jax's visit, well into darkness outside. When he spent time alone with me, it reignited the smoldering embers of our romance, making me question everything about how I lived my life. Somehow, I'd hoped talking about why Rob needed me would make me feel like my bond at home was stronger; instead, it shined a light on all our flaws.

I was quiet on the drive home, not practicing for an imminent argument like I used to; it would've ended with my telling Rob to leave. I didn't want to plant that seed.

A sharp draft blew through our apartment when I walked in. I huffed and went to close the many open windows. *I keep telling you not to do this.* My irritation grew when I leaned over a table and knocked some of my knick-knacks on the floor by accident.

Rob came out from the bedroom to the sound of my grumbling. "Babe? You okay?"

"Yeah, I'm...ugh..." I bent to pick everything up and tried to stifle my temper by talking to myself. *It's fine. It's just Rob. You love Rob. It's fine.*

His warm hand on my back made my stomach flip. "Can I help?"

"Well, you can stop leaving the windows open like I ask every damn day." I stood and charged away from him, toward the window in the far corner. "It brings in too much humidity, gets really cold by three in the morning, and then I'm awake shutting windows because you won't just put a damn fan by your side of the bed. I'm tired of paying for your hot flashes."

Rob stood in silence without trying to argue with me. Our roles were flipped.

"I hate that I can't eat what I want. I hate that we never go anywhere except Ethan's shop. I hate that you gripe about my binders, and I hate that you don't go with me to Mom's. But I swear to fucking God, nothing infuriates me more than when you won't close the damn windows." With the final one slammed shut, I turned and folded my arms. Expecting a fight, I put up my internal armor. *Here we go.*

Rob continued to surprise me and lowered his face instead. "I'm sorry, babe. I really am. I'll get some fans in here, if that's okay."

I squinted. *Why aren't you exploding at me?*

He walked up and held his hands out for me, which I took because I had no reason not to. "Thanks for saying these things. I need to know. I need to know what you're feeling and thinking if this is gonna work. And it can't work if you don't talk to me."

Now my guilt, fear, and anxious heart thumped loudly in my ears and head. A wash of cold over my whole body nearly made me shiver. I was disappointed with the serenity between us. Fighting would've given me an excuse to unload all the shit I kept inside.

He squeezed my hands. "Can we start over, babe? Right now. Right here. Just us moving forward?"

How could I say no? What kind of selfish monster would I be if I didn't stuff my insecurity in a box and lock it away? If he wanted a chance, I owed it to him. If he wanted the truth, I could give him that, too.

At least, most of it. "Yes. Let's do that."

He stepped a little closer and kissed me with the tenderness I imagined Jax would earlier.

I still love you, Rob. I swear I do.

one step closer

· · ·

Jax

OUR RELATIONSHIP SHIFTED, for better or worse. I slowly accepted that Tabby and I couldn't ever be more than the friends that we were. Instead of waiting for Rob to contact me, I reached out and offered up new things to try.

With his wardrobe change, Tabby started to wear tacky and fun ties like his casual shirts. It was easy to help him keep a signature style while still being work appropriate, especially when I sent links to Rob instead of buying them myself. That way, they were loving gifts from his boyfriend, and he showed them off with a beaming smile.

Look at this great one!

Tabby texted, with a picture of himself in a black button-down and a tie emblazoned with various insects.

You can be jealous if you want.

Oh, man. That's awesome. Just needs more moths. Or a rhinoceros beetle.

Nice knot, btw.

I was so glad he liked them. It warmed my heart to see him so confident. His dull scrubs were no comparison; the bugs were a winner.

I upped the ante and sent Rob even more ideas, one at least every other day. Tickets to the museum for the weekend. A drive up the coast to the beach at Bodega, where Tabby could talk about Hitchcock and his love for paranormal movies. I said, "Be sure to bundle up for the cold." A scheduled massage. A personalized pocket watch. Preparing for the Christmas season, I sent Rob a link to beard ornaments that I thought would make Tabby laugh.

Two weeks before Thanksgiving, as I walked to my car from the office after work, a cavalry horn went off in my pocket. Rob's ringtone, which heralded saving the day.

"This is Jax."

He barked, "Hey, knock it off with the texts, dude. You blow up my phone too much."

My heart rushed like I got my hand slapped. "Oh. Sorry. Just thinking ahead, I guess."

"I've got Christmas mostly covered, but this shit gets expensive, ya know?" Rob huffed with exasperation. "Wish you could give me some ideas that don't cost me anything but my pride."

It took every ounce of my self-control not to say, *if you had any pride, you could do that yourself.* "Not trying to make you go broke, Rob. It's just how I show affection, and apparently it works for Tabby. Gifts and quality time."

"Lucky for me, you have his same wavelength. I don't understand most of this."

"Then why are you doing it? Like, if you don't get it, why go along with what I've said? Doesn't he get suspicious that it doesn't seem like you?"

"I have that covered. I tell him Annie gives me the ideas. So, thanks for not busting it. All this shit—I do it 'cause he's worth doing it for."

Yeah. That's for sure.

"But seriously." Rob cleared his throat and softened his voice, as if someone else walked in the room. "If you have any ideas for me that I can do on my own without spending a dime? That's the kind of shit I really need."

I sat in my car and looked at my empty passenger seat, remembering how easy it was to talk to Tabby the first night we got to know each other. The same strange comfort I felt in his office whispered at the back of my mind.

Okay, Jamie. It's time to let go.

"I've got just the thing," I said, and gave Rob the greatest gift I could give Tabby: the gift of a new way to say *I love you*.

"TELL me you brought something other than peanut butter," Tabby said, settling into his office chair for our bi-weekly lunch meetup that Thursday. "I know you're picky, but you can't be *that* predictable."

"Predictable never hurt anyone." I sat with my paper bag opposite him, as usual. "You're right, though. I tried to be a little adventurous today. Check it out." Handing him one of the two creations, I bounced my brows while he opened it.

After eyeing me somewhat suspiciously and putting his pre-packed salad to the side again, he lifted the bread to look at the contents. "Jaxson Grady. Is this avocado?"

"The very same. Homemade version of your favorite sand-wich. Avocado, turkey, havarti, lettuce and extra mayo. Ta-da." I gave him an exaggerated bow in my chair and opened mine. "Personally, I think the usual place could use a titch more salt, so I have a couple packets if you agree."

He took a bite and swept his hair back while leaning in the comfortable chair. "Heaven. It needs nothing."

"Jax for the win," I said, relaxing and pulling out my phone to pick something stupid for us to watch in the meantime. Our growing routine was more than comfortable, now. It was easy, and like he said, predictable.

"You going over to Cordelia's for Thanksgiving? She makes so much food, it's astonishing. I'm sad to miss it this year." He barely gave himself room to chew before talking with his mouth half-full, which I didn't mind. The spot of mayo on his mustache distracted me, and I didn't point it out. It gave me an excuse to focus on his lips.

"I have nowhere else to be. My dad's made the feast every year since I was a kid…it's gonna be so weird not being at home for it. Do you have any special traditions this time of year?"

Tabby pouted for a minute as he thought. "Mm…not really. I'm going on vacation for two weeks on Saturday. Mom likes to see her sister in Chicago, and we do that every couple years. I wouldn't exactly call it a tradition. Rob's staying here. You?"

"As far as I'm concerned? All the family traditions are dead now that Mom's with Brian. I'm thinking about starting some of my own traditions. *Shit*—that reminds me." I navigated away from the comedy station to Google.

"What are you up to?" he asked, peering over the desk.

"It's stupid. I'm looking up the San Francisco ballet. Do they do the Nutcracker here?"

Before he could answer, Tabby choked on something and coughed uncontrollably.

"Whoa, don't die on me," I said, holding my hands up and lurched toward him. "You okay?"

He nodded, still coughing and turning bright red while he held up one finger and gathered himself. "Yeah, yeah I'm fine," he croaked.

"Good. My CPR's rusty."

Tabby tried to catch his breath, now teary from coughing so hard. "Sorry about that. Jeez." He sniffed and took a few deep breaths. "So, Nutcracker, huh?"

I went back to my phone. "Yup. My family's gone every year since I was five. I've never seen any show but Denver's."

"They do have one here. You've seriously gone all your life?"

"I know, it's cheesy. Not exactly the most *manly* tradition, so I don't talk about it with anybody. Even when I've gone with people outside of family, I pretend like I've never seen it."

"I don't think that's cheesy at all. You underestimate how many people like doing that—myself included."

I paused as a gentle smile crawled across my lips. "You do? You like the Nutcracker?"

He blinked a few times, showing off the long lashes I admired so much. "I *love* it."

"Right on."

As we stared at one another, the same sweet energy swelling between us that I'd felt so many times before, I considered asking him to join me. I couldn't deny how much I liked having someone at my side, especially this time of year.

Tabby beat me to it, though. "Jax, will you go with me?"

No hesitation. "Sure. I mean…if Rob's cool with it, anyway."

Tabby blew a raspberry. "He doesn't care. Not his thing whatsoever. He'd probably be relieved."

"Alright. Then yes, of course. Do you wanna check out the dates with me?" I leaned across the desk and we both scrolled through the options together. He cross-referenced the calendar on his wall to make sure there weren't other plans on his end.

"I can't believe it's already here," he said. "Feels like I went last month or something."

I laughed. "I can't believe you can't think of somebody to go with you. Gavin and what's-his-name aren't into it?"

"Not even a little. I think Gavin would rather die. Cordelia rolled her eyes once when I asked. Annie said it was too mushy for her."

"What? Too mushy for Annie? I mean, I get she isn't all that into lovey-dovey stuff, but the quintessential Christmas ballet is beautiful."

"True, but you underestimate just how much Annie hates romance. Like, she *hates* it." As Tabby said the words, he pulled back from my phone screen. His brows furrowed and eyes fell. "She…she hates romance completely."

"What's the matter?"

Invisible wheels spun in his mind. "My God." Tabby's gaze shot to me. "Annie would never advocate for something like that, would she?"

Huh? I felt hit by a train. "Advocate? For what? That's a weird thing to say."

He became progressively more flustered as the seconds passed. "Jax, I'll need to look at tickets later. Maybe when I get back from Chicago. Right now I need to make a call."

The lift I felt a few minutes before was gone, slamming me to the ground. "Um. Yeah. Okay. That's fine." Gathering my things, I tried not to fumble and drop stuff on the floor.

"You didn't do anything wrong," he said, standing and trying to backtrack.

"It's fine. I get it. You're busy." Patting myself down to make sure I didn't forget anything, I opened his office and slipped halfway through. "I'll hear from you soon though, right?"

Curtly, he said, "Yeah. Later."

"Bye." I closed his door behind me and left, barely shuffling out of his quiet office, unsure what just happened and dreading the answer.

peel

. . .

Tabby

I CALLED Annie the second Jax left the room. Her playback tone annoyed me. "Come on. Pick up the damn phone."

She answered with a huff. "You better have a good reason for calling instead of texting."

"Yeah. I do. Have you been helping Rob?"

Nothing for an anxious few seconds. "I'm sorry, what?"

"Rob. You know, my boyfriend, Rob. Since he moved in, have you been helping him? Don't bullshit me."

She scoffed. "Bullshit *you*? What the hell are you talking about? I never talk to Rob outside of D&D. Ever. What would I even help him with?"

"With me, with...with—" I spiraled in a panic. Of course she didn't help him. Why would I believe such a thing when Annie never liked Rob at all?

"Whoa, calm down, Tabby. What happened?" Annie's coddling tone brought the spinning room to a halt.

I was too upset to cry, too surprised to yell, too confused to make sense of anything. "You know how I've been saying he's changed since he moved in? Like he's another person?"

"Yeah, you've mentioned that. How?"

"He's flipped a fucking switch. I don't know why I didn't

think it was strange enough to dig deeper. He pays attention to me. Does nice things he never did before. He tells me he loves me and *shows* me to back it up. Started buying me ties, taking me places...he's still hung up on my weight, but it's not as bad as it used to be. Tries to like the things that I like. I thought he learned something, but when I asked, Rob said all the good ideas came from *you*."

"Me? Seriously? Uhh..." She lingered, and I saw her in my mind, jaw open, wide eyes searching for something to focus on. "I don't know why he'd say that. I've never told him to do anything."

"I know. I *know* you haven't, because this stuff...Annie, it's unreal. It isn't like Rob, it isn't like you, isn't like Ethan or Cordy or...goddammit, I've been using this stuff to fall in love with Rob all over again, and it's not him." I growled through my teeth and collapsed in my chair, leaving Annie on speakerphone while banging my head on the desk.

"Tabby?" she asked between my exasperations.

"I'm such an idiot. Why didn't I see it? Why did I try so hard to believe Rob was capable of becoming a whole other person after over two years of the same thing?" Though my heart knew the answer, my head couldn't believe it and hoped I was wrong.

Yet at the same time, I was elated. Dreamy. Floating. He was right in front of me the whole time.

"You better start speaking English. Right now."

"Annie, I know who Rob's been talking to. It's time to call him out on it." I hung up the phone without answering more questions and sent a hurried text to Rob instead.

Rob, tonight we need to talk. Just us. No D&D.

The afternoon of patients lasted longer than ever before. The fear that filled me was only eased by the balm of all the hope I had.

I prayed for all the guts required. *I love you, Rob; I really do.*

But I love Jax more.

bare

. . .

Tabby

I RUSHED home and tried to stop my left leg from shaking while I drove. I couldn't practice a fake speech or anticipate Rob's questions. All I could plan was to go in and do it.

How would he take it? My head hurt already, and I prepared for a screaming match. The optimistic side of me hoped Rob's sympathetic core could relate to how I felt about Jax and the confusion surrounding his reappearance in my life. Hell, we might even get closer as friends because of it. After all, Rob did love me.

At least, that's what I thought, anyway.

I stepped up to the front door and straightened my tie—the new one Rob bought me, covered in ornate leaves. I had matching contacts and velvet loafers. For my shifting aesthetic, it hit the mark. But if Rob didn't choose it, the gesture felt empty. Instead, he was a stranger who happened to do nice things. He didn't know me at all. We wouldn't stand the test of time this way.

"Okay. Breathe," I whispered, clearing my throat before going inside. Once past the threshold, my jaw dropped.

Candles everywhere, which gave off a warm smell of mouth-watering cinnamon buns. No other lights. Quiet music droned in the background. Jazz. The kind of thing I'd never listen to on my own.

"Rob?" I called out, only to get my echo in return.

He goosed me from behind and I yelped. "Hey, babe. Good to see you."

"Fuck." My hand went to my forehead, and I commanded my fast pulse to slow. "You scared the shit out of me. Please don't do that again."

"Okay, I won't." Rob turned me around and pressed our bodies together. The closest we'd ever been to dancing. "I'm glad you called off D&D tonight for us."

Yeah. That's why. "Mm-hmm."

"How was your day?"

"Fine. Easy. Slow. Yours?" Stalling wouldn't cut it forever. Why did the atmosphere have to be all wrong for what I had to say?

"Same. Nothing worth mentioning. Except my boyfriend looked great when he left in the morning, and I figured it would be worth burning up all these candles that he had stashed everywhere." He pointed to the dim jars on every flat surface surrounding us. "If you never light them, what did you think would happen? You'd just keep them forever?"

For all that the environment had changed, Rob's dig at my resistance to get rid of the candles was on-brand. He burned them in hopes to use them up so I wouldn't have them anymore. He noticed I was dressed nice but didn't do the same. His bright red, plain T-shirt clashed with everything and didn't do him any favors, even though his body was well-worth showing off.

"I don't know. I just like them, I guess."

"We'll break that habit. Like we're breaking your eating out habit, huh?" He smirked and led me to the couch. Every second in his disjointed dreamland was another obstacle.

Come on, suck it up. Say something, anything. I closed my eyes after we sat. "Rob, I—"

"Shh, I have something to say first." He took both my hands, and I opened my eyes again. His expression was like the apartment—soft, warm, and unexpected. "Tabby, you're so incredibly special to me. You know that, right?"

"Yeah." In half a second, my confusion turned to sheer terror. *Oh, God, please don't be proposing.*

"Can't believe we've been livin' together for five months already. Truth be told, until I moved in, I wasn't sure if this was gonna work."

Seriously? I cocked a brow.

"I mean, no offense, you kinda drove me crazy." Rob tittered. "Guess I'm glad you nagged me so hard."

I bit my tongue. "Uh-huh."

"Well, I…shit, you know I'm not good at this stuff. I never have been. But I found a great way to say how I feel." He shifted in his seat and leaned forward as if drilling his gaze into mine. Taking a deep breath, Rob made a decent effort. "Tabby Ross, I need you in my life. When you're not around, my life dries up. It's just…um…dry and meaningless. Like a drought or somethin'. But you come in and you fill in all the ditches and…no, not ditches…your love's like a stream or an ocean or… something."

It didn't make sense. "I'm sorry, what?"

"Ugh, *what was it?*" he said under his breath. Rob rubbed his temple like he'd forgotten the lines of a play. "It's just that… when I'm alone, and I'm dried out and dying, you give me life. Like the stream gives life. It can't go without it forever. The farms need the water or the crops will die. It's…ah, *shit*, it's…do you get it?"

I did. I got it. I heard it loud and clear. It was absolutely, indisputably, certainly not Rob. It was pulled from my memory and invented by my Wah.

"Are you trying to say, 'I need you like water'?"

"Yes. *Yes.* That's it, wow. See, I knew you'd get it." Rob sighed and patted his chest with one hand. "Was a little worried there that I fucked it up completely."

"Right." I shifted my body away from him and stared at the coffee table. *It's time. It's too late to pretend not to know.*

Rob touched my shoulder, trying to get me to look at him. "Tabby? Are you, ya know, gonna say it back?"

I huffed. "I might if you tell me where it came from."

He pulled his hand back. "What?"

"That phrase. That sweet thing you just said. If you'd made it up, you wouldn't have forgotten it." I fiddled with my fingers and felt his anger rising next to me. "So be upfront. Who did you get that from?"

He scoffed. "I—"

"And *don't* you dare say Annie. I know that's a crock of shit." I stood from the couch and folded my arms. "I didn't need to ask her to know. She thinks we're better off with other people."

"Well, fuck Annie then." Rob stood with an intimidating grunt. "Who's to say I didn't come up with this myself, huh? The candles, the pretty speech—I can do good things, too."

"Yeah, but you didn't. So knock it off and stop trying to be something you're not." I pulled on the knot of my tie and yanked it forward. "Like this. Did you pick this out? Do you know why I like this color? Huh?"

He stammered and couldn't answer before I cut in again.

"You come in and out of these moods where you're suddenly interested in things that I like, but the next minute, you're fucking bored. In all the pictures Annie took of you on my birthday, you looked so embarrassed by me, it was pathetic."

"I *was* embarrassed by you. You're still acting like a kid when you do shit like that."

"And you might know why if you bothered to ask me. You didn't ask me why I liked peacocks—and I bet whoever helped you tonight told you that. You didn't even ask what I liked while we were there. You couldn't give a shit if I begged you to. If you'd asked instead of implying I was just immature, you would've found out that zoo was the last family outing I went on with my dad before he died on the one-oh-one."

"Oh boo-fucking-hoo about your daddy, Tabs. Mine's still out there, and he *wishes* I'd get crushed beneath a semi." He stormed to the stereo and cut the music at the same time I flicked the switch for the lights.

"That isn't my fault," I yelled. "Stop punishing me for your family bullshit."

"You're the one who rubs it in that your mom still wants to see you every week."

"That's not rubbing it in. It's trying to welcome you into my family as a permanent fixture, but you don't give a damn. You *want* to be abandoned. You *want* to be nasty. You hope you're so unrecognizable that it'll be some sort of golden ticket to a new life. News flash, Rob, your past still exists no matter how much you want to get rid of it."

He held up his hands and tipped his head with a grin. "How would I know? You're the one who actually knows what support feels like, babe."

"Knock it off with that *babe* shit. I fucking hate it. I've always hated it. It's like you had a whole ocean of nicknames we might share, and you picked the bottom of the barrel. Do me a favor and never say it again, 'kay?"

"So that's on your laundry list of shit I can't do right, babe? Can't always be there to rescue you, babe? Don't make as much money as you do, babe? Nobody out of your friends likes me, *babe*? How about you cram all your constant complaints right up your ass."

I let go of all my hidden irritation and for once spoke my mind without fear of the consequence. "Great. I can finally stop asking you to do a better job when you're back there. Huh? How about that?"

"At least I can take off my shirt without people askin' why I've still got tits if I'm a dude."

I raged and knocked a candle off the table next to me. "Are you fucking kidding me? You have some serious issues if you think *my* body says something about *you*."

"It does. I'm gay and wanna be with a man. As you are, you're like a goddamn mutant!"

"Oh, good one." I gave a sarcastic slow clap, which only made things worse. "Thought your judgmental, asshole self went away when he swore he'd stop bugging me to have surgery. Did a decent job being hidden, but it turns out, policing my mayonnaise habits meant he never left. I'm not fat. I'm just too fucking feminine for you."

He flipped me off. "You're not trans. You're just a fucking poser with hormones." Rob terrorized the bedroom and threw open his few drawers, scooping armfulls for his suitcase. "You'll never understand all the pain I went through. Not this time. *This* time, I'm gonna leave first." Once it was decently full, he zipped it closed and rushed to get through the living room.

Maybe I should've stopped him or should've felt sorry. I couldn't get over the fact that two people who meant so much to me could be so very different. "Why the hell did you bring Jax into this, huh? Why ask him for help with things you don't even want to do?"

"I didn't," he said as he threw my shoes around while looking for his. "Your buddy called me first, right before I moved in."

"Why the hell would he reach out to you when you treated him like shit?"

Rob muttered, "The fuck if I know."

"Right. You didn't even think to ask, I bet." I opened the cabinet beneath our TV and stacked Rob's games and DVDs in a rush, clapping them together with each addition. "Just like you didn't bother asking why it threw me for a loop when he showed up at D&D and didn't know who I was."

"Why should I? And why anything else? I'm so sick of the passive-aggressive riddles you spew." He came to my side and grabbed the stack I already had and threw it in a brown paper bag by the kitchen table. "None of these better be scratched, I swear to God…"

"I just put them in a pile you moron. If they're scratched, it's only because you don't take care of them." I finished weeding his stuff from my collection and went to pick out whatever dishes he brought.

"You were supposed to take care of me, too, you know." His rage finally turned into tears, though he tried to hide them. "I said something nice, and you exploded at me. I don't deserve that. Nobody deserves that."

I stopped clanking my plates together and spoke to the wall. "No. We deserve to be with people who actually want to be with us, Rob. I don't deserve to feel like I have to do something I'm afraid of to be worthy." Slowly, I continued searching for the few things in the cabinet that were his. Instead of anger, a wave of sorrow made my fingers shake.

"Wait a minute. How did you know it was him? Did he bust me?" He came closer behind me.

"No."

"Tabby. How did you know?" He sniffed. "Tell me."

"It's a long story. Too long to tell now."

"Yeah?" He gripped my shoulders hard and turned me, pushing me against the counter.

"Ah—Rob, stop it."

"Tell me, dammit. Did you fuck him? Did you cheat on me?"

"No, I…ow, let me go, I mean it." I fought against him, but Rob was stronger. He moved from my shoulders to my forearms and held me still. "Rob, please don't hurt me."

"I wanna know why you're so damn attached to him. Did he tell you about all the calls and texts he sent me every week since he came here? I swear, he's fuckin' obsessed with you. *Why?*" Rob pushed me back even more, cutting the edge of the counter into my back and screaming in my face. "Why, Tabby? Tell me the truth!"

"You're scaring me. You're scaring me—"

"Spill it!"

I flashed back to the early days when he slapped me playfully before it escalated into something I couldn't control. One bad night, then two, then a handful, but he promised. Said it was a mistake. Said it was his T dose. Said it was stress. Excuse after excuse. And I let it slide because I couldn't do better. Couldn't find a man who'd love me as I was. I had no hope. No Wah. No father. Nobody willing to stand up for me against the boyfriend I thought would become my endgame but was really my worst nightmare. My guilt over him was truly a fear—fear of this exact moment, playing out in my kitchen, after nearly a year of nothing like it at all.

"You swore you'd never hit me again. You swore. Stop!"

"Say it, Tabby. Say it!"

In a moment of courage, I refused to cower. *I'm worth more than this.* Instead of surrendering to Rob's brute strength, I took a step forward. Pushed him off me. Watched him trip on himself and fall onto the tile. He crumpled with a thud.

"What the fuck?"

"I don't need you. Look at me. I'm a man, too." I opened the freezer and grabbed a handful of the ready-made ice from the dispenser inside. With each statement, I tossed one at him, chasing him closer toward his suitcase at the door. "You're not water to me. You're just a distraction. The asshole who hit me and hurt me—no more. I'm done. I was done a year ago. Done after you forgot Valentine's Day. Done after you refused to see Mom at Easter. Done when you wouldn't go with me to Pride. I was done when you asked Jax if he even belonged here and done when you asked if I was a child on my birthday. And now, right now? I'm done with you taking ideas from someone else and hoping I won't know the difference. I do." When I ran out of ice, I grabbed his keys on the hook and took off the one for my apartment. "You wanna know how I figured it out? He's my soulmate."

"You bitch," he screamed, standing to yell in my face.

"Right. I'm the bitch." I pushed the keys into Rob's chest and spoke calmly. "Jax fucked me long before I ever met you. Now get the hell out of my house. Don't come back." Opening the front door wide, I presented the hallway and stood as straight as I possibly could.

He glared at me, burning holes through my face. He only had power when I was defenseless. I didn't need Jax to be a knight in shining armor—I was my own. When I said I needed Rob, it was a gesture of my love. I allowed him to help me so he'd feel more valid. But when faced with reality, our broken bond wouldn't ever have the strength we both needed to thrive.

Rob left my life without another word. He moved back to the place where he lived when we met, with the landlord whose bridge never burned.

His escape plan wasn't such a bad idea after all.

unexpected

. . .

Jax

ETHAN and I were done with D&D night and locked up the store when he got a flurry of text messages. His phone buzzed out of control.

"What is it?" I asked, only half-interested.

"Oh, shit," he said, stopping on the stairs to write back. "Rob and Tabby broke up."

"What?" I whipped out my phone to make sure it wasn't on silent. No messages waited for me.

"Rob's pissed." Ethan cocked a brow and looked at me. "Says you have something to do with it."

"Me? I—"

"Whatever. Leave me out of it; I don't care either way. Those two have been at each other's throats for too long." He finished tapping and we made it upstairs.

Why the hell would Rob blame me? Despite how I felt about him, I was overly cautious not to cross any lines with Tabby. An anxious lump in my throat grew by the minute. I wanted to cower and defend myself, though it would've been pointless; words meant nothing at all if Rob already made up his mind. I certainly had no intention of trying to help them get back together. Ethan was right—they weren't a good fit. My selfishness was only a minimal player.

Minimal, but not absent. Rob had a shot, and he blew it.

To preserve my sanity, I blocked Rob's number, then agonized over texting Tabby or not. I wanted to drive out and check on him; thought about surprising him at work the next day. Had to slam my own brakes. The last thing I wanted after my breakup with Heather was to be bothered with anything, so I closed my eyes and attempted to put myself in Tabby's shoes.

In, then out. Filled my lungs, then exhaled. Sandalwood. Kindness. His soft voice and his laugh, which I wanted to hear more than anything—even better if it was because of something I said.

The answer disappointed me. If I understood him at all, he'd want to be left alone. Especially if Rob cut things off and left Tabby heartbroken.

I buried everything as my heart sank to a place filled with self-doubt. Of course he'd need space. Time, too. He might need forever. Who was to say, with a relationship like theirs, that Rob wouldn't be back within a week? In an effort not to keep my hopes up, I put my phone on *Do Not Disturb* so I wouldn't be tempted to reach out.

With some of my best moves wasted on Rob already, the many wakeful hours spent staring at the ceiling were filled with brainstorming new ways to bring Tabby close. There was nothing to lose except my pride.

ALMOST HALFWAY THROUGH FRIDAY, and my exhaustion thought it was Monday at dawn. I sighed hard and squeezed my temples. A tired headache from tossing and turning thumped with my heartbeat and made my ears ring.

Like a machine, I went to work fielding waste-of-time phone calls on my Bluetooth headset. Another rang in, still too loud despite constantly adjusting the settings, leaving me only a few minutes of peace after the last call.

My script was annoyingly simple. "Jaxson Grady, I-T."

The person on the other end couldn't print after the last user set their station to PDF default. An easy fix if they knew how to navigate. Torture because they didn't.

"Okay, let me help you with that...now that it's set right, what happens when you click *print?* Right. Did you turn it off and on again? Did you make sure it was plugged in first...? Uh-huh. Is there paper in it?"

Once the issue was fixed, my headache returned. Mini victories helped distract me and kept me from imploding over my silent cell phone. I rubbed my temples in tight circles and wished for noon to pass so I could escape the stuffy building and eat.

Twenty minutes. I can make it twenty more minutes.

The headset beeped again. I answered with an annoyed flick of the button. "Jaxson Grady, I-T."

"Yeah, this is the security desk. You have a visitor."

I sat up straight. "A visitor?"

"Told 'em to wait in the lobby. We aren't a concierge service, okay?" *Click.*

"Shit." *What if it's someone who needs to come up here?* I flew into a fury to straighten the papers on my desk, which was as disjointed as I felt. My knees became little more than half-set jelly.

On the elevator, I fidgeted and shook my legs while silently cursing every passenger who made it stop before the ground floor. Commanded myself to stay strong. Rob was as likely a candidate to seek me out as anyone else—he could've asked Ethan where I worked—so I prayed his face wouldn't be out there. I didn't want to confront him, and I certainly didn't want to risk having to comfort him.

The people in front of me took their sweet time flowing out to the elevator bank downstairs. I straightened my polo and made sure it was neatly tucked into my slacks, taking the extra minute to see if my hair was in place. The copper reflection of the elevator said I still needed a haircut.

Nervously, I went to the security desk. "Hi, I'm Jaxson. Somebody just called me about a visitor?"

The guard's stoic expression matched his dry purpose. "He's in the lobby. Blue shirt, pussyfooting by the entrance. If you want him cleared to go upstairs, you have to give us his name and a reason."

"Okay, thanks." I nodded and tapped the desk, then searched the lunch hour flood for a familiar face.

When I saw him, I froze, except for a smile that conquered my entire being.

Tabby had a cautious grin that shifted and shone when people passed him. With his hands behind his back, he appeared a bit taller than usual, which suited his formal outfit. The flattering deep navy button-down perfectly matched his floral tie—the one I bought him when we went to Macy's months ago. The knot wasn't quite right, and I wanted to fix it.

In an instant, the lobby was void of others and he stood out from the brightness outside. His gaze met mine. Tabby kicked his head back to invite me closer, still not revealing his hands.

I shook the headache away. Wished my shoes had four-wheel drive. The floor could've been black ice for all I knew, ready to topple me from the slightest wrong move.

"Hi Jax," he said coolly, taking a solid step forward.

I stammered through a bit of nothing first. "Wasn't expecting you."

"Yeah, well, I didn't announce it." He tipped his head.

I scratched at my temple and grimaced. "Ethan told me about your breakup. What happened?"

He shrugged. "Rob wasn't who I thought he was. That's all." His tone denoted no sadness. Tabby hid something in his mind as well as behind his back.

"I'm still really sorry. That's rough, especially right before the holidays."

"I'll be alright." Tabby took in a long breath and relaxed, looking much more comfortable than I was. "Anyway, I didn't forget what we were talking about yesterday. Went ahead and bought tickets. Nutcracker, first Saturday in December. Come get me at six and we'll eat after."

Snapping out of my daze, I fully realized what he said. "Wow. Yeah, sure. That sounds great, thank you. I almost forgot."

"Did you?" He took another step forward to shorten the gap between us. Barely a foot kept us apart.

I gulped. *What are you doing?*

"Jax, I'll be out of town the next two weeks. Chicago, remember?"

My lungs deflated along with my shoulders. "Right."

"I want you to know that I'm taking that time to breathe a little, okay?" Tabby shifted his gaze to the floor for a moment. "I don't want any calls, texts, emails, nothing. All I want is a couple weeks of space."

"Oh—of course. Space is fine. You need space from everything right after a breakup. I get it." I snaked my neck so I could meet his eyes again. "I'm sorry you felt you had to tell me that so I'd leave you alone."

"It's not that." He locked onto me, reading my mind as usual, shouting soliloquies while speaking no words. Tabby didn't need space to recover from Rob. He needed space to prepare for me.

Oh.

As we stared at one another, the room cleared again. Nobody existed but us. His sandalwood scent wrapped me like a blanket. My fingertips tingled. Did he feel the same? I was certain enough to believe it wasn't just me fighting against the urge to pull him in. Here in public, it would be too much. But for our souls, it wouldn't be too soon.

He didn't break our gaze. "You won't hear from me while I'm away. But I'll be thinking about you. I've been thinking about you a lot. I'll miss you when I'm gone, and I'm already excited to get back."

None of my many thoughts could respond the way I wanted to; since I couldn't hold him, I did the next best thing and reached for his crooked tie. "Can I fix this before you go?"

"Be my guest," he said with a cocked brow.

Our flirtation may as well have been hot sex for all that I wanted to take it off and keep going. Instead, I worked slowly so I could soak in his warm presence. Tied it in a single Windsor knot and pushed it to the top of his crisp shirt. My hands bent down his collar and rested on his neck when I was done. His light beard was as soft to my thumbs as I'd always imagined.

I wanted to pull him in right then. Anticipation would only make that moment sweeter when it came, especially if he was as fired up as I was.

"Very nice," he said, smiling wide enough to show his precious dimples while finally revealing the hand behind his back. Tabby passed me a single long-stemmed rose—deep burgundy and almost cartoonish with its perfection. "It's time for someone else to charm the charmer, Jax."

"Wow," I whispered, blinking in disbelief.

"See you in two weeks." He released the flower and turned to leave.

"Wait, Tabby, what does this mean?" I didn't want even the slightest confusion and reached for his shoulder. "When you get back—"

"It's a date." He took my hand and kissed it lightly, then strolled with better posture than usual toward his office, leaving me to stand alone with nothing but my high blood pressure to confirm I wasn't dreaming.

ready, set

. . .

Jax

"MISSED YOU FOR TURKEY SOUP, KID," Dad said, yammering on about work while I anxiously prepped for the night's date. His voice in the background distracted me enough to keep me from checking my text messages every five minutes to make sure Tabby hadn't canceled. "It was better this year since your mother wasn't around to leave the burner on and turn the bottom to sludge."

He'd said the same thing every year since she left. "Thought you liked how she overcooked everything."

"It was her signature style. Didn't mean I liked it. Wonder if Brian's enjoyed her hockey puck— I mean pot roast—yet." He chuckled, more lighthearted than I'd heard him in a while.

Despite his recent turn to feeling comfortable by himself, I worried. This would be his first year with nobody at home. Even if he didn't say he missed Mom terribly, the truth lingered. "How are you holdin' up for Christmas, Dad? Need me to come out and keep you company for a few days?"

He sighed. "Nah, I think I'll be alright. Besides, if your date goes well, you won't exactly have time to come out here, will you?"

A shiver ran up my spine. "Here's hoping."

"Your mother always dragged us to that ballet. Guess I'm glad for it. Helped teach you to be a gentleman."

"No, *you* taught me that."

"Damn right I fuckin' did," he said with a laugh that forced me to stop shaving so I could, too.

"I know you'd like this guy, Dad. Maybe I'll get lucky and bring Tabby home to meet you soon."

"Sure. You're a good judge of character. Truth be told, though, never did like Heather. Always felt something was off about her, knowhatImean?"

I rolled my eyes and patted my face dry. "You've said that about all my exes but one."

"Well, that's because Jamie was special, Jax." He yawned. "Hey, it's getting late, isn't it? When are you leaving?"

I sighed and picked up the phone, which had been firmly on the bathroom counter while I got ready. Shirt, pants, tie, all black, more serious than my normal palette. It felt appropriate for the occasion—confident, cool, and worth remembering. "I have about twenty minutes before I have to get in the car. I'm so anxious, I might leave now and circle the block a few times just to shake my nerves out."

"Hmm, that—*oh*," he coughed, like he stubbed his toe.

"You okay?"

"Yeah. Yeah, I'm fine, kid. Must've hurt my back earlier. I have a twinge in my shoulder. Let me know tomorrow how things go, alright? I'll be thinkin' about ya."

"I will, Dad. Extra hot, extra—"

"Cheese, extra crispy relleno, kid. Love you."

"Love you, too. Wish me luck." *Click.*

As if mercy smiled on me, a text from Tabby lit up my screen when the call ended.

Don't forget to be here by six.

Leaving now.

The man in my mirror was nearly a stranger with his crisp, dark outfit and visible nerves. I tucked the phone into my back pocket along with my wallet. My keys felt empty, lighter than they should've been since I'd finally purged the old one for the duplex back home. It represented the lock on my heart that kept me from opening up to anyone but Tabby. Now that he welcomed me on his own, I didn't need to guard myself.

I put on my father's double-breasted wool trench coat—one of the many relics from my youth that didn't fit him anymore. It was too formal for him anyway. The soft fabric used to swallow my lanky self; now, I filled it well. The green and black scarf Jamie made for me years ago waited in the side pocket, where it lived for its annual reveal. I unrolled it with care, wrapping it once around my neck before tying it in front.

With my courage bundled in the yarn down my torso, as if Jamie's blessing accompanied me, I hurried to the garage at the top of the street, ready for tonight to be the last first date I'd ever go on.

the nutcracker

. . .

Tabby

I WASN'T WEARING a green dress this time. Instead, I wore a forest green tie. It would suit Jax's dark eyes well in pictures, and I couldn't wait to see how he'd be dressed. I imagined something similar to the oversized suit the last time we went to the ballet together, but the image in my mind of an anxious teenager didn't fit with the man Jax was now. Growing frustrated with the fact that I'd purposely kept him at a distance for the past two weeks, I told my mind to shut up and stop trying to recreate him in my head. My imagination would never do him justice.

Tonight was the night I had to come clean. Waiting this long was a risk, and I couldn't hold the secret in anymore. Wah deserved everything I could possibly give him, starting with the truth. I prayed he would be as understanding as he'd always been, celebrate with me, and we'd make love until we couldn't move. Since he had experience with other men, I was excited to explore what he'd be open to.

Such was the plan, anyway.

I couldn't risk him finding out too early in the night, so I opted for a pair of contacts that matched my tie. Cleaned up the edge of my goatee and chinstrap with my straight edge, taking more time than I'd usually need. Everything had to be perfect.

After every step through my apartment, I thought, *How the hell am I going to tell him?* Only one thing was certain: it would happen here. Safe at home. I could tell him not to kiss me on the street despite—oh, how *badly* I wanted to. But one kiss in a lie would be like spoiling ten more in truth. It had to wait.

Dammit.

A knock at my front door shook me to my toes. I puffed out a quick breath and stiffened my back. *He's here. This is it. Another chance with Jax, at last.* After slipping on my favorite pair of sparkly black loafers, perfect for the special occasion, I opened the door and attempted to maintain the same suave air I had when I last saw him.

So much for composure. *Oh, hell. I don't stand a chance.*

My posture failed, deflating into nothing the second my eyes fell on the ancient creation staring me in the face. The scarf—the last gift I ever gave Jax—prominently draped down his chest, peeking out from his also-familiar coat.

My jaw hung open while I stared. Our date shifted into a museum exhibit for my youthful regret.

"Hey you," he said, absent the usual cadence that suggested we were friends. Instead, his breath lingered, as did his gaze, which didn't break from mine for so much as a blink until I said something.

"H-hi." As my strength wavered, faltering in his presence, I reminded myself that it wasn't Jax's job anymore to bring us together. It was mine. "Thanks for coming to get me. I hate driving at night."

He hummed and nodded, then peered into my apartment. "Nice place," Jax said with raised brows.

"Yeah. It is." I grabbed my coat and kept him in the doorway. "I'll, uh, give you the grand tour later. After dinner. Don't want to be late."

"Right. That works." He fidgeted as if nervous at the idea of being let in. Both of us knew what would happen if we were alone. Neither of us said it, though. The truth swelled between us like sticky bubblegum, and if it popped, we'd both be in it for sure. Caution kept up the illusion that we'd take things slow.

"You have the tickets?" he asked.

"Tickets?" I squinted, half-forgetting why he came here. "Yes, tickets!" I rushed for the refrigerator and plucked them from the magnetic clip. "They sent them in the mail like in the stone age. Shit, I'm glad you reminded me."

"I'm sure there's a will call," he said, not concerned in the slightest. Jax wanted to see *me*, not the ballet.

"Yeah, but I don't want to find out the hard way that they don't."

"Have more faith—if we couldn't do the show, we would've found something else to do." Turning to the side, Jax offered me his arm. "Shall we?"

I locked the door and patted myself down, checking once more that I had everything before looping my hand through the gap at his elbow. "We shall."

WE WERE STRICKEN with silence inside the car until parked underground behind the courthouse. Traffic left Jax stressed, and I opted not to distract him with idle chatter in my eagerness to speed the night up. The musty smell of exhaust bounced off the cool concrete walls as much as the sound of doors slamming shut around us. Once I closed mine, Jax eyed me from the other side.

I slipped next to him, knocking with my shoulder. He bumped me in return. We touched in progressive conversation on the elevator ride to the surface and over the striped lines of the crosswalk to the opera house. Outside, droves of people dressed to the nines congregated for the show. Flocks of small girls pranced in tutus and Christmas colors, throwing me back to memories of childhood when I despised dresses and putting my hair half-up in large bows. The view below of my festive shoes and well-fit slacks reaffirmed that my current aesthetic matched the person I was all along.

Jax stared up at the marble columns, admiring the beauty of the building, which echoed my view of him. The deepness of his chestnut eyes reflected the red and green lights flooding over the doors. His hair was tinged with the slightest hint of gray above his ears, proving his age and the passage of time. My Romeo, still beautiful, no less the man I wanted in my youth as I did now.

I took a step up toward the entrance and offered him my hand while time stood still. *Please take it, Wah.*

He met my gaze first and smiled, nearly blinding me with his brace-less teeth, so pristine and straight. His metal mouth of the past was worth the effort. When he took me, he did so with a confident firmness like his perfect handshake. His pulse beat against my palm. Our hearts alternated until we were in total sync. As one.

The crowd stalled again at the top of the stoop, leaving Jax and I to awkwardly wait our turn through the doors.

"You'd think people would know how to move forward," I muttered. "There's only fifteen minutes before the show starts. Why are they taking their time in the lobby?"

"I'm guessing...gift shop," Jax said with a smirk, "which I'll be stopping at, by the way."

"You would." I yanked him a little closer. "What're you looking for in a souvenir?"

"I don't know. Snow globe maybe. It's still weird not to have —" He paused, looking up toward the new white lights crossing the front of the building. "*Snow.*"

A black machine whirred on the balcony, sending a small flurry to everyone below. A manufactured spell, but no less endearing. I gasped along with him and felt oddly tearful.

"That's amazing," he whispered, reaching up for a few errant flakes. Distinct longing showed on his face, making his crow's feet collapse into nothing.

"Are you homesick?" I asked, certain of the answer.

Jax took in a slow breath and exhaled at the same pace. As he did, he released my hand, then grasped again with our fingers intertwined. Closed his eyes. "Not anymore."

I swallowed hard, and the people in front of us broke the traffic jam to get inside. We didn't stop to look for snow globes. I hardly listened to the usher helping us find our seats in the orchestra section. Jax let kids bump into his legs and politely smiled at everyone, always bringing his focus back to me.

It was happening. The spark. Magic. Second-chance romance.

"You're so handsome tonight," Jax whispered as we sat, tickling my ear and making me shudder. A rush of euphoria, lift, and disbelief took me far away—to a dream, a star, an island void of responsibilities, where money and family and the past didn't matter.

Keeping my hand tightly wound in his, I squeezed hard. "Nothing compared to you."

The look in his eyes was unmistakable. He was moving closer. Aimed at my lips. Couldn't escape. Three, two—

"Don't kiss me," I said, backing away a few inches.

Jax blinked a few times. "Huh?"

"Don't do it yet. Please." I gulped and brought his hand up, pecking ever so softly. "I want to kiss you, but not here. Don't... don't plan anything for it. Don't sweep me off my feet, surprise me in the dark, or pull me in by my tie. None of that. When it's time, I'll say so."

"I...I wasn't about to kiss you, but I'm glad you said something." He weaved through my hair. "I just wanted to say if you like to follow the music, it's okay to let go. I understand some people like to do that."

I sighed. *Of course you would remember that I tapped along, too.* Stuck with nothing else to say, I brought my focus to his chest and kicked my chin out at his scarf. "So...did you make this?"

The instant I said it, I screamed at myself. *What the fuck? "Did you make this?" Are you insane?*

He chuckled. "Nah, I can't knit for shit."

"Crochet," I corrected, still berating inside. *Shut up, shut up, you're making it worse.*

"Crobar? What?"

Goddammit, now I have to keep going. I pointed to a row and touched the loops. "The stitch—this is crochet, not knitting. Double crochet. Whoever made it used the yarns together. It's irregular, but green and black are pretty classic."

"Mm-hmm. Like your eyes tonight. And your tie." He reached forward and pulled me close by the blade, now teasing me because I gave us a set boundary. Jax rubbed our noses together. "I can't guarantee once you give the go-ahead that I won't do exactly this, by the way."

"Oh, Jax." I huffed into his skin while the lights flashed for the show to begin. "Please do…when it's time."

AT INTERMISSION, we toured the gift shops, and the second act buzzed by. We headed back to his car afterward, blending in with the sea of people as if the city's second wind just began.

"I know a good place to eat," I said, anxious to get back home but now more frightened of telling him the truth than ever. Stalling would only work for so long.

"So do I. Already planned for that." He greedily held me close to his left side now, much more brave than I'd ever been in public with Rob or anyone else. Jax was fearless and showed me off. A few other couples eyed us with judgment while we passed, but Jax didn't slow down or ease his grasp one bit.

The next car trip wasn't long—merely twenty minutes, though I recognized the neighborhood well. "Union square? Really? You forget something at work?"

"Hey, gimme a little credit. You love Cheesecake Factory, don't you?" Jax winked and laughed victoriously while pulling into a decent parking spot.

"I can't believe you remembered that. But right now?

Saturday night? It'll take hours to get in." I shook my head in incredulity but considered the longer wait to be a hidden blessing. "Happy to wait with you, though, if you really want to."

"Hell yeah, I do. Come on."

Jax and I tittered in the elevator to the top floor of the Macy's and joked about the last time we were here. Once free of the metal box, we were greeted by an impatient herd of people who were dressed like us—folks on dates that depended on this part going exactly right. The tension in the air was palpable and made me clutch him tighter.

The hostess passing out beeping squares had a frazzled expression, as if she'd been forced to smile too long and her lips began to hurt. A rush of guilt hit me when it was our turn to ask for a table. *If I had half a spine, we wouldn't even be here.*

Yet Jax wasn't through impressing me just yet. "Reservation for Grady, please. Two."

"Oh yes," she said, trailing her finger down the page until she found his name. "It'll only be a minute."

"You made reservations?" I asked.

He smirked at me. "Of course I did. I'm not a complete idiot. This place is hard to get into on a Tuesday afternoon, let alone a Saturday night after a show."

While the hostess walked away to fetch the server, I brushed my hand against his arm. "Jax—"

"Okay, you two, this way." A tall young man, early twenties, gave us a beaming, picturesque smile and waved.

"Wait," I said, bringing everything to a halt. "We, um. We don't need to be seated."

Jax stammered, "Tabby, what—"

"Just two slices of plain cheesecake. To-go, please." I nodded at the waiter. "I'll still tip you."

He turned slowly as if waiting for another instruction, but eventually picked up the pace again. "Okay, I'll be right back with that, sirs."

I brushed Jax's arm again. Too much time had gone by

already. Getting through dinner would've been torture, and I owed it to Jax to come clean. "We need to get back to my place. Trust me."

"Did I do something wrong?" Jax whispered, still stunned by my sudden change of plans. "Is it too much? Too fast?"

"No," I laughed, caressing his cheek. "It's nothing you're doing, and nothing you did. I have my own plans in mind. I'm charming *you* tonight, remember?"

He turned three shades lighter for a moment, then came back to Earth. "Right. Whatever you say."

Our order came and we rode the elevator down alone. A serious, suffocating fog replaced the flirtatious energy we had before. No turning back. It was fun, but nothing about our interaction felt like a first date. It felt like a hundredth date. A thousandth date. The kind of outing that resulted in a proposal and plans for the future, not the youthful try-out it would've been with anyone else.

"So, where to next?" Jax asked when we approached the car.

"You know where." I firmly met his gaze before we opened the doors on either side. "Take me home, Jax."

confession

. . .

Tabby

WHEN WE PULLED up outside my apartment, Jax engaged the emergency brake and tapped on the steering wheel for a moment. He stared straight ahead. "Are you sure you want me to come in?"

"More than anything." I directed his face toward mine with a single index finger. "I have something to show you."

"Do you..." He absently licked his lips and his voice dropped. "Do you have somewhere to be tomorrow?"

"Huh-uh."

"Me either."

"Good. Follow me." I hopped from the car and didn't wait for him while I approached the door. Our mutual excitement bubbled over.

God, I want him so bad. I just want him to take me. I unlocked the door with fidgeting hands. *Maybe just once...just once? Before telling him?*

Jax pressed his body against mine from behind and breathed over my neck. "Please say it's time."

"Almost." A forgiving click of the lock and we were in. I tossed my keys on the small table and we both kicked off our shoes. The lights were bright, but I needed them to keep me centered on the plan. *No, I can't touch him yet. All lies out first.*

He hung his coat neatly on the hook outside the closet and draped the scarf, too. Beneath, dressed in black, he was another dream. Bold and incredibly sexy. I already knew what he could offer me.

"This is my humble abode," I said, turning in a small circle with my arms out. "Take a seat. I need to do something real quick."

He took ginger steps toward the dining table and curved right to the couch without saying a word. Jax belonged there, like a piece of decor I'd picked out of a magazine. A perfect fit.

I smiled and ducked into the bathroom, closing the door and staring at myself in the mirror. My inner monologue was accompanied by an incessant, screaming ring in my ears from stress that never shifted.

What the hell are you going to do now? Give him an old picture? Tell him about Mom? I shook my head and splashed my face with cold water. *Think, dammit.*

Something got in my eye that made everything sting. The answer became clear: the contacts. No more. I removed them and loosened my tie, unbuttoning my white shirt to the second one down, exposing my chest hair and the top of my black binder. Assuming all went well and Jax could accept me, I didn't want my intentions to be lost one bit.

Besides my hidden coloboma, another old relic glared at me from the top drawer: his ring, the one I'd kept hidden since he moved to the city. It still fit, thankfully unaffected by my emotional eating after Rob and I broke up.

I let out a harsh breath and shook. *It's okay. It's time. It's Jax. It's just Jax. He loves you. He loves Tabby. It's alright. Just say it.*

When I returned to the living room, Jax presented the space as if it were his own. He'd placed our cheesecakes in their to-go boxes on the coffee table, along with our given plastic forks.

"Thought maybe you'd want dessert first." He bounced his brows effortlessly.

I flashed a quick smile, but my nerves were impossible, and I couldn't so much as snicker.

Jax scooted to the side, making room for me in the tight corner. "Come 'ere."

Approaching him, my heart thumped so hard I thought I'd pass out. Everything was hazy. Panic attack or brown out, who could say? Once my ass hit the seat, I wasn't going anywhere.

He loosened his own tie. "What did you wanna show me? Take all the time you need."

"Well, I—" I choked. *What the fuck do I do now?*

"Since you're a bit stuck, can I say something?" His scent filled my nostrils—so familiar, like home—enough to make me surrender to his every whim. It was citrus. Bright. Orange or lemon, maybe, with a light wash of lavender. It made me sleepy.

Jax thumbed my cheek and sighed. "Tabby, I didn't know I could feel like this again."

"Again?" I arched my brows. *Don't play dumb, you moron.* It was too late to take back.

"Mm-hmm. I'd given up on it." He took my right hand, which thankfully was sans-ring, because I wasn't ready for him to find out that way. "Tonight, you've proven all the more how great this could be. You're not just one of my people. You're my person, singular. A better fit than I could ever manufacture if I had all the tools and time in the world. It's no wonder my first love brought me to you."

"Jax, about that—"

"I know I talk about her a lot, and I'm sorry. After tonight, I swear I won't mention her again." While softening his expression, a distinct flush of pink appeared on his cheeks. True blush. "She's a guardian angel, this whole time begging me to open my eyes and really look at the kind of man you are."

"And...and what kind of man am I?" I sucked in a breath.

Delight pulled his sweet lips into a tender smile. "You're the perfect man, Tabby. Kind, sweet, driven. You've made something of yourself. You impress me. You—" Jax squinted.

Oh, no.

He stopped looking into my eyes and looked *at* them instead. "Is that..." He went from touching my face gently to holding me still in the light with both hands. "Is that a coloboma?"

I went mute. Words couldn't squeak by the fear. *It's all over.*

Jax grimaced. "Okay, maybe I should've eased up on mentioning her, but I hafta say—putting in a contact that looks like this isn't funny or cute to me, Tabby."

If I'd been any more of a coward, I would've taken the out and kept the secret all my life. But I couldn't hide Mom. Couldn't hide my ring. Couldn't hide the fact that one kiss might give me away. "It's...it's not. I just took my contacts out. This is me."

"Wait, so you have one, too?" His gaze still harshly focused on it. "Why didn't you say something? That's weird, right? Another coincidence?"

I clutched his wrists. My breath shuddered. "Not a coincidence, Jaxson."

Little by little, his eyes shined. "But...Tabby?" he whispered.

Please, God, let him forgive me. "I tried to tell you."

Jax's breath quickened. His grip on my face tightened so I couldn't escape as he stared ever harder. "T-tried to tell me what?"

"The last time Rob surprised me, I *knew* it was you helping him. He couldn't even say it right. Thank you for trying to give me a gift through his lips, but only one person is allowed to say that to me."

He slowed, but his tone faltered. "Say what?"

I gulped. "You know exactly what."

His eyes shot wide open. He panted with loud, harsh exhales —a metronome of doom to me. Pain fueled his last question, lacing an obvious hope to be wrong. "Hwa?"

My lower lip quivered, and a tear dropped over my cheek. "Hwa-Wah. I need you like water, too."

"Oh, my God," he yelled, backing away and pulling his hands into himself.

"Jax, please, let me explain—"

"Explain? I thought you were dead and now you wanna *explain?*"

Mayday. Mayday. The world crumbled around me. Turning back time wasn't an option, and I wasn't dreaming. My worst nightmare realized—Jax found out and greeted me with anger.

"Please tell me it's not true. This is a joke. *Please*, Tabby."

"I'm sorry." It was beyond too little, too late. The words all felt empty. "Wah, forgive me. I tried to tell you, but you didn't hear me. Then I was too scared to say it again."

"Are you fucking kidding me with this?" He shot up from the couch. "When did you try to tell me?"

"The night we stayed up talking in your car. I called you *Wah.*" I chased him and stood, too. "If you'd just listen for a second—"

He clutched his temples. "This isn't happening."

"I don't want to lose you again. I'm so happy you're here. We're meant to be, like you said. Now we can be."

Jax frantically took my shoulders and looked me over, searching for something. He didn't hold back. His hands swam over my body and bitter tears stained his eyes red. He shook, as did his breath, taking handfuls of my clothes. Jax's panic took a turn toward acceptance, and for a moment, I had hope he would come out of the shock and my lies wouldn't matter.

"It's you? It's really you?" Jax sniffed while kissing my hands, then pushed up my shirt to peck at my forearms. "Oh, God." Sliding his palms up to my face again, he grimaced in a half-smile, half-frown sort of way. "Tabby Ross. I would never have guessed that name. Where'd it come from?"

"Dad's nickname and Mom's maiden. A clean slate on all counts."

He coughed out a sob. "Hwa, I've missed you so much. Rehearsed this moment a hundred times, and I'm still not ready. Where were you?"

"I was here." I touched him in return, kneading his shoulders and directing him to sit again. "I was here, and I missed you too, Wah. It's time. Come on. Come here." Pulling on his collar, I aimed for his lips.

Jax startled and leaned away, keeping me at a distance. "How can you say that when you forgot about me?"

"What?" I shook my head and fear rose from my stomach, making the back of my throat sour with reality. "Jax, I couldn't forget about you."

"You did. You *forgot* about me. You moved out here and even though you said you'd keep in touch—you swore you wouldn't disappear—that's exactly what you did." He stood once more and glared at me. "I've spent all this time searching for you, and you didn't try to find me *once*?"

"And say what?" With my thumb and pinky outstretched, I mimed a phone at my ear. "Hey, Jax, it's been a long time. I miss you. I still love you. Oh, yeah, and by the way, I'm a *dude* now. Hope that's okay." I tossed the imaginary device and held my arms up. "Don't be so naive. You're smarter than that."

"Am I? Am I really smarter than that? Don't know why you're giving me the credit now when you obviously had so little faith in me." He wiped his face and raked through his hair, which I'd planned to do in a sensual sweep. Now, he nearly tore at his scalp. "You should've known I meant every word when we were younger. I said *nothing* could change how I felt, and I was right, wasn't I? I made a promise to you, but it didn't mean shit on your end, did it?"

"Don't paint me like that," I yelled. "I was scared. Fuck that —I was terrified. You had the luxury of thinking nothing could ever change because you didn't have a goddamned clue what I was going through."

"That excuse only works 'til I met you out here, *Tabby*." The way he said it was almost like a curse, as if my name alone was a lie. "Maybe not on day one. Maybe not on day two. But when I picked you up? When you laughed with me? When I told you I felt like I knew you *how many* dozens of times?" He scoffed. "No. You can't just whine and say you were scared. This," Jax said, pointing back and forth between us, "was too big to ignore, and you led me on to think you were a stranger from the cosmos of destiny, or some shit."

"Aren't I?" I pounded my chest with one hand. "Isn't it just as fucked up and strange that of all the cities, of all the clubs, of all the nights to look for D&D, you found *my* group?"

"Yeah, it would be magical and make for a decent story, if it wasn't for the fact that you let six months go by before telling me the truth. Why should I believe that you thought of me all that time in between, when you could just as easily have put me on some mental back burner. How can you prove this isn't just another lie?" He yelled to the ceiling, "Goddammit, I'm so sick of people lyin' to me."

"Here. You want proof? I've got it." I held out my left hand. "Look at this. It's my lucky D&D ring. You know, the one everybody thought I lost?"

"Oh, you conveniently found that while I was here, too?"

I bristled at the accusation and growled. "No. I always knew where it was, but I couldn't show you. Look."

He stayed where he was and pressed his lips together, then crossed his arms in an equally stiff way. Jax glanced at the ring, did a double take, and stepped forward to pull on my hand so he could really look.

I sniffed and wiped my eyes with the other hand. "See? I couldn't forget you. I thought about you all the time. Had it on the night we met, and I stuffed it in my pocket so you wouldn't find out by accident."

He rubbed over it with his thumb. "Is this what I think it is?"

"Yes." I hiccupped, out of my control. "You've been with me all the time."

"Some promise." He shook his head and released me. "You didn't say a damn thing."

"I'm telling you now. Jax, please—"

"You should've done better. If I didn't hear you, you should've said it again. Texted me, sent an old picture, something. Did you like watching me make an ass of myself going lovesick? Everyone knows I've been crazy about you, but you didn't care until Rob was gone."

"That's not true." I followed Jax as he went toward the kitchen to get away from me. "I've been a total mess since you showed up—over you, over Rob, over freakin' *Annie*, who knew something was wrong that night my car broke down and didn't stop nagging until I told her the truth. She's been begging me to say something ever since, and even called me out on my birthday over this shit. Can't you understand this has been killing me?"

"I swear to God, what the fuck is it with people who do shit they know will hurt me, but because they felt *bad* about it the whole time, that's supposed to make it better?" He turned around and gave me a dose of his usual self, which only drove the knife in further: "If I find somebody looking to buy fertilizer, I'll be sure to hook them up with you and Heather for your great supply of bullshit."

"Don't joke about this right now, Jax, *please*. I didn't know it would go on this long. The love of my life returned, and I wasn't single. I couldn't risk giving up what I had for the chance that you wouldn't want me anymore."

"But I would, and I did. Christ, I almost kissed you that night in the car, and you knew it. You *knew* it, didn't you?" His rage was an entirely different flavor compared to Rob's—I wasn't afraid he would hurt me at all. Instead, every word was another step toward self-destruction. Jax didn't want to yell at me, but it was all he could do to keep from breaking down.

I lunged to hold him still. "Stop this spiral and look at me."

"You were supposed to be different, Tabby. I trusted you." Jax broke down and pushed past me for his coat.

"Wait, where the hell are you going?" I blocked the door.

"Anywhere but here." He paused with his back to me and held the scarf, laying it flat between his hands before clenching it in tight fists.

"Wah, please," I begged, reaching for his shoulder.

Jax muttered, so calm and low, it frightened me. "I used to love this. Used to hold it and think about you. Imagined that, one day, you'd see me and think, 'There he is. He found me.'"

"I did," I whispered, barely getting over the pounding of my chest.

"No, you told me I couldn't kiss you yet, as if I hadn't kissed you a thousand times." He sniffed, turned around, and pulled the scarf tight, nearly taking it apart. "You took me to the Nutcracker and had the balls to ask me if I made this myself!"

Whether it was foolishness or desperation, I didn't care. I shoved Jax backward against the closet door with full intent to kiss him. My last shred of good sense kept me from doing the deed. "Stop. I love you. I *love* you, Jaxson Dale Grady. I always have. This...this is our chance to have everything. Our shot at happily ever after. Isn't this what you said you wanted?"

He bared his teeth and said, "Not anymore. Move."

My world was unraveling. I couldn't change what I'd already done. The plan for Jax to get to know Tabby failed because of one thing: I'd been Tabby all my life, and Jax knew it better than anyone.

"I can't let you leave like this," I said.

"And I can't believe I'm leaving, but watch." Jax jerked his shoulder to get away and swung open my front door so hard, it left a mark on the wall inside.

Before he was completely out of sight, I gave it one last shot. "Jax!"

He halted but didn't turn around.

"Tomorrow you'll wake up and remember you love me."

His head dropped while squeezing the bridge of his nose. Sobbing on opposite ends of the hall, we revisited that same cold night in December years earlier.

Come on. Come back.

Jax didn't answer. He left me to stew in the mistake that I'd been brewing for six months. Our perfect night, our second chance, was over.

Wah was gone.

unraveled

. . .

Jax

THE WHOLE WAY back to my place with Ethan, I screamed, "How *could* you?"

If it had been Denver, I would've taken the loop north and back again, like I did the night I caught Heather with Chris. With no straight highway, I got stuck in traffic and raged through the lights, barely careful enough not to be pulled over.

"You lying son of a bitch. Jesus, I can't believe it was you the *whole time*." I nearly ran into a pedestrian stepping into an underlit crosswalk and slammed on my brakes. It restarted the jump of my heart and I cried. *You're alive, you're alive, and I still fucking love you. I love you.* I folded over the steering wheel, spilling the agony from my lips and my eyes in equal measure. "You lied to me. *Lied.* Why? Hwa, how could you do this to me?"

The car behind me honked when the crosswalk was clear. I couldn't remember the rest of the drive and prayed I hadn't run any red lights in my grief.

One step. Then another. Don't trip. I stumbled my way from the parking garage to the shop and pulled myself up the metal staircase on the side to our front door. Every small sound was a clash in my mind until I could collapse inside.

Somehow the apartment was like stepping into another world. Ethan was watching a movie on the couch with Megan, and they turned the volume down when I came in.

"Hey, man. How was the show?" Ethan asked.

I sniffed and walked through the kitchen toward my room without saying anything. My heavy dress shoes squeaked beneath me, announcing every step.

Numb and lonely, I took off Dad's heavy wool coat and put it on the bed, glared at the scarf peeking out from the front pocket, then went for the rest of my loose tie. I moved so slowly, it didn't feel real. The whole night was a blip in time I wanted to wake from.

"Jax, you okay?" Ethan knocked on the door jamb since it wasn't closed. "What the hell happened?"

I shrugged and unbuttoned my shirt.

"Seriously, dude. You were so excited earlier. Was it not really a date?"

"No, it was a date." I sighed and looked at the ceiling as I folded my arms. "I can't believe—" The tears came again, and I clenched my jaw.

"What?" Ethan put his hand on my shoulder. "Talk to me."

"He spent six months lyin' to me, man."

"About what?" He shook his head. "I don't get it."

I wiped my eyes in an effort not to completely embarrass myself. "Did you have a high school sweetheart, Ethan? Somebody who got away?"

He blinked a few times. "Uh, yeah. Sure."

"Yeah? So did I." My lip quivered as I spoke. Saying it out loud helped me process everything. "I swore that I'd always love them, that nothing would change how I felt. I pined, and I searched, and I planned, trying to capture the same feeling I used to have, but they disappeared. So, I tried to move on. I thought I found somebody new I could love. Somebody who understood me the same way. Tabby had all the signs, and I still didn't see it. He lived here. His dad died. He—"

Ethan held his hands up. "Yo, you're talking in circles. What does this have to do with Tabby?"

"He *is* Tabby," I screamed. "Goddammit, he's the one. He just looked so fuckin' different I couldn't figure it out. Tabby knew and he lied to me!"

Megan came around the corner in her curiosity, while Ethan grimaced at my yelling.

"Do you get it, now?"

"So, Tabby was what, your old boyfriend?" he asked.

"Close. Try the other one." I shook my head and wiped my eyes again, out of words and still in shock.

"Oh, damn," Ethan whispered.

Megan chimed in with a cautious, "What's going on?"

Graciously, he figured it out and saved me the pain of more explanation. "I think Jax knew Tabby before he transitioned."

My phone buzzed in my pocket. Now with space between us, my heart was a mud pit of anger, sadness, and abject joy. *I found him. I did, right? Is it still too late?*

Not wanting to blow whatever chance still existed, I couldn't ignore it. Without looking, I answered, "Hwa, can I come back?"

A sobbing voice answered. It wasn't Tabby. "Jaxson, it's Mom."

"What? Mom?" I forgot Ethan and Megan still stared at me while I looked at the clock. "It's past midnight there, isn't it? What's—"

"Your father's in the hospital. He had a heart attack tonight." She sniffled on the other end. "Brian and I are here at Porter. Honey, I don't know if he'll make it."

My world ended. My heart stopped. Any pain from dealing with Tabby screeched to a halt and floated away. The only thing that mattered was Dad.

"Porter? Porter Hospital?" I grabbed the coat again and ran for the front door. "You tell them to keep Dad alive as long as you have to, alright? I'm coming to Porter. I'm headin' to the airport right now."

"Jax, what happened?" Ethan called behind me.

"I'm goin' home," I yelled, and ran five blocks north to hail a cab downtown.

crossroads

. . .

Tabby

I COULDN'T CALL ANNIE; she would've told me I was wrong to wait until now, and she was right. Couldn't call Jax, he was driving, and being pathetic wouldn't help my case. So I called the only other soul who wouldn't need an explanation and would almost surely not make me feel any worse.

"Sweetheart?" Mom answered, groggy, but concerned. "It's so late."

"Mom, I fucked up." I sobbed, collapsed on my living room floor after a full half hour of crying so hard I couldn't breathe. "I went out with Jax, and I told him the truth. Now he hates me for lying to him."

"Oh, Tabby." She sighed and clicked her tongue a few times. "Where is he now?"

"He left in a huff. I'm thinking about going after him."

"This late? Please don't, not when it's so dark. You didn't drive tonight, did you?"

"No, he drove. I was worried about him when he left, but Jax is careful." I sniffed and rubbed my temples, putting Mom on speakerphone. "I can't believe I let it go this far without saying anything. It got out of hand so fast."

Mom hummed in an understanding way, but she couldn't

offer me much comfort. We'd already argued about it more than once.

"Well, on the bright side," I said, trying to think like Jax and bringing something light to the subject, "I can get you his dad's number if you want it."

She snickered. "I don't think that will be necessary."

"Oh, Mom. What the hell am I going to do?"

"Well, put yourself in his shoes." She groaned as if sitting up in bed. It was well past her usual late-night movie marathon. "If somebody upset you, what would you want them to do to make it up to you?"

I closed my eyes and thought of all the times I wanted Rob to make up for something, and he never did. What was I hoping for? "I guess...I would want them to own it."

"Right. You're always looking for the good in all people. Doesn't Jax do the same?"

"Yeah. Yeah, he does. He gives everybody the benefit of the doubt." Talking to Mom helped calm me down so I could think more clearly. "First thing in the morning, I'm going over there. He just needs to sleep it off. Jax doesn't hold grudges. That's not how he operates."

"I suggest you get some good sleep too, so you're fresh to talk to him like an adult. Promise me you'll wait until the sun's up, and you'll drive safe."

"Of course, Mom."

"Goodnight, son."

"Night." *Click.*

MY ALARM WENT off at 6 a.m. It was still quite dark outside, but I couldn't wait to get ready to see him. I jumped in the shower and scrubbed the night off me the best that I could, and dressed in the book-print shirt I was wearing the first night he came here. We'd be at nearly the same place, and I could introduce myself again.

A clean slate. I just needed him to listen for five minutes.

Hope made my drive over lighter than ever. I hit every green light, even the pesky ones through the construction zone. Sunday made for a light-traffic day through the city. As if my mission was blessed by a guardian angel, I made it to him easily and found his car in the garage. When I got out of mine, I stroked his hood. *Thanks for making it home safe, Wah.*

Somehow, I had a feeling he would wake and be grateful to see me, even welcome me with open arms in spite of how we left everything. My gut said he needed me. I came to answer the call, hell or high water, across space and time. Whatever my soulmate needed, I would provide.

My hands and feet practically buzzed when I knocked on Jax and Ethan's door. It was too early for the store to be open, so either one of them could have answered. I stood with my hands meekly behind my back and regretted not picking up something else to offer besides myself.

To my chagrin, Ethan swung the door wide. "Oh. Hey, Tabby."

"Hi. I'm here to see Jax. Can I come in?"

Ethan blocked my way. "No. Sorry, he's not in."

My heart sank. "Look, Ethan. I know you're still pissed about me and Rob—"

"No, that's not—"

"But you don't understand what's going on between me and Jax, so you don't get a right to play goalie here. Let me in." I charged forward.

He slapped a hand on the opposite side of the door jamb, barring me completely. "Okay, number one, I'm not playing goalie. In fact, if I was, I wouldn't let you in anyway, because leading Jax on for six months was a real shitty thing to do."

Oh, no. I swallowed hard, wishing I didn't have to defend myself to someone else. "Did...did Jax tell you that?"

"Not exactly. But he told me he knew you a long time ago, and you didn't come clean. You were his, how did he put it? Oh, yeah. 'The one that got away'," he said in flippant air quotes. "Let me tell 'ya, if it were me, I'd be just as pissed as he was last night."

"Ethan, I'm trying to make up for it. Neither of you can imagine how terrifying it—"

"Number two, he really isn't fucking here, so bug off. I've got a girl in my room."

"That's bullshit. His car's here."

"He must've taken a cab to the airport then."

"The airport?" I scoffed. "Why the hell would he go to the airport?"

Ethan shrugged. "I don't know. Got a call and was really shaken up. Said he was going home to his dad. Headed to some hospital."

Colorado? "Did he say which one?"

"Yeah, but I don't know—"

I pushed Ethan inside and slammed him against the wall behind him. "Rack your brain, dammit. Which hospital?"

"Fine. Started with a P. Meg, do you remember that hospital Jax said last night?" he yelled, holding his hands up. I was a shrimp compared to him, but Ethan knew I was serious.

"Yeah, uh, Porter, I think?" Megan called from the back bedroom.

"There ya have it. Are we done now?" he asked, beyond annoyed.

"Yeah. Porter? Shit. *Shit.*" I ran down the stairs, hailing a cab like Jax did. Good idea in a panic.

Even if I was too late, Jax needed me. *I'm keeping my promise, Wah. I won't let you down.*

visitors

. . .

Dale, Jax's Dad

BEEP. *Beep. Beep.*

It annoyed the shit out of me, but I was somehow too exhausted to open my eyes. *What the fuck is that?*

A TV was on somewhere. Whoever watched it couldn't pick a channel and kept flicking through. Voices, music, and familiar jingles blared in short bursts before changing again.

I stretched my toes and felt a waffle-knit blanket and ill-fitting socks, slipping off me by the second. A hard, awkward-fitting monitor was clamped to my right index finger. An IV pulled at the hair on my left arm, making my wrist sore. Cool air puffed into my nose from a tube in each nostril.

Oh, hell. I'm in the hospital.

With a groan, I swallowed and opened my eyes to the obtrusive bright light from the hallway outside. Thankfully, my room was still dark. The digital clock on the wall said it was only 7:30 a.m., which was too early for me on a good day anyway. The neighbor in the room next door had the loud TV. Slumped in a chair at my side was a man dressed in black, and for a second, I nearly shit myself at the thought that the grim reaper himself had come to visit me, when I recognized his sleeping face.

"Jax...psst, hey Jax, kiddo, wake up," I said, unable to reach him from where I was. My craggly voice was quiet, so I cleared my throat to get his attention again.

With a jolt, Jax shot up in his seat and turned to me. "Shit, *Dad*. You're finally awake. Hold on, I'll get a nurse—"

"No, just wait a minute, will ya?" I held my hand up and smiled at him. "What are you doing here? Better than that, what the hell am *I* doing here?"

He gripped the railing by my bed and kept peering behind him, as if a nurse from the hall would see he was talking to me. "Mom called me last night, almost midnight. From what everybody's told me so far, you called for an ambulance 'cause you thought you were having a heart attack around seven. Somewhere between you calling and you goin' downstairs to meet them on the street, you fell and hit your head pretty hard. Concussion. They brought you here and all your emergency contact stuff was for Mom, and she blew things out of proportion. She called and made it sound like you were dying. I hopped on the next red-eye flight here. Had to layover in fuckin' Vegas."

"Aw, man? Just a layover?" I chuckled, then ended up coughing. "Well, glad I didn't die, anyway."

"I don't know if you were conscious or not when you were picked up since you're doing okay now. Docs say you only had a mini heart attack. It still wasn't good. Mom and Brian went home, and she's coming back around nine." He grimaced and shook his head. "Hate to say it, but I think it's time to say goodbye to extra crispy rellenos, Dad."

I slapped my chest. "Oh, no. Not *that*."

"'Fraid so. If you start having back pain like you did when I talked to you yesterday, you can't ignore that. It might not be a small one next time."

"Well, you've had to live without good food for a while now, kid. Think I'll survive?"

Jax smiled for a second, but his face fell soon after. It wasn't just fatigue. He twisted his hands together and cracked his knuckles. "I don't know. Maybe I should just come home and help you."

I squinted. "Things go that bad last night?"

He sighed. "It's complicated."

"Pssh, what's complicated? Did it go well or not?"

Jax must've figured I wasn't going to die without a nurse knowing I was awake, so he finally came back to the chair and gave up on trying to secretly flag someone outside. "Dad, I didn't tell you that Tabby's not...well, he's not like a typical guy."

I found the small remote at my side and propped myself up in the hospital bed with a slow, creaking whir. "Explain."

"He's...um...Tabby wasn't, uh, born a boy," he said, clapping his hands.

Like a reflex, my brows arched. What was I going to say about it? "Okay, and?"

"Look, that isn't really what matters here. It doesn't make a difference to me either way. What *does* make a difference is Tabby lied to me. Now I feel betrayed, frustrated, happy, in love, crazy, heartbr—"

"Whoa, whoa, whoa, kid. Back it up a second." I got tired of the air blowing into my nose and took the hose out, hanging it on the IV stand at my side. "Are you tellin' me you rejected him because he wasn't what you thought he was? I raised you better than that, Jaxson."

Jax shook his head frantically. "No, no, no. I knew he was trans when I met him out there. That's not the issue at all." He got misty-eyed and put his hands together, tapping his thumbs on his forehead as he leaned over. Reaching into his pocket, Jax pulled out a ratty old scarf and brought it to his face, almost muffling his words. "Dad, you were right. My first love *did* come back to me. I just thought...thought he would wanna tell me before trying to recreate our last date."

"Maybe I hit my head too hard. Gotta speak English, kid."

Jax met my eyeline and rolled up the scarf. "Tabby *is* Jamie. They're the same person. Dad, I don't know what to do."

Now his shock made sense, as did his apprehension. All my fatherly wisdom up to this point meant little. "You're shittin' me."

"Yeah. So. There it is." He chewed his thumbnail. "I feel stuck, Dad."

"Stuck? Come here," I said, getting him to lean over me, then I smacked him upside the head and laughed. "Get your head on straight. Jesus, I thought you had a *real* fuckin' problem, kid."

All the noise I made caught the attention of the nurses' station outside, and a stout woman with a magic marker came in and tried to burn my corneas with the bright fluorescent lights that she flicked on. "Good morning, Dale. I'm your nurse this morning. Your son already filled out a breakfast form for you a couple hours ago, and I'll tell them to bring it up now that you're awake, okay?" She scribbled something on the whiteboard by the door while Jax paced next to the window.

"When am I going home?"

"The doctor has to release you. Probably before this evening if you're feeling alright." She handed me the oxygen tube with a stern glare until I put it back on again. "That's it. Buzz if you need anything."

I carried on with Jax as if our conversation hadn't been bull-dozed. "This is why I don't like hospitals." My smile fell when I looked at Jax again. "Aw, now what's this about?"

He shook his head and put his hands on his hips, looking older and more like me than I'd ever realized. Maybe it was the coat, or maybe it was the fact he still had hair, but my son was a better man than me, even if he couldn't see it. "I walked out on him last night. Didn't listen. I was so angry about his lies that I didn't care why he lied in the first place."

His worry made me proud. "So go make it up to him now." I pointed to the chair again to get him to sit. "Seriously, you're making this harder than it has to be. Forget anything you were angry about—you and I both know you tried your damnedest to find someone else and it didn't work out."

Jax snickered. "Wish you weren't so right about that. I feel like everything I can do now would feel cheap. I need it to be big enough for Tabby to know it's the end of the line for me."

I felt struck with ancient inspiration. Why not try a recycled idea? "Well, when you were just a kid, you got Lisa's blessing. Why not do it again?"

He sat up straight. "Seriously?"

"Sure. I mean, she was so young, only my age. I bet she's still around, right?"

Jax blinked a few times. "Yeah, she is. Tabby talked about his mom. My God—she lives north of the city. *Shit*, that's why he didn't want me meeting her. I would've known her instantly."

"Well, there ya go." I nodded at him with slow approval. "You owe me five bucks or something for being right about this, I think."

We stared at each other for a minute. He chuckled first, then we both cracked, full-on laughing so loud that a nurse poked her head in to shush us.

"Get the hell outta here, Jax. You've got a job to do now."

"I can't leave now; I only just got here."

"Kid, I'm a grown man and can take care of myself, thank you very much. Besides, if your mother panicked enough to call and say I was dying last night, I bet she'll be here much earlier than nine. You shouldn't waste time." I patted his hand. "Go home, Jax. Go to California. Make a new home with Tabby."

His tired eyes had fear behind them—fear that he'd already wasted his shot.

"Tell me—have you even tried to talk to Tabby since last night?"

He sighed. "No. I was too focused on you, and it's an hour early there."

"Good. Don't call Tabby—surprise him. Show up and tell

Lisa you're sorry you doubted him. Any good man would make amends the best way he knows how. This is yours."

Jax pulled out his phone. "He said she does real estate in the bay, so it can't be too hard to find her office, right? I can't believe I didn't try to look *her* up all these years, but I thought that would cross a line or something."

"Forget that. Check flights before you run outta time."

He nodded and went downstairs for a slightly higher hope at a faster internet connection.

In the meantime, a nurse brought the breakfast plate in, making me wish I could stay a little longer. I wasn't getting any younger and this was too close of a call. Slowly waking with each bite, I took stock of everything I had to be grateful for, starting with the son who would drop everything on a dime to be here with me.

Jax returned with his hands in his pockets. "Got the last seat on a direct flight that leaves in two hours. Gotta go now."

"Good. Seeing as I'm the one stuck in a hospital bed today, I've got nothing better to do. I'll find her. You get to the airport and get your ass home. We'll tag-team it. Deal?"

He deflated, openly disappointed to be leaving so soon, but he had a job to do. "I love you. I'm glad you're okay."

"Extra hot, extra cheese—"

"Extra *avocado*, Dad. I'll call you when I land in the bay." Jax waved as he sauntered from the hospital room, trying to linger a little bit more.

I was proud of my son; of the man he'd become. His future was just beginning.

JUSTINE, Jax's mother, drove me nuts the whole time she was here, overly concerned and bringing up things from the past that I didn't want Brian to hear. He was gracious and spent most of the time sitting in the hall while she treated me more like a mother than an ex-wife. The more time she spent fussing over my bed, the less comfortable I was. Thankfully, the kind young nurse who came to deliver my lunch tray could sense my growing annoyance, and she told Justine and Brian that I'd had enough visitors for now.

Enjoying the last little bit of quiet while I gathered my strength after lunch, I flicked through the endless loop of TV channels myself, as I'd heard earlier. A few minutes were all it took before I saw why my neighbor couldn't decide on anything in the morning. *Swear to God, there is nothing good on. They really don't want people stickin' around here, do they?*

The phone beside my bed rattled me with a sudden ring. I even jumped before realizing what it was—nothing like the quiet harmonica of my cell phone. The ER doc cleared me for release at six p.m., and I was milking it for all it was worth. Half-dreading Justine's voice on the other end, I answered, "You know, this loud-ass hospital telephone isn't good for heart attack patients."

"Uh...Mr. Grady?" the man's voice asked.

"Speaking."

He was shaky on the other end. Unsure. "Mr. *Dale* Grady? Jaxson's father?"

That's odd. I squinted. "Who is this?"

"Oh, God. I'm so sorry. I called to see if you were actually here and...I wasn't expecting them to transfer me to your room instead of telling me yes or no. Are you feeling alright? Is Jax there?"

I turned off the television. Whatever was happening on the phone was much more amusing. "I'm fine, son. But I'll ask again, who is this?"

"Well, Mr. Grady, my name's Tabby Ross."

"Wow, no shit," I whispered in surprise. "I'm, uh, afraid you just missed Jax. He's heading back to San Francisco as we speak."

Silence, then a scoff of humiliation. "Of course he is. Figures he'd already be on his way back just when I get here."

"Wait—did you hop on a plane to follow Jax to Denver?"

Tabby took in a breath. "Sir? I'd follow your son anywhere."

I held in my urge to joke with him, too charmed by his hope-less confession. "I'm sorry I don't have better news for you. Where are you now?"

"No, it's fine. My fault, really. I'm standing outside Porter Hospital with nothing but the clothes I put on this morning. I forgot how damn cold it gets out here." Tabby stammered a bit before getting to the point, which I guessed was equal parts temperature and frazzled nerves. "Since I'm here, would it be alright with you if I came inside for a visit?"

"Come in? To see *me*?" I found myself caught in a strange place myself, like on the opposite side of a principal's desk. "Sure, I guess, if you really want to."

"Yes, sir. I'll be right up." *Click.*

My hospital room wasn't ready for anyone who wasn't family. I snapped into action to flatten the sheets and stacked all the trash on the hospital lunch tray. It wasn't much; might make for a better impression. What the hell was I nervous for, anyway?

The same voice from the phone spoke with a nurse outside, and I eyed the heart monitor. *Stop giving me away, you stupid machine.*

A young man peeked his head in and gave me a wave. His arms were bright red from the cool air outside, not protected enough by his short-sleeved shirt. Tabby's hair was dark, not what I expected, but when he stepped into the light, it emerged —the strong resemblance to my friend from the past, even if it was only a faded memory. His nose and lips gave him away.

"Mr. Grady?" he asked again, just as apprehensive as on the phone. "I'm Tabby. It's nice to see you." Extending his hand, Tabby gulped loud enough for me to hear.

I shook it without thinking and chose not to acknowledge the past just yet. "Yeah, thanks for coming by. Come sit down."

The boy nodded, straightened his shirt, then took a few strides to sit in the chair where Jax was only hours before. "So, um, are you sure you're okay? It's not exactly normal to hang out in a hospital."

I chuckled. "Funny story. Cracked my head open, and Jax's mom made a big deal out of it. Blew things out of proportion. Jax has something waiting for him at home, so I told him not to hang around here for a boo-boo."

Tabby smirked. "I'm glad to hear that. I'm not surprised he didn't wait to find out if you were really hurt." His eyes, so youthful and wide, shone for a moment. He slowed, wanting me to really listen. "You should know, sir, your son loves you very much. You're the most important person in his life. He misses you."

"Thank you," I said, well aware of Jax's family loyalty. Hearing it from someone else made it all the more real, though. It warmed me.

I couldn't pretend like the young man at my side was someone I didn't want to reach out to, because I knew too much and was too old to play bullshit games. Enough was enough. "If your ol' man was still around, I bet you'd have done the same thing, Tabby. I'm sorry he's been gone so long."

Whatever shell of false strength around him quickly crumbled. "You know who I am?"

"Of course I do. You're Lisa's kid." I smiled, not able to hide my excitement. "Shit, you've really grown up, haven't you?"

"Afraid I've grown into a real mess."

"Nah, life'll do that to you."

He pieced back together all the cracks in his composure, sniffed hard and set his strong jaw. "Mr. Grady, I need to apologize to you. For not being upfront with Jax when I met him again, and for not believing in him." Tabby shrugged while biting his lower lip for a moment, staring at the ceiling instead of me. "I should've known he wouldn't judge me. Should've trusted when he said he wouldn't change. I was scared."

"Sounds like you had every right to be." I cocked a brow. "Jaxson spent a really long time heartbroken. Ended up dealing with some really bullshit people. But when he met you...he was happy again, ya know? He'd call me and wanna talk about something other than work. I don't understand that IT shit that he does. I understood him when he talked about you."

"Do you think I blew it?" he asked, wiping his eyes with his thumbs.

I couldn't risk revealing too much, so I tried to give Jax the best chance at his surprise. "That I don't know. I do know it takes guts to get on a plane and follow somebody, even if you aren't sure where they're gonna be. Takes guts to do what you're doin' right now. It carries some weight, I think."

Tabby blushed. "I really hope you're right." He stood from the chair again, burning our short time together so his nerves wouldn't short out. "Mr. Grady, I'm in love with your son. I've loved him all my life. Right now, right here, I'm asking for your blessing to find out if he loves me, too. If he'll still have me."

So, this is what it feels like. Having no daughters, I never thought I'd ever be put in this position. It was so cliche, so beyond awkward, I was almost embarrassed on his behalf. It meant more than words to see Tabby step up. My son was the target. The one Tabby wanted. Regardless of however I answered, they'd charge forward, so which side would I ultimately like to be on?

"I can't give you a guarantee what Jax will say, or if he'll forgive you. But I can give you that blessing to ask, Tabby Ross. That, I'll do for both of you." I held out my hand, which Tabby took gladly, shaking it with the same technique I'd once taught Jax. It was firm, not too strong, with no hesitation. A binding contract.

Tabby couldn't waste time and flurried his feet, not sure if he should run downstairs for a cab or try to get plane tickets first. "Oh, I almost forgot," he said, erasing yesterday's white board notes after picking up the magic marker on the desk.

"What's that for?"

He wrote down a phone number I didn't recognize, then

turned and gave me a mischievous smirk. "I couldn't get you connected before. If Jax didn't know, you *couldn't* know. Mom hopes to catch up." Tabby tossed the marker on the desk again. "Thanks, Mr. Grady. Wish me luck." He saluted, then jogged out of sight.

I smiled and put my hands behind my head with a laugh. "I knew those kids would work out someday."

redo

. . .

Jax

DAD DID GOOD. Got me an address, even. I slept for a few hours once I came home so I wouldn't be a complete mess in the evening, but there wasn't time to waste. It had to happen tonight. The rest of my life, of *our* life, was waiting.

To calm my nerves, I wrote to Annie, just to make sure Tabby was still okay. She only confirmed she'd heard from him and nothing else. I prayed I wasn't already too late, and that my reaction didn't ruin us for good.

Like I did when I was a teenager, I bought Tabby's mom a bouquet of carnations—simple flowers, so happy and colorful. Their scent was what I preferred over roses. The florist wrapped it in a ribbon of gold. As I left the shop, a shiny, right-side-up penny caught my eye on the sidewalk—it blessed my voyage, and I tossed it in the air before adding it to my collection.

It was dark when I arrived at the house north of the city. The horizon glowed in a misty haze from the fog. Compared to the biting cold of home earlier in the day, it might as well have been a spring evening. Christmas lights adorned every house I could see, and in Lisa's front room, a large tree twinkled with a white and silver motif through the window. To keep from announcing myself too early, I parked around the corner and opted to have some distance to breathe first.

The day had been a whirlwind from sunup to sundown, and I still couldn't believe everything I'd done in the past twenty-four hours. Dad texted me when he left the hospital and sent me a picture of his pathetic dinner: a salad with extra avocado. I smirked at his message before leaving the car, grabbing the flowers and facing my destiny.

Her doorbell was a standard *ding-dong,* audible from the outside. My heart nearly jumped from my chest while I waited for an answer. I resisted the urge to peer in the window or knock, certain she took her time for a reason. Who was I to demand instant attention on a late Sunday night?

Tabby's mom opened the door with a wide smile. It wasn't one of pure shock or surprise—she knew something, but what, I couldn't quite tell. "Hello there, young man. Can I help you?"

Wow. She wasn't any different from the woman in my memory, except her hair was shorter and speckled with more gray. A waft of cinnamon hit me in the face from the open door, orienting me again to winter despite the lack of snow. Her mere presence reminded me of home, just like Dad did.

"Yeah—yes. Hi." I held my hand out for her. "I don't know if you remember me. My name is—"

"Jaxson Grady," she finished for me, taking my hand with a light touch. "I couldn't forget you if I tried. My, my. You're all grown up."

"Yes, ma'am." I wasn't any less nervous than I was the first time I met her, shaking all the way to my toes.

She released my hand and leaned against the doorway, folding her arms. "What brings you to my house so late after all these years?"

"Something that can't wait until tomorrow." I cleared my throat and tried to stand up straight. Being taller than her felt unnatural. Relaxing my shoulders, I let the nerves flow through my fingertips, buzzing until I could focus enough to remember all I had rehearsed. "Ms. Nova, I have a question for you."

Lisa's open and attentive eyes shone. "I'm listening."

I paused for a deep breath, as if my future depended on the next few sentences. "A long time ago, I asked for your blessing. See, I loved your daughter, and I wanted nothing more than to tell her so. But things changed. We got older. Grew apart. I spent half my life praying I would feel the way I did in those days, searching and falling for anyone who might take me. On the way, I found someone who filled my soul in ways I've never known."

"You deserve that," she said, filling the space where I paused at the end.

"I'm really glad you think so, 'cause that's why I'm here again." Like she did when I was only a kid, her words made me feel worthy. Gave me enough courage to finish the thought. "Lisa Nova, I'm madly in love with your son."

She closed her lips in a tight, though quivering, smile.

I nodded as I spoke, choking back my emotions. "Tabby's incredible, just like he always was. He's everything I've ever needed or wanted. Maybe I've already blown it, maybe it's already too late, but he's not just someone I wanna be with for now. I mean it forever. Can you forgive me for any upset I caused him so I can give him the same fulfillment he gives me? Will you give us your blessing like you did before?"

"Of course I will." She sniffled and wiped a few tears away, then opened her arms to me. "Oh, Jax. Thank you for loving him."

I hugged her tightly, no longer caring about the status of her flowers as I let them fall to the floor behind her. "Dad taught me well, what can I say?"

Lisa patted my back and welcomed me into her home, where we sat on her couch and talked about the lost years. We ordered a light dinner and crafted a plan.

The clock chimed in the hall. It ticked down to nothing. Then, a light knock.

The familiar *ding-dong*.

It was time.

finding him

. . .

Tabb

WRITING to Jax felt like too dangerous of a game. I didn't want him knowing about my trip to Colorado since I'd missed him, and his dad would likely bust me anyway. All I could hope was to intercept him somewhere at home, if I could get there before the day was over.

Annie helped calm me. Though she still didn't approve of how long I'd waited to come clean, she supported the fact that I did so at all. Messaging her kept me sane until the plane boarded —a merciful direct flight that would land before nine. Enough time to still find him before having to concede that making up would have to wait until Monday.

I took a cab from the airport to Dragon's Lair since my car waited in the parking garage anyway. Anxiety made me bang on the apartment door harder than I should have.

Ethan answered with an annoyed, "Seriously?"

"Hey, is he home yet?"

"Home? Are you shittin' me? Didn't you hear me this morning?"

I rolled my eyes. "He came back already. Are you telling me he hasn't been here?"

Ethan shrugged. "I don't know, man, I ran the store all day. Can't you just call him?"

"No, I—" I pulled my hair and backtracked down the stairs. *Where the hell are you?* I yelled behind me, "Call me if he comes home, please."

In the garage, Jax's car wasn't next to mine. It made my stomach drop—he did come home, but where else would he go? Maybe he saw my car and figured I was already waiting for him. Or maybe, because his apartment was empty, he thought to intercept me before I left, too.

The city seemed to grow by miles after every block. Unlike this morning, I hit every red light. Pedestrians filled and abused every crosswalk. For how late the hour was, San Francisco was awake and alive, even worse than what we saw last night after the show.

My apartment was as cold and empty as ever before, with no Jax outside to give me hope. I ran out of options.

Should I break down and call him?

At that moment, my phone rang. The name on the screen— while comforting—still wasn't his. "Hi, mom," I answered, defeated and tired.

"Hi, sweetheart. Did you get home safe?"

"Yeah, I'm here now." I sighed and plopped onto the couch. "I can't believe I've been on two planes today, and I still missed him. Thank God for those credit card points."

"Aw, I'm so sorry, Tabby." Her tone wasn't overly cloying or false, but it had a hint of something else. Mischief? "Have you eaten? I know it's late."

"Other than shitty airport food? No."

"Do you want to join me? I ordered from that Japanese place you love. The one with the amazing sushi. There's too much here for me."

My stomach rumbled—true hunger, not nerves. I'd avoided eating to keep from getting sick, and now I regretted it. "That… sounds amazing, actually."

"Promise me you'll be careful, okay? In fact, can you get an Uber so you don't have to drive?"

Her presence would calm me enough to think clearly. Enough to plan a new strategy the next day. It was exhausting just thinking about more travel, but I had nothing more to lose. "Sure, Mom. I'll be up soon."

On the way there, I wondered where my Wah could be. Every black sedan we passed that looked like his took my breath away. My phone nagged in my pocket, tempting me to message him. I resisted. If Jax wanted to hear from me, he'd say so. The ball was in his court if he saw my car at his place.

Mom's street was lined with Christmas lights from all her neighbors; thankfully, they all had good taste and shied away from inflatable monstrosities. It was a classy winter wonderland, only absent the dusting of sugar from the sky that adorned Denver's streets.

Intense loneliness stuck me when I paid the driver and walked up to Mom's door. I considered staying over—not like I could work tomorrow anyway when I still didn't know where he was. Ringing her doorbell, part of me wondered if Jax's dad took the bait and called her already so she'd have an idea what to do next.

She opened the door and pulled me into a tight hug. "I'm so glad you're here safe."

"Of course, Mom." I squeezed her. "Most of me is intact."

"What does that mean?" She released me and took my face in her hands.

"My heart's broken. I can't find Jax. I'm worried if I call him, it'll only make things worse."

"You can't make things worse by telling someone you love them, Tabby." She ran her fingers through my hair, which brought my blood down to a low simmer. Mom was a good antidote to my panic. "Come inside."

I did as she asked and stood in her living room, admiring the tiny bells and angels on her Christmas tree. The strong smell of cinnamon and sugar made me feel like her home was made of cookies—inviting and comforting, like she was. "I thought he'd reach out to me, but he hasn't. That's not like him."

"Have you tried reaching out yourself?"

"No. Too many things to say that I haven't practiced." I shook my head, clutching my temples and groaning. "Don't ask why I think him calling me first will somehow fix that."

Mom stood at my side and adjusted a few off-kilter ornaments. "So, you're still scared?"

"Of course I am. I know I shouldn't be. God, I wish he were here right now."

She hummed. "Why not practice all those things you say you need to, and I'll tell you if it needs adjusting."

I took a deep breath and closed my eyes. "I'd say I was sorry again, wouldn't I? That, and the million little things that make me love him."

While I stood before her tree, weeping for my lost first love, I imagined how his smile looked last night. How close we were when he squeezed my hand under the fake snowfall. I remembered his teenage self, desperate for me, and how hard it was not to call him when we first moved out. I needed him. Wanted him. So many lonely years were spent hoping he was happy, when all I really wanted was for him to reappear.

"Go on," Mom said as she stroked my back. "Talk to him."

Still locked in my fantasy conversation, I imagined the warmth of Mom's house was his presence, and the hand on my back belonged to him, not her. In an instant, we were together again, sharing our hearts as I wanted to last night.

"Wah, I'm sorry. I'm…beyond sorry." While I spoke, weight lifted from my shoulders. It flew away into the ether. "I'm sorry for not telling you the truth, sorry for doubting the man that you are, and sorry I couldn't tell you why I disappeared so many years ago. You see, when I left, I tried to get by on memory alone. I had all these reserves to keep me going—your ring, your words, the image of you in my head—but I didn't realize what a drought I'd been in until you showed up again."

The hand on my back swirled in circles and splayed. It tickled and grounded me all at once.

"Rob tried to say that, and he wasn't any good at it. Still, I knew. You were my water, and now...I was drowning. In too deep. And I understand why you were upset—it wasn't my lie, or how much time I'd wasted. It was because of the years you spent searching, and I hadn't reached out to you. I guess...part of me thought wearing your ring was enough, but that's bullshit, Wah." My eyes went hot, enough that I felt my words pouring like tears. "The truth is, if I'd found you, I would've dropped everything to be with you. I would've changed my life, moved away, done *anything* to be at your side. When you met me that first night and shook my hand, it was over for me. I gave Rob a chance because I thought I owed it to him, not because I didn't want to give you a shot. You already won."

The one hand on my back turned to two. They moved up to my shoulders and kneaded me gently. The familiar touch was pulled from the depths of a hope long since lost, and the bright scent of citrus cut through the warm cinnamon ahead of me.

Is it my imagination, or...?

As a prayer, I released everything from my heart. "You deserve to be chased, Jax. You deserve everything. I told your father today that I'd follow you anywhere. That was no lie."

A quiet sniff behind me forced me to pause. Fingertips swam over my arms to my hands, then laced with mine.

I gasped. "Is it really you? Are you here, Wah?"

"Yes," Jax said, just as broken and tearful as I was. "Did you really talk to Dad?"

"I did. I just missed you at the hospital." Wrapping his arms around me, I leaned back into his chest, soaking up every bit of his warmth. "Mom didn't say you were here."

"I'm beginning to think they're conspiring against us."

"Against you, or for you?" Dale said on speakerphone.

We both turned around to find Mom with her phone face out, and Dale on a video call. They both had beaming smiles of victory. All four of us laughed at the ridiculousness of it all before Jax released me so we could be face to face.

He wiped his eyes, then did the same to me and took a breath. "Tabby Ross, you're my Hwa."

"Wah, you're everything." I admired him in the twinkle lights, which sprinkled him like glitter. "I wouldn't change you at all."

"Me either." Jax hummed a sweet sigh while he looked over me.

I finally took the chance to trail through his hair and send goosebumps over his arms. "My greatest regret is every lost moment since you came here. How can I make that up to you?"

"Well, it wasn't a total loss. Now we can share all those great ties I got Rob to buy."

I burst with laughter. "You have that right. Definitely some winners. Though now that begs the question…why did you help him at all?"

Jax shrugged. "I wanted to see you happy. If I could help make that happen, it was enough."

"Do you think, deep down, you knew? Was that why?"

"No. I didn't know your secret." He relaxed, revealing a new depth of honesty. "But I knew I loved you."

"Hey Lisa, why don't you show me your beautiful kitchen again?" Dale said, signaling that it was time to give us some privacy. Mom jumped and left the room.

I tickled Jax's ear and flitted my gaze over his mouth. "I think it's time."

"You sure? Because once this happens, that's it for me. I mean business."

"Yeah." I sighed and melted into him. "I'm ready for forever."

His deep brown eyes lit from within while he leaned down to

me. When our lips met, my chest caught on fire with joy. We were one once again, meant to be, fitting too well to be anything but soulmates.

keeping him

. . .

Jax

IT WASN'T enough to have him in my arms at his mother's house; that was far too awkward, and we held back what we could. The three of us—four, with Dad on video—caught up on all the years we'd missed over a small dessert, since it would've been rude to skedaddle so fast.

Hwa squeezed my left thigh under the kitchen table, making my temperature spike. When Dad clicked off the phone and Lisa took the plates away, Tabby whispered, "Take me home."

"Yes, sir," I said, rising and pulling out his seat.

"Are you leaving?" Lisa asked, returning with a grin.

"Yeah, Mom. Jax is a great driver. We'll be careful." Tabby kissed her on the cheek before we left with our hands together. I don't remember saying goodnight to her, though I'm sure I said it. My brain was focused on one thing alone.

Tabby blared music from his phone while we drove back to the city, claiming it was to make sure I stayed awake. I knew better. He was equally as anxious as me to rediscover our dynamic and answer a different kind of appetite.

Over the Golden Gate, past the park, up the now-familiar street where I parked last night and thought that was the end. Now it was real.

I pulled the car against the sidewalk and admired him, much the same way I did that first time we sat and talked together.

Tabby turned off the music and turned to face me. "I, um, called in sick tomorrow. You know, because I flew today and wasn't sure if I'd be back in time."

I nodded, then pulled out my phone to do the same. My text had a typo, but I figured it made my claim of being ill look more legitimate since it would be midnight soon.

"Can I come in?" I asked.

He snorted. "Didn't you just call off work so you could?"

"I don't know...I'm nervous." I laughed and let the tension bleed away. "You could change your mind at any moment and send me packin'."

"Nah...not when I know exactly what *you're* packin'," he said with a bounce of his brows. "Come on."

We left the car, and I chased him up the steps, impatiently standing back a few feet while he unlocked the door. The second it opened, Tabby grabbed my hand. He made no stops along the way. Straight to the bedroom.

Finally.

"Kiss me," I said, keeping him still before he could push me back onto his mattress.

Tabby looked up at me through his thick, sweeping lashes and let out a breath. I expected him to say something poetic, but he did as I asked instead, using both hands to pull my face toward him. He moved against me again and again, unable to satisfy the hunger within, and I did the same.

Releasing my face, Tabby worked down my buttons, pecking the bare skin he exposed each time until he pulled my shirt out from my waist to make me topless. His strong hands claimed me as his territory, touching every bit of me that was no longer covered. I opened my arms so he could take me in.

When he stepped away and placed my hands on his shirt, I asked, "May I see you?" before touching the first button.

"As much as you want to see." His eyes, staring deep with

the key to my heart within, were as I remembered them in youth. Like I always said, he couldn't hide from me, and now he didn't want to.

Down I went. One, then two, popping each one to reveal his hirsute chest until I reached the stretched, black material hiding beneath.

"Don't mind the binder," he whispered. "Keep going."

We finished undressing, bare before one another, save for the binder he kept on his top. I didn't remove it, nor did I ask, because it meant more than just clothing to him.

"You swear you forgive me?" he asked before we began. "This is it?"

"Of course I forgive you." I trailed my fingers over his shoulders and tipped his chin toward me again. "I'm so in love with you, Hwa. Handsome Hwa. It was always meant to be this way."

He blinked quickly and nodded, then brought his lips to mine.

That night, we made love all the ways we knew how, making up for lost time. Tabby fit in my arms as I fit into his. He started just as soft as he ever was, then flipped the script and dominated me. I loved every minute. He made me feel secure, protected, loved, chosen, and downright starved for.

Now my reserves were built up forever. We'd never have a drought again.

one of us

. . .

Tabby

JAX DIDN'T HESITATE and brought over a load of his things the next morning. He and Ethan had an agreement since things were going well with Megan—as he moved out, she moved in. It worked out for all of us.

He picked me up after work that Thursday and we agreed to announce to the group our new status. I hadn't even told Annie the news, and Ethan wasn't a gossip, so chances were high that it would be a surprise to everyone.

I clutched Jax's hand while we walked from the garage to the store, eyeing him with a dreamy gaze at his side. He playfully bumped me with his shoulder on the way. Jax brought a change of clothes for me in his car so we wouldn't have to detour back home before coming—while I'd gotten used to dressing nicely at work, being casual for D&D was still important to me.

"You ready for this?" I asked him before we went through the doors.

"Are you kidding? I can't wait to see the look on Annie's face." He winked, then charged through, yanking me behind him.

Gavin and his boyfriend were loudly laughing when we made it to the table, showing off a new set of dice. Cordelia set up a few hand-painted decorations for the board. Ethan locked up behind us and found his seat, clearing his throat before he sat to draw attention to us.

When everyone looked up, they went quiet. A moment passed.

"So, we have a bit of an announcement," I said, glancing between Jax and the rest of them.

"It's about fucking time," Gavin said, breaking into applause.

Everyone laughed and clapped along while Jax and I turned bright red and chuckled into each other. So much for declaring our love as some big surprise.

Annie hurried over and hugged us both. "I'm so excited, I can't see straight."

"Aw, and you're the only one of us who can," I said, bringing her close. "You're just happy to know I'm not with a complete asshole."

"Well, that, and…" She cocked a brow at Jax.

I squinted at her. "What are you two up to?"

"Nothing that concerns you. Yet." Annie pecked me on the cheek and went back to her chair.

"But she hates this kinda thing," I said to Jax with a scoff.

"You have that wrong. She just hated Rob." He put his forehead against mine. "Actually, I've found she's quite useful."

"You're hiding something. I demand to know what it is."

"Oh, you'll find out soon enough, Hwa. Patience, *grasshoppa*." He kissed and lifted me slightly off the ground.

"Okay, now you two are making *me* sick," Gavin's boyfriend said.

"You know, I still don't actually know your name," retorted Jax, keeping his arm around me. "Every time I think about you, I still say *Hawk* in my head."

The group practically erupted with more laughter. "The jig is up, man. Spill it," Gavin said, displaying his open hand as an invitation.

He sighed and folded his arms. "My name's Toby. I don't like being confused with Tabby, alright?"

Jax snorted. "Seriously? That's the reason?"

"I'm still partial to *Stationary*," Annie said, winking at him.

Toby stood from the table and flipped us all off, then sat on Gavin's lap and shook his dice for us to begin. "Enough of this mushy bullshit. Like Annie says—to the death!"

acknowledgments

Many thanks to all the early readers of this book; without you, it wouldn't have become what it is, and I wouldn't have, either. There are far too many of you to name, but I will single out a few:

To my children, Tesla and Edison, who were patient and forgiving when I spent hours typing away, bringing these characters to life.

To Makenna Albert, who always had so much faith in me as a writer and whose comments helped push me to be better at every step.

To Kat Sinclair, my first real reader and writing friend, who saw the first drafts of this story and reminded me not to repeat myself so much.

To my sister and father, true Colorado natives, who were always on my mind when I took Jax places we all knew so well. There's no green chili in California, which is such a tragedy, I had to chronicle it.

And to my husband Steven, who proposed to me after the Nutcracker on 16th street in Denver, and whose response to my first questions about who I was inside was to ask if he could help me learn to tie a tie. You've always been the real key.

about the author

Jo Morgan Sloan is a proud Colorado native and a Northern California transplant. They've been actively writing since late 2013 and began as many writers do: with unhinged fanfiction. From contemporary romance to fantasy and literary fiction, Jo is passionate about realistic and heartfelt relationships on the page as well as torturing readers in the best ways. Writing *The Key* was integral in Jo's journey of self-discovery, proving that life only gets more interesting north of thirty.

Keep eyes out for their sophomore effort, Stableshoes, an MLM twist on classic Cinderella.